SUNSHINE &

Sammy

NEW YORK TIMES AND USA TODAY BESTSELLING AUTHOR

MELANIE MORELAND

ABC
CORP

BOOK 5

D1430723

Dear Reader,

Thank you for selecting the Vested Interest: ABC Corp series to read. Be sure to sign up for my newsletter for up to date information on new releases, exclusive content and sales.

Before you sign up, add melanie@melaniemoreland.com to your contacts to make sure the email comes right to your inbox! **Always fun - never spam!**

My books are available in both paperback and audiobook! I also have paperbacks available at my website.

The Perfect Recipe For **LOVE**

xoxo,

Melanie

ALSO BY MELANIE MORELAND

The Contract Series

The Contract (Contract #1)

The Baby Clause (Contract #2)

The Amendment (Contract #3)

The Addendum

Vested Interest Series

BAM - The Beginning (Prequel)

Bentley (Vested Interest #1)

Aiden (Vested Interest #2)

Maddox (Vested Interest #3)

Reid (Vested Interest #4)

Van (Vested Interest #5)

Halton (Vested Interest #6)

Sandy (Vested Interest #7)

Vested Interest/ABC Crossover

A Merry Vested Wedding

ABC Corp Series

My Saving Grace (Vested Interest: ABC Corp #1)

Finding Ronan's Heart (Vested Interest: ABC Corp #2)

Loved By Liam (Vested Interest: ABC Corp #3)

Age of Ava (Vested Interest: ABC Corp #4)

Sunshine & Sammy (Vested Interest: ABC Corp #5)

Men of Hidden Justice

The Boss

Second-In-Command

The Commander

The Watcher

Reynolds Restorations

Revved to the Maxx

Breaking the Speed Limit

Shifting Gears

Under The Radar

Full Throttle

Insta-Spark Collection written by M Moreland

It Started with a Kiss

Christmas Sugar

An Instant Connection

An Unexpected Gift

Harvest of Love

An Unexpected Chance

Following Maggie (Coming Home series)

Mission Cove

The Summer of Us

Standalones

Into the Storm

Beneath the Scars

Over the Fence

The Image of You (former title My Image of You)

Changing Roles

Happily Ever After Collection

Heart Strings

Sunshine and Sammy
Vested Interest: ABC Corp #5

Copyright © 2022 Melanie Moreland
Registration #1193844
ISBN Paperback: 978-1-990803-01-7

MORELAND
B O O K S   I N C .

Edited by:
Lisa Hollett — Silently Correcting Your Grammar
Proofing by:
Carissa Riggs, Carissa's BooksnCoffee Proofreading Services
Cover design by Karen Hulseman of
Feed Your Dreams Designs
Photographer Eric D Battershell — O'Snap Media
Model Burton Hughes
Cover content is for illustrative purposes only and any person depicted on the cover is a model.

This book is a work of fiction. The characters, events, and places portrayed in this book are products of the author's imagination and are either fictitious or are used fictitiously. Any similarity to real persons, living or dead, is purely coincidental and not intended by the author. The author acknowledges the trademarked status and trademark owners of various products referenced in this work of fiction, which

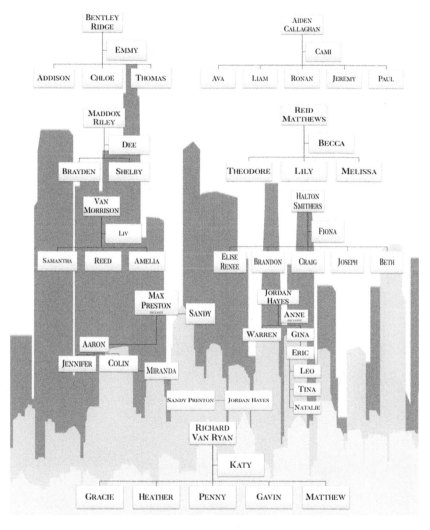

FAMILY TREE

The Contract **VESTED INTEREST**

NEW YORK TIMES AND USA TODAY BESTSELLING AUTHOR

MELANIE MORELAND

DEDICATION

Carol—you asked for this for so long,

And now he is yours. Enjoy!

CHAPTER ONE

SAMMY

I slipped my key into the lock, opening the door and walking into the house. Immediately, I was surrounded by the familiar scent. The one that reminded me of my mom. Of home. Sage and citrus. Fresh, clean, and warm.

"Dad?" I called out, hearing noises from the back of the house.

"In here," his voice returned my greeting. "In the garage."

I headed to the back of the house and out the door leading to the garage. My dad, Vince Morrison, or Van to everyone who knew him, was standing amid boxes, scratching his head.

"Hey," I greeted.

His face broke into a wide smile. "Hey, Mouse."

I couldn't stop my own smile at his greeting. He had nicknamed me Mouse when he'd started dating my mother and had never stopped calling me that. I could still recall that day as vividly as if it were only yesterday. Van, standing tall and broad in my mother's office doorway, smiling and friendly. Taking me to his office

1

and coloring with me, feeding me a lemon Danish so Mom could finish her work. Coming with us to lunch. Listening to me as I talked his ear off. I was convinced he was a giant. The truth was, he was only a man—but to me, a great one. He married my mom and became the best father a girl could ask for. Loving, protective, kind, and fun. He adopted me, then he and Mom adopted my brother Reed, and finally my sister Amelia. Together, we became a family.

"Hi, Dad. What on earth are you doing?"

He chuckled, shifting another box. "Believe it or not, there are still boxes we haven't unpacked since we moved out here to Port Albany permanently. Your mom suddenly remembered a cookbook she hadn't thought of in years and wanted a recipe from it. I was looking for it."

I laughed. "Probably easier to look online."

He shook his head. "It was her mom's and handwritten. She searched everywhere in the house for it. I thought I would find it in one of these boxes."

I smiled at him. When my grandmother had passed a few years ago, my mom had been incredibly sad, and my dad had helped her through that terrible period. It didn't surprise me that he would dig through boxes looking for a recipe for her; that was the sort of man he was.

"Can I help?"

"She says it was in a small notebook. Spiral-bound—she thinks yellow."

"Oh, I remember that. Grammie kept it on the shelf in her cupboard."

He nodded. "Most of this is design stuff and things you kids made that Mom couldn't part with. But a couple of boxes are labeled 'Kitchen Miscellaneous.'"

"I'll look through one."

He lifted a box down in front of me, then kissed my cheek. "Thanks, Mouse."

Ten minutes later, I held up the faded yellow spiral-bound notebook. The cover was bent and torn, stained with splashes of water and various ingredients. "Got it!"

He grinned. "Awesome. Liv will be thrilled. I have a feeling I'll be having a new dish for dinner later."

I returned his grin, then clapped my hands in delight when I saw what was by his workbench. "Is that my old bookcase?"

He nodded. "I'm giving it a fresh coat of paint and sparkle."

I laughed, running my hand over the smooth wood. He had made this bookcase for me when I was a little girl and loved everything pink, glittery, and princess-y. Since then, it had been used by other girls in the family and was well loved. "It needs some fresh glitter."

He grimaced. "I never thought I'd still be in the glitter phase all these years later. But here I am."

I nudged him. "You love it."

He shook his head, but I knew I was right. He loved seeing the bookcase in a new room, being used all over again.

He held out his hand. "Come have coffee with your old man and catch him up."

"You don't want to clean this up?"

"No, it's time to go through it and either get rid of it or get it in scrapbooks. Your mom always planned on doing that. I'll help her sort through the stuff, and it'll give her a project to do." He smirked. "Maybe I can get a little more room in the garage, then."

I laughed and took his hand, following him to the kitchen. He puttered around, making coffee as I filled a plate with cookies. Mom always had cookies on hand. Dad had a sweet tooth, and he ate them daily. He still worked out every day so he could afford the treats.

He set down a mug of coffee in front of me and reached for a cookie, biting down with a satisfied hum.

"Where is Mom?"

"Out with Emmy, Cami, and Dee. Apparently the boys were wrestling a little too enthusiastically last Sunday, and we need a new sofa in the Hub."

I lifted one eyebrow. "*The boys?*" I repeated. "You know they're all grown men. Including you."

He winked. "They'll always be boys to me. It was the triplets. Then Aiden joined in. I might have helped. A sofa may have been sacrificed in the name of fun."

I laughed. "I missed it."

"We were all scolded thoroughly, then the women decided it was time to replace the furniture anyway. We'll donate all the current stuff. Your mom already found a place that needed it."

"Good."

"Now, what is your news, my girl? Mom said you had a new offer on the table—you were waiting on final details to decide whether you would accept it."

I nodded around a mouthful of cookie and took a sip of the strong coffee. "I accepted this morning."

"Where are you off to and for how long?"

"Alberta. And I'm not sure. Six, maybe eight weeks?"

"Alberta. Nice place. Lots of mountains and great scenery."

I crossed my legs, swinging my foot in excitement. "It's a family-run ranch. Mostly cattle, but some other things as well. A brother and sister team. They want to add a tourist element to the ranch. You can go and be a cowboy or cowgirl for a while. Herd cattle. Work in the fields, camp under the stars. There are a couple of buildings on the property that would make great accommodations. I'm going to go in and design them. Help them plan out the menu, so to speak. Make sure a city slicker like me could handle it. Gathering eggs, picking apples. Going overnight camping. Sleep in the bunkhouse." I grinned. "Milk the cows. I'm really excited about this one."

Dad took a sip of coffee, looking amused. "Pretty sure dairy cows don't leave the pasture by the barn. Hardly herding."

"They have beef cattle as well—that's the main focus of the ranch."

"Ah. Makes more sense." He scrubbed the back of his neck. "Mouse, you haven't been on a horse since you were a kid. You decided you didn't like it. It was, if I recall correctly, 'not like the horses at the fair.'" He chuckled. "In other words, these were big and actually did more than move in a circle. You ended up on my saddle with me the whole ride."

5

"Dad, I was eight."

"Have you been on one since then?"

"No."

He chuckled. "Kinda my point."

I laughed with him. "I'm pretty sure I'll be okay. They don't go far. I've been talking to the sister, Rachel, a lot. She is sort of spearheading all this. The brother, Luke, stays pretty busy with running the ranch and the staff, I gather."

"How old are they?"

"Luke is forty. Rachel is thirty. They inherited the ranch from their parents." I slid my phone toward Dad. "It's a great place."

He scrolled through the photos. "Nice setup. River Rock Ranch. Great name. I like it."

I nodded. "Been in the Adler family for three generations. They want to keep it going."

"Either of them married?"

"Rachel is engaged. She never said anything about her brother, and there is no spouse listed on the documents. I, ah, gather, he is a bit of a grump. All business. All farm. That's why I've been dealing with her."

"That could be tricky."

I shook my head. "He signed all the forms and is on board. He just doesn't have time. I'm happy to deal with Rachel. She has some good ideas. The network is excited. It'll be featured as soon as I have it ready."

"Awesome. When are you going?"

"A week."

"Quick."

"Right time of the year."

"Of course." He drained his coffee cup, his voice mild. "No crew?"

I withheld my grin. My dad both loved and hated what I did. I was an independent DIY business starter. It had happened by accident when I helped a local business get off the ground and it was featured on a TV show. Since then, I had grown my company into a successful, sought-after ally. I received hundreds of letters a year from people with business ideas that needed some help with the details, the execution, and often some financial aid. I worked with the chosen project and the person or family, filmed the process, used my knowledge and expertise to help shape the foundation, and assist financially. When complete, the show was featured on a national TV network.

Every business I had chosen had flourished and grown. My reputation was solid and so were my unorthodox methods. I had a business degree in marketing and design. Plus, thanks to my dad and my family, I could wield any power tool there was and loved the entire building or demolition process. I preferred the hands-on approach and refused to pin myself to one kind of business, a steady crew, or even a locked-in contract with a single network. I took on small projects, big jobs, simple two-week ones. Some never saw any TV time, simply a new foundation on which they could build with my backing on my website and social media. But the network I liked to work with gave me a huge platform and a free hand, often helping with the financial end when required. They liked my work, I liked their ethics, so it was a win-win for us both. I gave them three shows a year, and they were happy.

My dad worried about me on every project.

I shook my head. "You know how I work. I run the camera myself, and I use local crews to do the work." I met his eyes, shaking my head. "You worry too much, Dad. I've been doing this for years. The clients are thoroughly scoped out, and I check in with people regularly. With today's technology, I don't need a huge crew following me around. I love how the shows look, and so does the network—and the viewers."

"I still worry, you going to strangers' places."

"As I said, you worry too much. The network does its own check as well as what I have done. I make sure everything is on the up-and-up."

"But you didn't fly there ahead this time to check things out?"

"No, time precluded it. I have Zoomed with Rachel several times. Her lawyer, as well, when he went over the agreements. Everything is fine." I patted his hand. "I'll call every few days."

"Every second day," Dad bartered. "And a text every morning."

I hid my grin. "Done."

He grunted and took another cookie.

"How's your sister?" he asked, letting the subject drop.

"Deep into the script. I can't believe Mila's book is going to be a movie."

Dad beamed, proud and happy. "She deserves it. It's a great book. I mean, they all are, but that one is spectacular. Who'd have guessed our shy Mila could write something so powerful?"

"And sexy," I added with a wink.

"We don't think about that," Dad replied. "I can't."

I laughed at his reaction.

"She'll miss you," he said, changing the direction of the conversation.

"I know. But it's not forever. Did you know she plans to go on location when they shoot the movie?"

"She told me. Do you think she can do it?" he asked with a concerned frown.

"I think it's great. It will help with her shyness, Dad. Andi, her agent, will be with her. She'll make sure Mila is okay."

"You know I worry. Especially…" He trailed off.

I patted his hand. "She hasn't had an episode in a long time, Dad. Andi knows what she's dealing with. She'll be fine."

He nodded slowly. "Both my girls off into the world."

I shook my head. "Your *girls* are in their thirties, Dad. I don't even want to think about how high into my thirties I am. We're hardly girls anymore."

"You'll always be my girls. That will never change."

"And you'll always be the greatest man I know," I replied.

He smiled. "I'm glad you think so."

"I know so. We all do, Dad."

He reached across the table and squeezed my hand. "Easy when you have awesome kids."

The sound of a car made him look up, and he smiled. I loved how pleased he looked, knowing Mom was back. Their love was still strong and a joy to witness.

"Your mom is home. She'll be excited to hear your news and want to know all your plans. Plus, she'll want to see your designs."

"I was counting on it."

He stood and winked. "I better go see if she has bags to carry. Tell her I found her book. I bet I get a reward for that."

"Um, I found the book."

"You wouldn't deny your old dad kisses from your mom now, would you?"

I shook my head. "Heaven forbid."

He nodded sagely. "That's what I thought."

CHAPTER TWO

SAMMY

I strolled home, enjoying the quiet of the area. I loved it here. It gave me the peace and tranquility I needed to create and, once a project was done, to wind down and relax. I had a small place in Toronto that Mila and I shared as well. On occasion, one of us had to be in town, and it was easier to have our own place—we both preferred the comfort of it to a hotel. We had bought a small one-bedroom apartment in one of the many buildings built and owned by BAM, and between us and all our "cousins," it was used frequently. We even had an app to make sure no one overlapped. Everyone chipped in on the maintenance fees, and Mila and I had priority over the calendar, but often someone crashed there if they were working late. It worked out great for us.

I had to admit, there were times I yearned for something else, but what it was, I didn't know. I figured, when I found it, I would know. Until then, Port Albany was home.

I opened the door, hearing Mila's soft voice in the kitchen. I headed there to see her at the table, her laptop open as usual.

Her phone was tucked against her shoulder, and she was typing furiously as she listened. I wasn't sure if she was taking notes or writing. When a scene hit her, she typed it out fast, so it could be either.

I grabbed a glass of water for myself and refilled her empty glass, then sat down. I studied my little sister with affection. We may not have been related by blood, but our bond was strong. Our parents adopted her when I was about seven and she was three. She was neglected and starved for affection, terrified of her own shadow, and timid.

She still suffered from shyness. My entire family sheltered her fiercely. She had been picked on in school because of her quiet nature, and our brother Reed had been sent to the principal's office more than once protecting her. She had gotten braver, but to this day, she was demure and quiet. She preferred books and music to people. Solitude to noise.

But we, as a family, knew a different Mila. She was funny and droll. Sweet and kind. Always giving. Loving. She had the ability to make a person laugh so hard they cried. She could hold her own with the fastest of comebacks and quips once she was comfortable with you.

That was the trick. Getting her comfortable.

I grinned as she hung up with a barely mumbled goodbye and kept typing. A scene, then. I kept quiet until she finished and hit the save button.

"Whew," she muttered, raising her gaze to mine. For someone adopted, she looked strikingly like my mom, with the same golden, intelligent eyes and honey-colored hair. She was tiny —the tiniest of the whole family—which added another level of protectiveness to us all. But underneath the shell of the quiet, small person beat the heart of a lion. I adored my baby sister.

"Got out the words?"

"Yeah. They wanted to change a pivotal scene in the book for the movie, and I disagreed strongly. So, I wrote it differently, but the same, if that makes any sense."

"Nope."

She laughed, the sound light and airy.

"You will when you see the movie."

"When does filming start?"

Her eyes lit up. "In a month. They finally cast the male lead. I'm so excited."

"Who?"

"Nicholas Scott."

The name was familiar. "Isn't that the guy you told me was in your dream cast?"

"Yes."

I searched my memory. "Wait, wasn't he in rehab recently? Isn't he there a lot?"

She shrugged. "He has the right intensity to play Duncan. And I think there's more to the rehab than they report."

"What do you mean?"

She glanced over my shoulder with a frown, looking thoughtful. "There is something incredibly deep and troubled in his eyes."

"It's called addiction."

"No." She shook her head. "It's more. He is going to be the perfect Duncan. I know it. I really pushed for him. And I'm thrilled with the woman they chose to play Roxie. It's going to be amazing."

"And you're going to go on set?"

She hesitated, then nodded. "Andi says it's important. I can give insight into the characters to help the actors. And I want to see the process."

"You'll do great."

"Andi will be with me. And I have to do it."

I patted her hand. "Yeah, you do."

She sighed. "When are you leaving for the farm?"

"It's a ranch," I corrected gently. "A week from today. I have a ton of stuff to get ready. It's going to be crazy."

"I can help."

"Thanks, kiddo. I might take you up on that."

Mila yawned and I chuckled. "Were you up all night writing?"

"Most of it. I had a great idea for a new series. I wanted to get it outlined. Then I kept going." She stood. "I'll go grab a short nap, then we can have dinner if you're around?"

"Mom offered dinner for both of us around seven."

She grinned, her dimples showing. "Even better."

She wandered down the hall, already lost to her thoughts. Living with a writer was odd. I never knew what to expect. Some days, her schedule was semi-normal. Other times, she was up all night writing, sleeping at odd hours. It was always different.

Chuckling, I reached for my laptop on the counter and opened it. It was time to make more lists.

My next adventure waited.

———

Sunday was the usual brunch at the Hub with whichever family members were around. I filled my plate, looking around and smiling. Ava and Hunter were in the corner, still in the throes of newly married bliss. Addi and Braydon were chatting with Maddox and Dee. Gracie and Jaxson were sitting on the sofa, laughing at something Ronan had said. Everywhere I saw groups and smiles. Lots of teasing. There always was when we got together. I made my way to the table where my mom and dad sat with Bentley and Emmy. I sat down, my dad pulling out my chair for me. "Where're Nan and Pops?"

Bentley smiled. "At Colin's place today. It's his daughter's birthday."

"Oh, I wanted to say goodbye. I'll pop over later."

"Your father tells me you're headed west to make over a dude ranch?" Bentley asked, lifting one eyebrow in question.

I chuckled and took a sip of coffee. "It's a cattle ranch. But they want to try having people stay and be part of the experience. Ride a horse. Help herd the cattle. Nothing dangerous. Sleep under the stars, eat by the fire—that sort of thing. They have a couple of buildings that would make great sleeping accommodations. I think it could work well. People love that sort of hands-on involvement. Something different."

Emmy looked interested. "That sounds like fun. Maybe we should try that, Rigid."

15

Bentley pursed his lips. "If that was something you wanted, Emmy."

Aiden snickered. "Unless it's five-star all the way, Bentley considers it roughing it." He waved his fork toward Bentley. "I can't see your snooty ass sharing a bunk, sleeping on the ground, or eating beans off a tin plate."

Everyone chuckled.

"Rachel, the sister I've been dealing with, assures me the guests would be very comfortable and well-fed, but I agree, not sure I see you there, Bentley."

Emmy grinned. "Maybe a girls' adventure weekend."

Cami, Aiden's wife, lifted her hand. "I'm in. I think it would be fun for a weekend. Go see some cowboys do their thing." She winked at me. "I've always been a sucker for a man in a Stetson."

"Sunshine," Aiden said, sounding surprised. "You never told me that. I can go get a hat. A lasso. You can run, and I'll chase you. Rope you like a little calf and carry you back to my bunk and—"

Cami covered his mouth before he could finish that sentence. Bentley looked horrified then grateful as she stopped him. Everyone else burst into laughter, used to Aiden's inappropriate conversations.

"I think we'll stick to that weekend. You tell your client to expect us, Sammy," Cami said dryly.

I wiped my mouth, meeting my dad's amused eyes. "I'll do that."

Mila joined us, sliding in beside me. "Hey, kiddo," I greeted her.

She smiled at everyone. "Sorry I'm late. I was on the phone with Andi."

"Ironing out more details?"

"Yep. And she read the first draft of the next book. She loved it."

"You'll send it to me so I can read it while I'm gone, right?"

"You'll have time?"

I nodded. "I expect most evenings I'll be on my own. I'll do some video edits, but I'll have time to read."

"Great. You know I love your notes."

"I'm all in."

She squeezed my hand. "Thanks."

I winked. "Anytime."

―――――――――

My afternoon flight was uneventful the next day. I enjoyed the quiet time, listening to music and getting ready to start the project. When we touched down in Calgary, I turned my phone back on as I waited for the luggage. I had only one large suitcase, plus a box of well-packed equipment. I grabbed a cart, waiting patiently. My phone beeped, and I looked down in dismay at the message from Rachel telling me her fiancé had been in an accident and she was on her way to the hospital with him. She wouldn't be at the airport to meet me but would send a driver to pick me up.

I quickly replied, assuring her that wasn't a problem and hoping her fiancé would be all right. I found my luggage, piling it onto the cart, and headed past security to the area where people waited for their loved ones. I glanced around, expecting to see a driver with a sign. Not spying any, I headed to the side to stay out of the way. The flight was a little early, so perhaps they hadn't arrived. I glanced around in curiosity, my gaze sweeping the terminal. My sight landed on a fine specimen of a man, standing to one side. He was tall. Thick. He had his arms crossed, and he looked uncomfortable in the space around him. He wore a plaid shirt over a T-shirt and a cowboy hat—not an unusual sight here, but somehow on his tall frame, it helped him stand out. He took it off, sweeping a hand through his hair, then placed it firmly back on his head. I caught a glimpse of dark hair, and suddenly, I locked eyes with the cowboy, his intense gaze meeting mine. His appraisal was as frank as mine, his lips curling up slightly in appreciation before he frowned and shifted away, his profile now on display, the scruff on his sharp jaw the same dark color as his head. I tried not to stare at the size of his arms under his tight shirt. I dropped my eyes, taking in his jeans that hugged his wide thighs and the dusty leather boots on his feet. I found myself envying whomever he was waiting for. I stepped back, leaning against the pillar, hoping to witness the reunion. Would he smile and grab someone, lifting them high, then kissing them? Or was he the sort to simply hug someone or give them a curt nod, saving their reunion for a more private setting?

I shook my head. He could be meeting his brother. Sister. Mother. A friend. Maybe all there would be was a slap on the back and a smile. Or a grunt. He didn't really look like the smiley type. He was serious and impatient-looking. I tore my gaze away. I had other things to think about.

I smiled at the woman beside me trying to keep her kids close. She caught my eye with a rueful grin. "Their dad has been away for a week," she said by way of explanation.

I bent close to the little girl. "Are you excited to see your daddy?"

She nodded fast, her curls bouncing. "I draw him this!" She showed me the paper with the colorful marks. I admired it. "He'll love it," I assured her. "But you have to stay close to your mom because it's a big place, and he'll see her, but he won't be able to spot you since you're so little."

Her eyes grew round, and she stopped trying to break away. Her mother shot me a grateful smile, and I returned it before glancing at my watch. I hoped the driver would be here soon. The crowd was beginning to thin out, and there was no sign of him. I pushed my cart over to the information area to ask if there was a place for drivers to wait, then went outside, but no one had my name. I went back inside, noting the cowboy was still there. He was pacing now, looking displeased and impatient. I struck up a conversation with a woman who was also waiting, and she kindly agreed to watch my luggage as I ran to the washroom. When I returned, the cowboy was gone, and I was disappointed I never got to see his reunion. I pushed that thought out of my mind, unsure what to do. I didn't want to contact Rachel since she had far more important things on her mind. I decided to hire a car. I knew the name of the ranch and where it was located. I would simply get myself there and find Luke.

Except as I headed toward the doors, the cowboy walked back in. Our eyes locked again, and something struck me as familiar, as if I'd seen him before. His irises were a clear blue, as bright as the sky on a summer's day. I'd seen those eyes before—a few times during Zoom meetings with Rachel. For a moment, I was puzzled, then I stopped walking and spun around. "Luke?" I called.

He stopped and turned, a frown on his face. He eyed me up and down, his slow gaze somehow warming me inside.

"Who's asking?" he demanded.

I stepped closer. "I'm Samantha Morrison."

"I'm sorry?"

For some reason, I wanted to touch him. I laid my hand on his arm, feeling the band of muscles flex under my touch. "Sammy. The person Rachel sent you to pick up."

His expression said it all. He wasn't happy. I'd probably interrupted his day. Rachel said he was busy all the time.

"I'm sorry to have taken you away from your work. I could have hired a—"

"You're Sam?" he interrupted me, looking angry.

"Sammy. My friends call me Sammy."

"My sister said Sam. You're a *woman*."

My hackles rose. "Thanks for the information. I'm well aware I'm a woman."

"Does Rachel know this?" He flicked his fingers as if I were a bug. "That you're—" his eyes focused on my breasts, then met my narrowed gaze "—that you're not a *Sam*?"

I tilted my head to the side, studying him. *What was his problem?*

"Since we Zoomed several times, I think she figured it out."

He shook his head. "Well, I don't think so."

Then he turned and stormed away.

CHAPTER THREE

LUKE

I stomped to my truck, jumping in and peeling out of the parking lot as quickly as I could get through the paid gate. The woman claiming to be Sam didn't follow—thank God. I wasn't sure what I would have done if she had.

She had caught my eye the second she walked through the door, pushing her luggage cart. She scanned the area, looking for whoever was picking her up, not looking particularly upset they weren't there. She simply stopped by one of the pillars and took out her phone. I couldn't stop staring. She was very pretty, even if she was a city slicker. Her dress pants and blouse were stylish and well cut, her feet encased in nice-looking shoes. Her hair hung down her back like a ribbon of honey, the light glinting off the strands. I wondered if the color was real or came from a bottle. These days, most women seemed to prefer something different, as opposed to what they were born with. She wasn't tall, but she held herself with an easy grace that made her seem so.

I watched as she helped a mother who was trying to corral her children, both of whom, it seemed, were anxious for the arrival of their father, I surmised. She bent and spoke to the little girl, smiling and open. She had an amazing smile. Her full lips stretched wide, showing off her teeth. It was quite something, and it transformed her face from pretty to stunning. It reminded me of when the sun would break from the clouds and brighten the sky. I had to look away before she caught me staring. The last thing I was interested in was someone from the city. Especially someone who looked like her. No doubt, despite the sunshine smile, she would be high-maintenance.

Been there, done that. Never again.

I waited, growing impatient as the travelers seemed to be done coming through the door. I patted my pockets, cursing under my breath when I realized I had left my phone in the car. I needed to call Rachel and make sure I had the right flight number and check on how Tyler was doing. He'd rolled his tractor on his farm this morning and had been in pretty bad shape. Rachel was with him and had left me a message to call for a car service, but when I had contacted them, they had no one to go into Calgary. The other company I called wanted almost double the cost, and it simply wasn't in the budget. I decided to do it myself. I wasn't big on this project Rachel was taking on, but if it helped save the ranch, I had to be cooperative at least.

I headed to the truck and got my phone, then went back to the terminal. I wasn't prepared for the pretty woman and her words.

I certainly had zero idea that the Sam Rachel talked about was a woman.

That woman, in particular. The one with the pretty smile. She spelled trouble with a capital *T*.

It wasn't fucking happening.

I stewed all the way back to the ranch and headed into the small town that was close instead of going home. I hit the bar and ordered a scotch and a cold beer. I flung the shot back fast, feeling the heat of the liquor as it hit the back of my throat and trailed down. I shut my eyes and took in a deep breath. I wondered for a moment what Sammy was doing. No doubt, she got a hotel room or was on her way back to wherever she came from. She could talk to Rachel when she got home. I'd pay for her inconvenience myself. Then we'd move on to another solution.

"Another?" the bartender, Rick, asked.

"No, thanks. Gimme a burger, though. Fries."

"Coming up."

I calmed down as I ate. I sent Rachel a message asking about Tyler, not mentioning the woman. She replied and said he was in surgery. Her next line made me grimace.

Rachel: Be nice to Sammy. We need her.

Had she always said Sammy? I was sure I only heard Sam. I shook my head. It didn't matter. She was gone, and I would face Rachel's ire once she found out what had happened.

I didn't reply.

I did my best to put Sammy out of my mind. How pretty she was. Her lovely voice when she spoke—low and well modulated, almost sultry. The unexpected warmth in my chest when I looked at her. Her beautiful smile that lit a room. How much I had wanted to cover her hand with mine when she touched me. How much I wanted her to touch me again. Simply recalling her closeness made my body tighten with desire. I forced all the thoughts out of my head. Instead, I thought about the repairs needed on the barn. What assistance I could give Tyler and his family to help out. Who I could spare on the ranch to make sure their farm was managed. I pulled out the little notebook and pencil stub I kept in my back pocket and jotted down ideas as I ate. It gave me focus.

Feeling more normal, I paid my bill and headed to the truck. I drove out to the ranch, smiling as I always did at the sight of the entrance. The huge willow trees on either side of the gate stood tall and full, constantly swaying in the air. The sign had been made by my grandfather and still hung there today—a testament to his workmanship. I pulled up to the house, cutting the engine and climbing from the truck. I headed up the steps, stopping in bewilderment at the sight of a large suitcase sitting on the porch by the door.

Who did that belong to?

I got my answer when the screen door opened, and the woman I now knew as Sammy walked out, holding a glass of water. She sipped it, looking at me calmly.

"Took you long enough."

"What the hell are you doing here? How did you get in?"

"Rachel told me there was a key in the flowerpot."

"You spoke to my sister?"

"Yes."

"I told you to leave."

She flashed me a smile. It was still beautiful, but this time, it was wide, dangerous, and somewhat scary. She set down her water and held up a file she took from her bag. "I have a contract, Mr. Adler. Signed by your sister and you. I'm not going anywhere."

I gaped at her.

"I told Rachel there was a mix-up with a car and I got myself here. I also said you were out. She told me how to get in and which room was mine." She smiled. "I didn't mention what *really* happened."

"You are *not* staying in the house."

"Then point me to your guest rooms… Oh wait, that's why I'm here. I guess I am staying in the house. And you are going to accept it."

I stepped forward, almost growling in my anger. I jabbed my finger at her. "I don't fuck—"

The next thing I knew, I was flat on my back on the porch, Sammy bent over me, smiling down sweetly. "Careful, Luke. I have a protective father and an uncle who made sure every girl in my family could defend themselves from men who like to point their fingers and talk down to them. Never mind about showing me to my room. I'll figure it out. I'll leave the equipment box in the kitchen. I'll need it later."

She stood and brushed off her hands, looking around. "What a gorgeous place you have here. I'm looking forward to working with you!"

She took her suitcase and rolled it into the house, never looking back.

I blinked.

What the hell just happened?

I headed to the small space I used as an office. When I'd grown up here, this was my mom's room. She sewed in here all the time. Constantly adjusting hems, patching shirts, pants, recycling flour sacks into aprons, dish towels, whatever other inventive idea she came up with. Rachel could hem a pair of pants and stitch a seam closed, but that was it. I only used a needle and thread if an animal was injured. I doubted I could sew anything.

The room had sat empty for a long time until we cleaned it out and I began using it as an office. There was a lot more paperwork now than there had been in my dad's era. He used to have an old accordion file box he kept all his papers in, and he would sit at the kitchen table at night with my mom and do anything required, then file it away or give it to her to deliver or take into town to copy. Nowadays, a computer was a must, plus a printer. And still, my filing wasn't done. There simply weren't enough hours in the day.

I sat down at my desk, feeling tired and far older than my forty years. I looked around the room—the walls needing painting, the boxes of unfiled papers overflowing. Instead of agreeing to Rachel's idea of using the ranch as a tourist destination to bring in extra revenue, I should have sold some of the land and used that money to hire an assistant and purchase some more dairy cows.

Except the thought of selling land that had been in my family for generations sickened me. Knowing the land would be turned into housing or, worse yet, industry, destroying all the peace and tranquility of the area and upsetting the ecosystem—I simply couldn't do it. I had to figure out a way of making it work. Keeping the land, the ranch.

For whom? a small voice in my head whispered, but I ignored it. Rachel was getting married, and I knew they planned on having children soon. Her fiancé's farm butted up against our land on one side. The ranch would go to their offspring, and they would keep it going. They would be part Adler, and that was good enough. I doubted I would ever marry or even settle down. Children were not an option. That chance had come and gone, and my life was the ranch and running it. Saving it for the next generation.

A noise brought me out of my thoughts, and I lifted my head.

Sammy was in the kitchen, no doubt getting something to eat.

What the hell was I going to do about her?

She was right. I had signed a contract. I sat back, rubbing my face in vexation. Maybe leaving her stranded at the airport hadn't been the best move. Or being rude to her. My mom always said you attracted more flies with honey than vinegar. Perhaps if I sat and talked to her, calmly, we could reach an understanding and she would agree to leave.

I would have to apologize. That was something that didn't come easily to me. *Stubborn*, my mom used to say. *Pigheaded*, Rachel insisted. She was probably more accurate.

My phone rang, and I answered it when I saw it was Rachel.

"Hey, Rachel. How's Tyler?"

"Out of surgery and in recovery. Stable," she replied, her voice strained with relief.

"Good."

"I'm staying here."

"I understand."

"I need you to handle Sammy."

Handle her? I doubted my sister would want to know how I wanted to *handle* her.

I drew in a deep breath. "Do we really need her, Rach? Is this idea solid? I mean—"

She cut me off, sounding exasperated. "Yes, we do, and yes, it is. It's expand what the ranch does, or sell some of the land or the entire thing, Luke. You agreed to this. Why are you being so obstinate suddenly?"

"*She's a she*," I hissed into the phone. "I thought you said Sam— like a man. Not Sammy like a stubborn woman who refuses to listen to me."

And looks like a wet dream come true, I added silently.

There was silence for a moment, then Rachel began to laugh. "You are such a moron. I should have known you were only half listening to me. I told you Sammy, as in Samantha. The very first day we discussed this. It's not my fault—or hers either—you have a memory like a sieve. Oh God, have you been rude to her?"

I paused. "Define rude."

"Luke Jonathan Adler!" she yelled into the phone. "What did you do?"

"I might have left her at the airport after telling her off."

"You *left* her at the airport?" she repeated. "Have you taken leave of the little good sense you had in you?"

"She found her way here anyway and informed me we had a contract." I defended myself. "And you call me stubborn. Now

28

she's in the kitchen getting herself something to eat, making herself at home."

"Moron," she muttered. "I'm related to a moron."

"So that falls under rude?"

"You are a complete ass. You go down the hall, and you apologize. Nicely. Then you sit down and listen to what she has to say, you overgrown idiot. Her ideas are amazing. The publicity is exactly what we need to start this off. You ruin this, Luke, and you can kiss the ranch goodbye."

"Fine," I snarled into the phone. "I'll go make nice. She better not flip me again."

"What?"

"She took exception to me pointing my finger at her, and she flipped me onto my back."

"On my God," Rachel breathed out. "You have completely pissed her off. What have you done?"

"I'll apologize."

"You do that." Then her voice softened. "Listen to her. She is amazing. I trust her. Completely."

I sighed, the fight draining out of me. "Okay. I'll apologize and get on board. Let me know how Tyler's doing."

"Did she really flip you? You're twice her size."

"Like I was a gnat. I have to admit, it was impressive."

She giggled, the sound making me smile. "I would have liked to see that."

"I have a feeling it might happen again. She's feisty."

"And you're pigheaded. What a combination." She sighed. "I love you, big bro."

"Love you too."

I hung up and let my head fall to my chest. The scent of coffee wafted down the hall, and I knew I had to go and talk to Sammy. Apologize. Let her crow about what an idiot I was. I knew Rachel would contact her later, so I had to do it now.

Pushing myself up, I braced my fists on the desk and took in a deep breath. I just had to remember to stay far enough away that she couldn't get her hands on me. I had a feeling both her smile and her moves were her deadliest weapons.

It was like lassoing a spirited filly. Patience and determination. I could do this.

I ignored the fact that a spirited filly never caught my eye the way Sammy had. Nor had I ever wondered what it was like to kiss a spirited filly.

I ignored that fact completely.

CHAPTER FOUR

SAMMY

I heard his footsteps coming down the hall, and I braced myself. I thought I was prepared for when Luke entered the room.

I was not.

His hat was gone, his dark hair gleaming in the light. The few silver strands only made him look more handsome. He'd pulled off his plaid shirt, leaving him in a tight white T-shirt. His muscles flexed and bunched as he walked toward me. The cords in his arms were thick, his biceps the size of my upper thighs. I swore his muscles had muscles.

His thighs were massive, his jeans strained tight around the flesh. Everything about him spoke of strength. Determination. Power.

Yet when I met his eyes, the hostility was gone. Instead, they were steady, the clear blue brilliant against his tanned skin.

He looked at the plate in front of me and grimaced. "I'm sure we can find you something better to eat than that. You must be hungry."

"No, it's fine. I, um, made coffee. Kind of addicted to the stuff."

He chuckled, the sound low and throaty in his chest. "I hear you."

He opened a cupboard and took out a mug, filling it. He took a long sip and nodded in appreciation. "Good. Strong."

"No point in drinking it unless it is," I said cautiously.

He hummed in agreement as he took a chair, turning it and straddling the wide seat, his jeans stretching farther to accommodate the strain. He rested his forearm on the chairback and took another sip, then set his mug on the table.

"I believe we got off on the wrong foot."

"What part? You leaving me behind, or me taking you down on the porch?"

He chuckled again, smiling this time, the movement changing his whole face. I'd thought he was handsome before. Smiling, he was downright dangerous. His eyes crinkled, small laugh lines appearing. A deep dimple popped high on his left cheek. One side of his mouth lifted higher than the other. He displayed an easy charm in the way he pushed his hair back from his forehead. Then he winked at me.

He was devastatingly sexy.

"Impressive for a little filly like you."

I sniffed. "It's not your size. It's how you use your strength."

He nodded and looked thoughtful. "I'm sorry for leaving you stranded and being rude."

I pursed my lips. "Rachel tell you that you had to say that?"

"She might have made the suggestion."

I smiled at his honesty. "You really thought I was a man?"

He drained his mug and set it on the table. "I have a habit of half listening to Rachel at times. If she says I should have known, then I should have known. It's on me. But yes, I expected a guy with a beard, not a pretty woman with, ah…" He dropped his eyes to my chest and trailed off. "Not a woman."

"You thought I'd have a beard?" I teased.

He grinned, making that sexy dimple appear again. "The name Sam sounded as if there would be a beard, yes."

"Well, sorry, no beard. And no dick."

He gaped at me, then flung back his head in laughter. It was loud, honest, and real. It made me smile. He slapped the table and shook his head.

"Well, Lady, for not having a dick, you got some cojones on you, I'll give you that."

I shrugged. "In the family I grew up in, you needed to have balls to survive."

He wiped his eyes. "I'll remember that. Now, are you going to accept my apology?"

"Since you were so sincere, how could I refuse?"

He leaned forward, suddenly earnest. "I am sorry. I know how much Rachel has set in store for this to work. I shouldn't have overreacted, and I certainly shouldn't have taken my shock out on you. I'm glad you're so, ah, tenacious and found your way here. Give me another chance."

I met his intense gaze. His eyes were as blue as the ocean on a sunny day. Fathomless. His heavy eyebrows and long lashes set them off. They were also direct and honest.

"Why did you agree to have me here?" I asked.

He sighed. "I love this ranch, and I don't want to lose it. The beef industry has changed drastically. Prices and demand are down. Yet my costs are up. We've added a dairy aspect, but it's still a struggle. Our beef has a strong reputation of excellence and our dairy will as well, but it takes time."

"Why is demand down?"

He stood and filled his mug, bringing the pot over to top up mine. He grabbed an apple from the bowl and sat back down, rubbing the red fruit on his shirt before taking a bite. He chewed and swallowed before answering.

"There is a huge vegetarian/vegan trend. The whole cow flatulence thing. Beef took a beating with the mad cow disease scare. Consumption has gone down overall. Chicken farmers feel the effects of the trends as well. So do pig farmers. We all have to manage and bend as the world changes."

"And you have chickens too."

"Just a small brood. I also have sheep and goats. We have a few crops, but mostly for our own use."

"I see. So what changes have you seen?"

"For me, my herds are smaller. I sell fewer cattle for an even smaller profit. The grasses my animals graze on are free from insecticides. We let them roam freely over the ranch. We rotate where the cows eat so the grass has a chance to regrow. I use a technique to help spur that growth with hens."

"Hens?"

He chuckled. "I'll get into that another day. We use no growth hormones or any additives. It takes them longer to mature, which costs me more money. But I refuse to lower my standards. We have never been part of a tainted meat problem. Never had mad cow affect our livestock. But we still suffer."

"How long does it take a cow to, ah, grow?"

"About two years on a grass-fed diet."

"Wow."

He nodded, and I heard the frustration in his voice. "I want to keep the ranch producing the finest cattle. The best beef. We are completely free-range, no additives. Organic. Have been for years before it was another trend. Beef is still needed. Still wanted. It's a high source of iron and part of a healthy lifestyle. It's leaner and more nutritious now than ever—especially the grass-fed cows. Beef contains every nutrient you need in order to survive. Not many people realize that."

"I didn't," I replied.

"I assume from the snack you're eating, you're not a beef eater?" He indicated the crackers and cheese on my plate.

"No. I like beef. My whole family does. But the truth is, I was so hungry when I got off the plane, I had the driver pull into a drive-thru, and I ate in the car. But I'm snacky, and I love cheese and crackers." I flashed him a smile. "I didn't really want to rummage in your kitchen too deeply in case you tossed me out again."

A grin pulled on his lips. "You got the driver to pull into a fast-food place?"

I lifted one shoulder. "I was hungry."

He chuckled. "Okay, then."

I ate another cracker, chewing slowly.

"So, you dislike vegetarians."

He laughed. "No. To each his own. I dislike fish intensely. But I don't hate the fisherman. And I know many feel the same about beef." He narrowed his eyes. "How do you feel about fish?"

I chuckled. "I eat it on occasion, but it's not my favorite." I finished the last cracker. "So, I'm here because…?"

"Bottom line, we need more income to supplement what we bring in now. Rachel thought the idea of adding a tourist element was a good one. I wasn't big on it, but when I looked at the numbers, it made sense. The profit was good compared to the outlay, and it can happen quickly. She was the one who got in touch with you."

"It could work very well for you. I haven't seen much of the place, but I was going to go for a walk in the morning and scope it out. Start sketching more ideas. I had planned on sitting with Rachel over designs and the filming, but I guess for now, you'll have to put up with me."

He rubbed his eyes. "Does your crew arrive later?"

I shook my head. "No film crew. I do it all myself. I help with the design, the setup. The vision. Your show will feature all the renos from start to finish and promote the business."

"All yourself?" he asked, looking surprised. "I'm impressed. Again."

"I prefer the control."

"So what do you need from me?"

"I know you're busy. Rachel told me you run the show, which is why it was always the two of us talking. I can bring you up to speed fast. Show you my thoughts. I'll oversee it all. But I need some ideas from you on the things your guests will be part of. The overnight camping. The dinner under the stars. What they'll experience as a 'hand' here."

He rubbed the back of his neck. "Ideas, as in telling you or you experiencing them?"

"Experience is best."

I saw the indecision on his face. Heard the weariness in his voice. I had a feeling he was juggling so many balls in the air, he had no idea how to handle anything else. Rachel being gone with her hurt fiancé was simply another ball for him to manage.

I leaned forward. "I'll make this as easy as possible on you, Luke. I promise. I won't get in the way, and I'll try not to add to your list. Once Rachel is back, I'll deal with her."

He sighed and nodded. "Okay, then, let's do this."

I held out my hand. "Tomorrow, we start fresh, yes?"

He eyed my hand with trepidation, and I laughed. "Friends, Luke. I promise."

He wrapped his large hand around mine, his touch surprisingly gentle. "Friends. And tomorrow."

I tried not to notice how his gaze lingered on my face. How warm my hand felt in his. How sexy he was across the table from me in his T-shirt and bulging muscles. How handsome he was when he was simply being Luke.

I failed totally. But I shook his hand, trying to keep my voice calm.

"Tomorrow."

I left Luke in the kitchen, and I got ready for bed, washing my face and slipping on a tank and shorts. The room was warm, but I couldn't get the window to open, so I would have to make do until the morning. It was a nice bedroom, the wide wooden floors like silk under my feet. It was painted a pretty shade of blue with white wainscoting on the bottom half of the walls. The old-fashioned bed was high off the floor, the iron headboard gleaming in the light. The furniture was antique, and so was the throw rug that graced the polished wooden floor. A club chair was in the corner, complete with cushions and a table with a nice light to read by. The windows were big, and the view I had seen earlier was spectacular. Wide-open fields, cows grazing, wheat dancing in the breeze in the distance. I could hardly wait to get out and explore in the morning.

It was still early, so I opened my Kindle and read for a while, but with the door closed, the room became stuffier. I got up and pulled on the windows, but they both remained stuck. I opened the door, hearing nothing but silence. I crept to the kitchen and poured a glass of water, amazed at the difference in the temperature of the rooms. It was so much cooler out of the bedroom. I opened a couple of drawers, hoping to find a screwdriver or something I could use to help loosen the windows, but I came up empty-handed. I slid the drawer shut, then recalled the back room I had peeked in earlier. It looked like a storeroom of sorts. A hodgepodge of odds and ends. I bet I could find something to help loosen the window.

I opened the door leading to the room off the kitchen. I pulled on the string that led to the bare bulb overhead, but nothing happened. But I found a flashlight, and I turned it on, casting the light on the shelves. I saw a basket with a screwdriver handle sticking out of it and, pleased, I set down the flashlight, dragging over a small step stool and reaching up for the basket. I was about to step down when a sudden sound startled me.

"What the hell——" a voice growled. I twirled, gasping at the sight of Luke, holding a baseball bat high, ready to swing.

I stumbled, falling off the step, the basket flying from my grasp. My head glanced off the shelves, and I cried out as the metal connected with my skin, an instant throbbing headache starting. I shut my eyes as the floor rushed up to meet me, shocked when a set of strong arms prevented me from hitting the floor. I blinked up into a pair of confused, bright-blue eyes.

"What are you doing?"

"It's hot," I gasped, a wave of dizziness rushing over me. "Window."

Then I blacked out.

LUKE

I was lying in bed, dozing, when I heard it. A noise coming from the kitchen. I sat up, listening, about to lie back when I heard it again. It wasn't coming from the kitchen, but the back storeroom.

I heard the sounds of movement and items being shifted. I highly doubted it was Sammy. Why would she be poking around in a storeroom at midnight?

Was there a burglar? Had an animal gotten in?

Both seemed highly doubtful, but I had to go and check. Holding my baseball bat, I crept down the hall, looking toward the other end. The master bedroom and my office ran off the left side of the kitchen, while the two guest rooms ran off the right side, along with Rachel's room. Sammy's door was shut—or at least pulled closed. Another noise drew me toward the storeroom. I saw the beam of a flashlight moving, and I lifted the bat higher, wondering what I would be met with and what the hell they were looking for in the storeroom.

Nothing shocked me more than to find Sammy on a stool, holding a basket of gardening tools.

"What the hell?" I demanded.

My voice startled her. She gasped and swung around, the tools going everywhere as she pitched forward. I dropped the bat, grabbing her before she hit the floor but after her head smacked the side of the shelf. The sound of her skull meeting the metal edge sickened me.

"What are you doing?" I demanded, swinging her up into my arms.

She gazed up at me, dazed and confused.

"It's hot. Window," she muttered, then went limp in my arms.

Cursing, I carried her out of the storeroom and down the hall to the room she was staying in. I pushed open the door, noticing the temperature of the room. I laid her on the bed and hurried to the window, unlocking it and opening it wide, letting the cool night air rush in. Then I returned to the kitchen, grabbing an ice pack from the freezer and a wet cloth.

Back in her room, I ran the cloth over her skin. I had felt how warm she was as I carried her down the hall. Then I took the ice pack and wrapped it in the cloth, laying it on her head. A lump was forming on the skin, and I knew she was going to have a bad headache when she woke up.

I stared down at her, swallowing deeply. She wore a skimpy tank top and shorts—neither of them doing much to cover her or hide her from my greedy gaze. She was tiny but perfectly formed. Lush breasts filled her tank top, her nipples showing through the thin material. Her hips were rounded, highlighting the indent of her waist. I wondered briefly what it would be like to hold those hips. Watch her ride me. Suck those nipples into my mouth and flick them with my tongue as they pebbled and stiffened under my touch.

Jesus, I needed to stop thinking that way. Because of me, she'd fallen and hurt herself. Now I was having lustful fantasies about her?

"Get a grip, asshole," I muttered to myself.

I shook my head to clear the thoughts and grasped her shoulders, shaking them gently. "Wake up, Sammy."

She stirred, mumbling, and I let out a relieved breath. "Sammy," I repeated. "Wake up."

Her eyes opened, and she frowned. "Luke?"

41

"Yeah, it's me." I searched her confused gaze. "Are you okay? Do I need to take you to the hospital?"

She frowned. "Why would—" Her eyes flew open wider, startled. "Why are you in my room?"

"You were in the storeroom. I thought there was a burglar, and I startled you. What the hell were you doing in there?"

"I was hot. I couldn't open the window. I was looking for a screwdriver."

I indicated the windows. "That wouldn't have helped. There's a locking mechanism in the handle. I should have told you, but I didn't think."

"Oh God," she said then sat up, holding her head. "Ouch, that hurts."

"Let me see."

With a frown, she tilted her head back, and I brushed the soft hair away, examining the lump. "No broken skin, but it's a nice goose egg." I met her gaze. "I'm sorry I startled you."

Something passed between us as we studied each other. Something warm, intense, and new. I was even more aware of how few clothes she was wearing. The fact that I only had sleep pants on. Two layers of clothing easily removed. I realized how close I was to her—another couple of inches and our chests would brush each other. Our mouths could connect. Her eyes widened, and her breathing picked up. She felt the same thing—the same draw. I moved a little, bringing myself nearer. She inhaled sharply. I narrowed my gaze to her mouth. It tempted me. Strongly.

Except as she lifted her head, she whimpered. It wasn't a sound of pleasure but one of pain. I pulled back, shocked at how close I had come to kissing her.

"I'll get you some Tylenol."

I rushed from the room, heading to the kitchen to get the pills. I poured some water for her and took a minute to calm my raging body. My heart raced as if I'd run a mile. My blood strummed through my veins, pulsating to its own beat. My hand shook as I opened the bottle. My cock was heavy, erect, and ready.

I hadn't expected this sort of reaction at being close to Sammy. If she hadn't have whimpered in pain, I had no doubt she'd be under me right now. I wouldn't be wondering how her mouth would taste. I would know.

It was unacceptable.

I dragged in long breaths. Thought of unpleasant things. Cleaning the barn. Shoveling manure. Anything to stop the other thoughts from staying in my head. Once I was sure I was under control, I returned to the bedroom, grateful to find Sammy had pulled a light blanket over herself. I gave her the pills and watched as she took them.

"I'm sorry," she whispered.

"It's not your fault. I should have thought about the fact that the room would be warm. It always is since it gets the last of the sunlight."

"I meant—"

I cut her off. "I know what you meant. Nothing happened. Nothing will. Now, you go to sleep. I'll check on you in a few hours."

"You don't have to do that."

"Yes, I do. The last thing I need is you dying on me the first night." I offered her a grin, wanting to lighten the atmosphere. "Rachel will definitely think I had something to do with it."

She chuckled, holding her head when the action caused her some discomfort.

"I'll leave the hall light on and the door open. It'll help with air flow."

"Okay."

The last thing I saw before I snapped off the light was the sad look on her face. I didn't like it.

I touched her cheek in the dark. "Everything is good, darlin'. Just go to sleep. I'll watch over you."

Then I left her, shocked at how hard it was to do so.

CHAPTER FIVE

LUKE

I left her, but I couldn't relax. Ten minutes later, I was back
in her room. She was sleeping, her breathing deep and
even. With a huff of air, I sat in the chair in the corner,
already knowing there would be no sleep for me tonight. Her
Kindle was on the armchair, and curious, I opened it, chuckling
as I read a page of the book she had been reading. Historical
romance. Not what I had figured her to read. My curiosity grew,
and I searched her library, finding a variety of genres. Seeing a
new murder mystery book I had been wanting to read, I opened
it and settled back. Might as well take advantage of the time.

I spent the night reading and checking on her. Every two hours, I
gently woke her, made her tell me her name and mine, had her
drink some water, and let her go back to sleep. By the third wake-
up, she was grumpy and out of sorts, almost snarling when I
shook her awake, not even giving me time to ask her anything.

"Dammit," she cursed. "Luke Adler. Sammy Morrison. It's Tues-
day, for heaven's sake, and I hit my head." Then she pushed away
the water, rolled over, and began to snore. I straightened, trying

not to laugh. Little Miss Mouthy was back, which, I was certain, indicated she was fine, but I stayed and finished reading the book. I had to be up soon anyway.

The morning air was chilly, and I made sure she was tucked in, leaving her sleeping, figuring she'd have a headache when she woke up and needed the rest. I showered and changed, drank a cup of coffee, and headed out to start my chores. I sighed as I stepped outside, inhaling the fresh air deeply. I set my hat on my head and sauntered toward the barn, already tired. I had a feeling today was gonna be a long-ass day.

SAMMY

I woke up, confused and buried under a pile of blankets. I yanked them off me and sat up, looking around. It took me a moment, and then yesterday came back to me.

All of it.

The airport. The altercation with Luke. The apology. The storeroom. Gingerly, I touched my head, wincing at the lump. I padded over to the mirror and looked at the bruised flesh. Luckily, the skin hadn't broken, but it was going to be sore for a while. Behind me, the curtains waved in the breeze, and I walked over, studying the ingenious locks I'd never noticed. I had flipped the ones on the sash open, but these were hidden in the handles. Clever.

I recalled looking for the screwdriver. Being startled by Luke's voice. How he had caught me. The strength of his arms cradling me. The warmth of his skin seeping into mine. How he had woken me in the night, checking on me. Glancing down, I felt myself blush. My tank top and shorts didn't leave much to the imagination—and he had seen it all. And thanks to my little fall, I knew he'd been up all night, waking me, making sure I was okay. No doubt he was the one who had bundled me up like a burrito in the blankets.

What an impression I must have made on him. I wouldn't be surprised if he asked me to leave again later today.

I got ready in jeans and a light T-shirt and headed to the kitchen, realizing it was past eight. I assumed Luke was long gone and thinking I was being lazy. I was surprised to find him at the table, eating a plate of eggs and toast.

"Morning," I muttered, slightly embarrassed.

"Well, if it isn't my little cat burglar. Going for the gardening shears, were you?"

I huffed out a laugh. "Sorry about that. I thought I saw a screwdriver handle. To help open the windows."

He waved me off, grinning around a mouthful of eggs. "Nope. Trowel. Wouldn't have helped you much unless you decided to head outside and weed the garden." Then he frowned. "I'm sorry for startling you. How's the head?"

"A bit sore."

"No doubt." He indicated the stove. "I made eggs. You'll have to look after your own toast."

I scooped some eggs onto a plate and waited for the toast. I carried my plate and coffee to the table. He finished his breakfast and grabbed an apple, biting into it.

"Thanks," I said, indicating the food on my plate.

He smiled. "I always eat after the first round of chores."

"I don't expect you to cook for me."

"I eat a big breakfast every morning. A decent lunch. Supper too. I work hard. We all do."

"How big is the ranch?"

"Over six hundred acres."

"Wow."

"That's considered an average size."

"Hmm. How many cattle?"

"I have five herds—about eighty in each. The number varies as they are born, sold, et cetera."

"What does a typical day look like?"

"Up early, coffee. Rotating the herds, checking the health of all the animals, mending fences, milking the cows, gathering eggs, checking on the sheep and moving them, to name a few. Plus, there is paperwork, sales, budgets, running the ranch, payroll, and so on."

"Wow. You have help, I assume?"

He nodded, chewing the last of his apple and swallowing. I tried not to notice how his neck muscles shifted and pulled as he ate. The way his Adam's apple bobbed and moved. It was surprisingly sexy. "I employ lots of people. The numbers vary, but I have a foreman, two, in fact, plus other full-timers. My dad always believed in working smarter not harder. I can spend all day mending fences, or have someone do it and concentrate on other, more important things. Some things I can't hand off, like the paperwork or budgets, but I work on those with Rachel, and I have an accountant who helps."

"And cooking meals?" I asked, finishing my eggs. "This was delicious."

"There's a cook and a cookhouse. Everyone works hard, and I feed them breakfast and lunch. Dinner when need be or snacks. But the cookhouse is open all day so the crew can eat."

"All men?" I asked, curious.

"No. I have cowgirls too. Some of them are better than the men I hire. I believe it's your heart, not your dick, that makes you a cowboy." He winked.

I laughed.

"What are your plans?" he asked.

"I'm going to scope out the ranch. Look at the buildings Rachel thought would make great bunkhouses. Gather some ideas and then meet with you or Rachel and get a plan together."

He nodded, draining his cup. "Rachel says people are willing to pay a lot of money for an experience like this."

I nodded. "They are. But you have to give them what they want, plus some unexpected perks."

"Like?"

"Rustic but modern. Ride a horse, but a comfortable bed. Easy meals, but delicious. Sleep under the stars, but no snakes. A real campfire, but marshmallows to roast. Glamping."

He frowned. "Glamping?"

"Glamorized camping."

He shook his head. "But that's not real."

"We're not selling them real, Luke. We're selling them an escape. They don't want to shovel shit in the barn. They want to walk the fields. Eat under the stars and listen to cowboys tell stories of the old days. That's what they want."

He shook his head. "Anything else?"

"Yes. Cowboys who tip their hats and say 'howdy' and 'ma'am,' but know what the Wi-Fi password is. Someone named Cookie making their breakfast. The illusion of being a ranch hand for a week."

He lifted an eyebrow. "I see."

"The beauty is you can decide the limits. Four people max. Ten people. One week. Three days. You can build the package. Tell them what they get. Then you surprise them. Add in a couple unexpected things. Their own cowboy hat. A bathtub under the stars that looks like a horse water bowl—"

"Excuse me?" He laughed. "A horse water bowl? You mean a trough?"

"Yes. A simple romantic fantasy many have about a ranch."

He shook his head. "There isn't much romantic about a ranch. And my biggest fear is the interruption of the work. Or someone having over-the-top fantasies about cowboys."

"Like I said, you can decide. You can structure where they are allowed to go. Rules can be set in place. We can start small and build up. Assign certain staff to the tourists. But if you make them happy, word will spread. They'll return. Some are simply looking to escape their daily grind."

"Life is a grind here as well."

"But to them, it's different. And they'll only see the beauty and peace of this place." I winked. "You hide the business behind the façade. Like Disney."

He stood and stretched. "This all makes me uncomfortable, Lady. But I'm going to do as my sister asked and keep an open mind." He paused by my chair, lowering his face. I blinked, my heart rate picking up.

Was he about to kiss me?

Instead, his long fingers tilted my chin up, and he looked at my forehead. I inhaled, smelling straw, fresh air, and something distinctly masculine. He touched the lump, his fingers gentle, and shook his head. "Be careful today, Sammy. Wear a hat. And sunscreen. You'll burn." Straightening, he placed his hat on his head, looking sexy and worried. "The cookhouse has a weathervane on top of it. You can't miss it. Callie will feed you when you get hungry."

Then he walked out.

I put the dishes in the dishwasher and looked around the house, feeling curious. The sizable living room had a beautiful fireplace, all done in river rock, the stones smooth and almost glossy in the sunlight. A thick wooden mantel held a few pictures, and I studied them. There was a family portrait, and I smiled as I saw how much Luke looked like his dad. Tall, strong, and handsome. Rachel resembled their mother, but they both had their dad's blue eyes. Their mom was tall, blond, and willowy. They were a nice-looking family.

The same wide wood floors were throughout the house. Worn, comfortable furniture. Old, hand-braided rugs were scattered around. A TV in the corner was the most modern item in the room. The kitchen was expansive and lined with lots of cupboards. A huge island with a butcher block top was well used. There was a massive table in the dining area and French doors that led outside to a deck that was home to a monster grill and a smoker. My dad had one just like it back in Port Albany.

I turned back to the interior. Everything was homey and warm. Two hefty fans moved slowly, keeping the room cool. I peeked in the other rooms on my side of the house then, after hesitating a moment, walked into Luke's room. I told myself it was part of my tour, but mainly, I was curious about it. The furniture was heavy and masculine. A king-size bed with a sturdy frame. A tall dresser. A large chair in the corner, with a pile of books on the table beside it. There was an en suite, and I peeked in. His damp towel was thrown over the top of the door, and the room smelled like him. Crisp. Clean. Fresh air mixed with spices. Sage, maybe? Something subtle but pleasing. The room was neat, the walls white and the bedding navy. All simple, organized, and somehow, very Luke. His closet door was open, and I saw a variety of plaid shirts hanging inside, and on top of his dresser was a folded pile of T-shirts. Obviously, his standard "uniform" for the day. I resisted sniffing them.

Barely.

His office held boxes of paperwork. Files. A computer with a large screen. It wasn't messy, but it wasn't neat either—a work in progress, my dad would say. A pair of glasses sat on a pile of paperwork. I picked them up. Classic, straight black frames— they would highlight his blue eyes perfectly. I could only imagine how sexy he looked in the timeless eyeglasses. I wasn't sure I'd survive that.

I hurried down the hall and chose a light sweater in case it became cool. After taking another couple of Tylenol, I put on some sun block and grabbed my phone, a sketchbook, and a camera, putting all the items into my knapsack. I stopped and grabbed a bottle of water and an apple, then headed outside, gazing around. Everywhere was busy. In the distance, I could see people on horseback. I heard the cows, the sounds of distant conversations. Faint music playing. Muted machinery. I saw the cookhouse not too far away, and I could smell something sweet on the air. Farther past the cookhouse were the structures Rachel had talked about that she thought could be revamped into sleeping quarters for the guests. I slung my knapsack over my shoulder and started exploring.

A couple of hours later, I sat by the river, still in wonder at the beauty around me. The sounds, the scents, the peace—all so different from Port Albany, where I spent most of my time. It was lovely at home, but the expanse of space here—the rolling hills and green grass, the blue of the sky—it was breathtaking. I had walked for what felt like miles, crisscrossing the ranch several times. I had stopped by the cookhouse and introduced myself to Callie, who handed me a cinnamon bun the size of my head that I munched on while I walked. I checked out the buildings. Saw the cows. The large stable that held the horses used on the ranch. The barn. The huge chicken coop. And I knew I hadn't seen everything. It was an impressive operation.

I scanned the area but couldn't see the ranch from here so decided this was a good place for a break. I'd find my way back in a short while. I pulled out my sketchbook and scrolled through the photos I'd taken of the buildings Rachel had directed me to.

They would work perfectly for the ideas I had. I jotted down notes, ideas, and thoughts. Started lists, created must-have scenes for filming. I took a drink of my water and rolled up my jeans, sitting on a boulder by the river with my feet in the water. I realized where the ranch got its name. River rock filled the bed, the banks, and larger boulders and pieces were scattered all along the winding waterway. It seemed to circle a big area of the ranch before branching off into the distance. I would have to ask Luke about it. Rachel had mentioned an area where the water flowed into a natural swimming hole they used in the summer. People would love that. For now, I enjoyed the coolness on my feet.

I began to draw. The property had three structures that would be perfect for Rachel's plan. The largest one could contain sleeping quarters and a common area for people who wanted to sit and relax. I could easily fit six bunk beds in the back area. I was thrilled to find the buildings already had plumbing since they had been living quarters at one time. I would have to discuss all the requirements with Luke regarding septic tanks, or maybe we used composting toilets. I scribbled a note. The second building was smaller—one large room and a bath. I could do another six bunks and a few chairs for sitting. The smallest building could be for those who preferred privacy or a small group that liked to be on their own. Four bunks, a bathroom, and a table and chairs. The structures were sound, even the roofs in good shape. Some floors, updated wiring and fixtures, the furniture and touches, as well as plumbing, were the main things needed. I couldn't help but think of my dad and how much he would enjoy a project like this. I could see him, Aiden, Ronan, and Hunter working here—enjoying the sun, riding the horses, eating at the cookhouse, and building the sleeping quarters. Even at his age, my dad still loved everything to do with construction. I tucked that idea away to think about later. I worked for a bit, then slipped the book back into the knapsack.

I sipped the water I'd brought, warm now, but it helped with the thirst. I took out the apple and set it on the rock, taking off my hat and lifting my face to the sun. I leaned back on my hands, enjoying the peace and warmth. With a sigh, I stood and carefully waded into the river. It was shallow at the edge, barely coming up to my calves, but the rocks were slippery so I moved slowly. I walked around, enjoying the cool water, eating the apple, and planning in my head. I was already excited about this project, and now that I had seen the ranch and breathtaking vistas, I was eager to start.

As usual when I was in deep planning mode, I lost track of time and my surroundings. My head was filled with ideas, colors, ways of marketing the ranch. I would definitely be talking to Richard and picking his brain. He would love to give me his opinion— Richard always liked to share his thoughts—and he would have a lot of them about this place.

A noise startled me, and I pivoted, the sight of a cowboy standing beside a horse by the edge of the river unnerving me. I had been so deep in thought I hadn't even heard them approach. My foot slipped on the rocks, and I threw up my arms, trying to right myself, but it was too late. With a loud yelp, I went backward into the water, the cool suddenly cold as my entire body was submerged in the deeper part of the shallows. My apple flew from my hand as I went under, but I barely had time to be startled before I was yanked back up, Luke's frantic expression greeting me.

"Jesus, woman. Do you try to kill yourself daily?" he demanded.

I sputtered. "I think you keep trying to. You scared me again."

He narrowed his eyes. "I called to you. I've been looking for you for half an hour."

"Looking for me?"

"No one has seen you for two hours. I was worried." He dropped his arms. "This isn't the city, Sammy. You have to pay attention to where you are and your surroundings."

"Are there many lions prowling about?" I asked dryly, wiping my face.

He bent closer, the brim of his hat throwing a shadow between us. "There are coyotes. Bears. Even some snakes."

I shivered. I hated snakes. "I was fine. Nothing was around. Until you showed up." Something caught my eye, and I frowned. "My apple is floating away."

He looked over his shoulder, dismissing my words. I pushed past him and waded carefully, following my apple. It was good, and I had barely eaten half of it.

"Leave it," he growled.

"No."

"I said—"

I didn't hear what else he had to say. Again, I slipped, going under. And once more, he appeared beside me, dragging me up to the air. "Goddammit. I said leave it. I'll get you another damn apple. Stop trying to drown yourself!"

"Stop telling me what to do!" I yelled back, then without thought, pushed him.

He hadn't expected me, and with the slippery rocks beneath him, he went under with a big splash. I covered my mouth with my hands, shocked at my behavior. He stood slowly, dripping wet, glaring at me, obviously as surprised as I was by my actions. I tried not to laugh, but I failed. A wide smile broke out on my face, and I started giggling. I covered my mouth, but it was no use.

"You find this funny? Me all soaked?"

I nodded in silence, unable to talk, the peals of laughter getting louder.

Until he stood taller, shedding his plaid shirt, leaving his T-shirt in place. It and his jeans clung to him like a second skin, lovingly wrapped around his muscles and showing them off. I spied a tattoo on his right shoulder, and I had a sudden, burning desire to know what it was. I swallowed, my throat feeling dry as I stared at him, unable to help myself. He was a work of art.

His gaze never left mine as he tossed his shirt to the bank. His hat followed with a lazy flip of his hand. My apple floated by, and he bent, plucking it from the water and taking a huge bite, chewing slowly.

"Hey," I protested. "That was my apple."

He polished it off with another large bite, tossing the core far into the field where a mouse or bird would pick at it.

He shrugged. "Whoops," he said.

I bent, swiping at the water, splashing it into his face.

A wide, wicked grin appeared on his face as he wiped away the water.

"You're going to pay for that, darlin'," he said, his voice low and threatening.

"Bring it on," I replied, my gaze darting around, looking for an escape route.

In a flash, he moved, and I ducked with a squeal. He went down again, coming up out of the water like an angry bear, his growl impressive and deep. I turned and tried to run, but my feet slipped, and he was on me before I could go anywhere. He lifted me, tossing me into the middle of the narrow river channel, and I went under, coming up this time on my own, laughing and trying to find my feet. I pretended to flail, and I gasped. "Luke, it's too deep!"

He lunged, and I moved so he went in face first. I was laughing so hard, I found it difficult to move, but I headed to the bank, rushing as I heard him behind me. Once again, I was lifted out of the water, but this time, he tossed me onto the bank, hovering over me.

"Now where you gonna go, Lady? I got you trapped."

My response died in my throat as our eyes met. His gaze darkened, dropping to my chest and back to my mouth. My nipples were cold and wet from the water, hard pebbles under my thin shirt. I ached to feel his mouth on them, warming the buds but keeping them hard for another reason entirely. My breath caught as he lowered his chin, rubbing against one, his gaze never leaving mine.

"I might buck you off," I threatened, my voice weak.

"I'd like to see you try," he responded, sinking lower, his chest pressing into mine. His heat was shocking through my wet clothes, his power and strength evident. Yet I felt no fear.

Only desire.

I wanted to feel his lips on mine. His hands on my body. If I was honest, I had wanted to feel that from the moment I saw him across the airport.

I shifted my hips, and he groaned, the sound erotic. He rolled his hips, and I felt him, hard and big, through the layers of fabric.

I couldn't resist. I didn't want to.

I pulled his mouth to mine.

CHAPTER SIX

LUKE

J esus, her mouth. I thought her smile was pure sunshine, but nothing compared to the heat that hit me when I slid my tongue inside to meet hers. Desire, hot and potent, licked up my spine, turning my cock into steel. I slanted my head, going deeper into the wetness of her kiss. She tasted of apple, sweet and tart, and something unique—something I was certain was just Sammy.

I knew I shouldn't be kissing her. But I was powerless to stop.

I had caught glimpses of her all morning, walking, exploring. Talking to Callie and some of the hands. Peeking at the cows and horses. She had a book in her hands she wrote in constantly. My curiosity raged, wanting to know what she was writing. I got busy with a hurt horse and then realized I hadn't seen her for a long time, so I went searching.

I had seen her on the boulder, her head lifted to the sun, her honey-colored hair a mass of brilliant gold falling behind her. She stood, walking into the water, her hands on her hips, seemingly lost in thought. I was certain she would have heard me walking up with Maverick trailing behind me, but once again, I startled her. When she fell into the river, I rushed to get her, worried she had hurt herself. What happened after was as unexpected as it was delightful. Her surprising push. Her teasing. The laughter she had brought to the surface. No one could make me laugh the way she seemed to.

It was that damn smile of hers. Pure sunshine.

And now with her under me, I wanted to feel her heat in a completely different way.

She whimpered in pleasure, her arms tightening around my neck. I sat up, bringing her with me so she straddled my lap. The wet denim covering our legs was coarse and rough. Her mouth was smooth, her tongue silky and sweet. I slid my hands under her wet shirt, tugging on the hem. I wanted to know how her skin felt against mine.

Until I heard it. The sound of a horse approaching. Maverick whinnied, and with a low curse, I stood, pushing Sammy away. She stumbled but remained upright, her gaze confused.

"Someone is coming," I said, heading toward my shirt and hat lying on the bank.

I looked toward the hill, Jeff appearing at the crest. He waved and trotted over. "Found her, did you?"

"Yep."

"Went for a swim?" he asked, lifting one eyebrow in question at our wet clothes.

"I slipped in the river, and when Luke tried to help me, he fell too," Sammy said, extending her hand. "I'm Sammy, by the way."

He bent, shaking her hand, then with a wink, tipped his hat. "Howdy, ma'am."

Sammy laughed, clapping her hands. "Perfect!"

Jeff laughed, and I felt a grin pulling on my lips. I had told him what she had said as we were patrolling the borders, checking fences. He had chuckled, finding it all as confusing as I did. But he had obviously listened.

He straightened in the saddle. "Okay. I'll, ah, leave you to it. Callie saved you some lunch, Sammy. It's her homemade stew— you don't want to miss my wife's stew."

"Thanks," Sammy replied.

Jeff met my eyes. "She saved you some too, boss."

"Great. I'll be along shortly."

He nodded and turned his horse, moving away.

Sammy and I stood watching him, then I turned to her. Her mouth was swollen, her eyes bright. Her hair was a mess and her cheeks were flushed, but all of that could be put down to a dunk in the river.

At least that was what I told myself.

"Should I apologize?" I asked.

"For what? Kissing me?"

I rubbed a hand over my chin, feeling the thick stubble under my fingers. "Yeah."

63

"Well, since I kissed you right back, I would say no."

"It was just an impulse. I got caught up in the moment," I informed her. "It shouldn't have happened, and it won't happen again."

She frowned. "It won't?"

"No. You're here to do a job, and I'm not looking to start anything. Or interfere with your job."

"So basically, you *are* apologizing."

"I'm setting the rules."

She pursed her lips. "The rules. Right. No kissing. Okay."

A beat of silence passed, and I found myself unable to look her in the eye.

"You should change out of those wet clothes and get lunch."

She nodded. "Point the way to the ranch, and I'll head back."

I called to Maverick, who was standing under the shade of a tree, chewing grass. He walked over, and I grabbed the reins and held out my hand. "Get your stuff, and you can ride back with me." When she hesitated, I frowned. "It's perfectly safe."

I took her knapsack and wrapped my arm around her waist, lifting her to the front of the saddle. I swung myself up behind her and handed her back the knapsack. I felt a shudder run through her, and I pulled her into my chest. "Don't be afraid, darlin'. We'll go slow."

I urged Maverick forward and, in an instant, realized what a huge mistake this had been. I could feel every inch of her pressed to me. The top of her head was right under my chin, and I could smell the soft fragrance in the waves of her hair. My cock roared back to life and was trapped between us. Every step Maverick took, every roll of our bodies, connected us.

Perfectly safe?

I was totally fucked.

SAMMY

Oh my God, he was huge. He surrounded me, his muscles rippling, his breathing heavy. I felt his erection, hard and pressed against my lower back. I heard his low, muttered curses. The desire I had felt when his mouth was on mine hadn't abated. It was only heightened now. He felt it too.

His laughter and teasing in the river had been unexpected. His kisses even more so. He tasted of the apple he ate, coffee, and mint. He was delicious.

And the man could kiss. His tongue was addictive, his mouth a hidden treasure I wanted to explore over and over again. I was sure if his foreman hadn't shown up, I would have been naked with him on that rock, writhing in ecstasy as he took me. Riding that stallion would have been far more pleasurable than this one. Maverick seemed like a nice horse and all, but I was certain what was trapped between us would be even better.

He had said no more kissing. It was a mistake.

He was lying. I knew it. I felt the heat between us. Felt the desire in his kiss and the need his body pushed into mine.

I wasn't a young girl, crushing on a cowboy, thinking she'd found her Prince Charming. I was a woman, quite capable of deciding whom she slept with and when. I was well aware of the differences between us and our worlds, but I had zero expectations. I saw nothing wrong with a little romance, a fling, while I was here.

I simply had to make him understand that. From the feel of his erection, part of him was already on board with it. I only had to make the rest of him comprehend that.

We were quiet on the ride. I was surprised at how far I was away from the ranch and grateful Luke had come to find me. He went directly to the house, swinging off Maverick and holding up his hands to help me down as if he had done it a hundred times. I slid from the horse, landing on my feet with a little oomph of air escaping.

"That's a long way up," I said to break the tension between us.

He snorted and rolled his eyes. "That's because you're so short, Lady." Our eyes met and locked, the heat flaring between us instantly. He stepped back, shaking his head. "Go change and get your lunch." He turned and walked away, heading for the door.

"Hey," I called. "Don't you need to lock your horse?"

He stopped and turned, his voice incredulous. "*Lock* my horse?"

"Tie him up or something. Someone could take him, or he might wander off."

He shook his head. "Unlike you, Lady, he listens to what I say. He doesn't need to be tethered to stay in place. You, on the other hand…" He trailed off. "Might not be a bad idea."

Then he turned and headed inside. But he was laughing and muttering about locking his horse. I grinned. I knew that would get a reaction.

But what I hadn't expected was the spread of warmth in my lower belly when he mentioned tethering *me*.

I probably wouldn't object.

———

Luke was gone when I came out of my room. I tried not to feel disappointed. Maybe it was for the best and he was right. I was here to do a job, not have hot sex with a cowboy.

Although, I would consider that a perk.

I wandered to the cookhouse, feeling hungry. Callie was busy rolling out dough when I walked in. She smiled at me, wiping her hands. "There you are. I was wondering if we lost you the first day!"

I shook my head, and she bustled around, handing me a tray. "Sit and eat."

"Can you join me?"

She nodded. "Let me get a cup of coffee."

I took a mouthful of the stew she ladled into the bowl, groaning at the flavor. "Oh my God, this is so good."

She chuckled and sat down. "With all your exploring, you must be hungry." Her lips twitched. "Not to mention your swim in the river."

I had to laugh as I dipped the soft, fluffy bread she'd given me in the thick, rich broth. "Luke startled me, and I fell in."

"Is that how you got that goose egg?"

I shook my head, swallowing before I replied. "No, that was last night. I'm not usually so clumsy."

She shrugged, her eyes dancing. "Something got you distracted, honey?"

I met her gaze. She was about my age, pretty, with soft brown hair and dark eyes. Tall and slender, she was also strong. I had watched her lift a fifty-pound sack of flour that morning like it was nothing. Slap a huge piece of beef onto the cutting board like it was a loaf of bread. Her arms were toned and tight. I wouldn't mess with her.

"Um, no?"

The door opened, and Luke walked in. He was in fresh jeans and a tight T-shirt that showed off every delicious muscle on his torso and arms. Remembering how his chest felt pressed into mine, the power and strength in his arms as he tossed me, hovered over me, made me blush, and I dropped my eyes, spooning more of the delicious stew into my mouth to cover the whimper that wanted to escape.

Callie stood with a grin. "Never known the boss to swim midday before either."

"She pushed me," Luke said, sitting down. "I'm hungry. You got any stew left, or you too busy gossiping with the city gal to get me some lunch?"

She shook her head. "Always so charming. Are you telling me this city gal pushed you into the water?"

"I am."

"Hmmph."

"What?" He narrowed his eyes at her.

"Bowled over, I suppose some would say."

"Get me my lunch," he growled.

She walked away laughing. I kept my eyes on my lunch, eating and keeping my mouth busy.

"You got all you needed this morning?" he asked.

I resisted telling him I still needed to have him inside me. Instead, I nodded.

"Got some ideas?"

I nodded again, stuffing bread into my mouth to stay quiet.

He tilted his head. "Nothing to say, Lady? Cat got your tongue?"

I shrugged.

Callie called over. "Come get your tray, Luke. I'm not a waitress."

Luke unfurled himself from the chair. "I'm coming. Keep your shirt on."

He stopped by my chair, bending low, his voice a whisper in my ear. "Lucky damn cat."

I fought not to choke on my bread. He patted my back in mock concern. "Careful, Lady. Don't want you to hurt yourself." Then he sauntered over and took the tray from Callie. "I'm eating outside. I got some calls to make."

I glared at his retreating back.

I owed him for that one.

———————

Callie sat back down, shaking her head. "That man. Pain in my ass. Him and my husband."

I laughed. "Aren't they all?"

She chuckled. "Probably."

"Have you been here long?"

She smiled and took a sip of her coffee. "I grew up not far from here. Met Jeff when I was twenty, and we got married. Jeff has known Luke his whole life. He worked here for a long time. I worked in town at the diner, and when Luke decided to start up the tradition of a cookhouse again, I took on the job."

"You enjoy it?"

"I love it. I love cooking and baking, and there is only so much I can cook for us at home, which was one reason I worked at the diner. Here, I get to feed all the hands, and it satisfies me." A sad look crossed her face. "We were never able to have kids, so looking after all the people here helps."

"I'm sorry."

She shrugged, smiling again. "I accepted it a long time ago. I love it here."

"Do you know about the plans Rachel has?"

She nodded. "I have so many ideas for menus and cookout plans. I was hoping to maybe teach a class or two. Cowboy food. I can hardly wait to see it happen."

"Awesome idea. That's great." I was thrilled with her enthusiasm. "I hope Rachel is able to be part of it, once her fiancé is on the mend."

"I talked to her this morning. Tyler is awake and doing well. He needs time to heal, but he should be home soon. She's like Luke, and she'll have it all under control."

I finished my bowl of stew. "That is great news, and that was the best stew I have ever eaten. I hope that's on your menu."

She nodded. "Yep. I'm even planning some vegetarian meals." She wrinkled her nose. "Although I'm not sure you'd come to a cattle ranch if you don't eat meat."

I laughed. "You never know. To be on the safe side, yes, some vegan and vegetarian options would be good, just in case. The guests will have to provide all that information ahead of time so you won't be surprised."

"Good. Dessert?" she asked.

"Dessert?" I responded. "You have dessert?"

Luke walked back in, his tray in hand. "Did I hear dessert?"

She stood. "Jam roly-poly."

He groaned. "Give it to me."

She cocked an eyebrow at him, waiting.

"Please," he added.

She nodded. "Better."

"What is it?" I asked.

"Think of a hot jelly roll. With custard."

"Sounds wonderful."

He nodded, taking his bowl with a muttered thanks before disappearing again.

I tried to hide my smile. She treated him like a wayward child, even though I thought she was a few years younger than him. And the cute part was that he allowed her to do so.

I had a feeling there were many layers to Luke Adler.

I looked forward to peeling them all back.

CHAPTER SEVEN

LUKE

I walked into the house around six. I was tired, sore, and hungry. In other words, a regular day on the ranch. With one exception. The house wasn't empty.

Sitting at the table in the kitchen was Sammy. She had a laptop open, papers scattered around her, and she was writing furiously on a notepad. Her brow was furrowed in thought, and her pink tongue stuck out the side of her mouth in concentration. Her hair was gathered into a knot on the top of her head, and I saw the reddened skin on her neck and back where her loose sweater slipped from her skin.

"I told you to wear sunscreen," I announced, heading her way. "Are you in pain?"

She blinked at me, tapping a pencil on the end of her nose.

"Hello, Sammy," she drawled. "How was the rest of your afternoon?"

"Don't be giving me lip, Lady. You'll be sorry. Your neck is sunburned."

"I'm aware. I missed the back of my neck and top of my back. Hazard of having short arms. It's fine."

I huffed out a sigh. "Okay, what—" I stopped, drawing in a deep lungful of air. Something smelled incredible. "What have you done?"

"I asked Callie, and she said you usually stopped around six. I dug some stuff out of the freezer and made dinner. It's just a casserole—one my mom made all the time and my dad loved. But I thought you'd enjoy coming home to something to eat."

Somehow I wasn't shocked at her thoughtfulness. Everyone she had spoken to today had commented on how lovely she was. "Polite and friendly," some said. "Cheerful and smart," others commented. The "fucking sexy" comments from some of the crew got my back up, and after the look I shot them, I doubted they would repeat themselves. They knew they'd have to deal with me. My little speech on respect and under my protection might have guaranteed it. I had no idea why I said it, but I did.

Probably because I knew Rachel would want me to. That had to be it.

Or at least so I told myself.

"I didn't expect you to make dinner, but I'm grateful."

"You want to wash up?"

"I'm going to grab a shower. I'll get a bottle of wine with dinner if you want?"

"Okay," she agreed easily, going back to her notebook.

I headed down the hall, glancing over my shoulder. She looked oddly right sitting at the table, surrounded by her project.

I shook my head. I'd obviously had far too much sun today.

"This is delicious," I said around a mouthful. Her "just" a casserole was accompanied by a huge salad and warm bread.

She smiled, the warmth of it making me smile back at her.

"What do you usually do for dinner?"

"Rachel or I would make dinner. I like to barbecue. When she got engaged, I was on my own more, and I started cooking big meals a couple times a week and having leftovers. It was easier. Sometimes Callie takes pity on me and fills the freezer with things I can pop in the oven. Rachel leaves me meals too."

"So, you're out of the house by five and work until six every day?"

"Yeah. Usually. Somedays, I let my foremen handle it, and I hunker down with paperwork. But I like the hands-on approach. It's my ranch—if I don't care enough to work hard, what message does that send to my ranch hands?"

"Do you get vacations?"

"I have taken a day or two on occasion. My parents always made sure we had a week as a family. My dad would trade with a couple of other ranchers, and he would look after their places when they were gone, and they would look after ours. I took a week a couple of years ago. Last year, I went to a conference, and Tyler stayed with Rachel and made sure everything was okay. I also have great foremen who help."

I wiped my mouth and sat back. "A ranch is like a well-run office. We have to look after the animals and the land. You don't just put on a cowboy hat and saddle up. You learn growing up on a ranch or you take courses, or both."

"You can take a course to become a cowboy?"

I laughed. She had a way of making me do that constantly with her techniques of asking questions. "We're not really cowboys, Sammy. We're ranch hands."

She shook her head, tapping her notebook. "Nope. The brochure says cowboys."

I had to chuckle again. "You can call us anything you want. But yes, you need knowledge to be one. You get it by education and/or hands-on learning. But we're all hard workers. You don't pull the line, you don't stay. You can't be a slacker and be a ranch hand. It simply doesn't work. I pay fair wages, and I expect fair work. I make sure you're looked after, so you look after what is important to me."

"You run a tight ship—or a ranch, I suppose."

"I have to. My animals are valuable. I need them cared for. They're the priority—the lifeline of the ranch. That's why it's so important this idea of Rachel's comes with rules."

"Of course." She reached over and grasped my hand. "I understand completely."

I believed her reassurances. I looked down to where our hands were touching. Without thinking, I flipped mine over so I held hers. The skin was smooth and soft as I stroked my thumb on her wrist, where the flesh was pale and thin. Her pulse jumped, and I looked up, meeting her lovely eyes. I realized how close I had bent over the table, and I quickly released her hand and pulled back.

"I need some more of that casserole," I muttered, taking my plate and heading to the stove. "After dinner, you can show me some of your plans."

"Sure." Her voice sounded breathless.

When I sat down, I purposely kicked my chair to the right, giving myself a little more space.

I needed the distance, and I refused to question the reason for it.

SAMMY

Luke disappeared briefly after supper, and I organized my files on the table. I hadn't failed to notice his shifting his chair farther from me at dinner. I knew he was feeling the same strange draw to me as I was to him. I had no idea why he affected me so much. As soon as I saw him, the energy around me picked up. I became focused on him. His movements, the sound of his voice. The way he took command of a room when he walked in. The broadness of his shoulders, the power he exuded in his stance. He simply mesmerized me. I had never felt a draw to someone the way I did to Luke.

I had never felt the same amount of passion and desire when he kissed me earlier. Or been so aware of someone when he sat behind me on his horse. The urge to melt back against him, feel the heat and strength of his body molded to mine, had been intense. I was certain he felt the same sensations I was experiencing.

But he seemed determined to ignore it.

He returned, heading to the fireplace, and moments later, a cheerful blaze started. He situated the screen in front of the flames, wiping his hands, and returned to the table. "Supposed to get chilly tonight," he explained. "Rain tomorrow." He sat down. "You might want to rethink that little outfit you call pajamas and wear something decent..." He trailed off and cleared his throat. "I mean warm to bed."

I ducked my head, trying not to laugh. He *was* affected. "I'll keep that in mind."

"How's your head?" he snapped, obviously angry at himself.

"Fine." I took pity on him. "Any more news from Rachel?"

"Tyler's doing well. It'll be a while before he recovers. I'm meeting with his brother tomorrow to see what he needs."

"You're going to help on his farm?"

"Of course. We help one another here. The Johnstone farm butts up to the eastern edge of my ranch. He's my neighbor, friend, and soon-to-be brother-in-law. I get on well with his parents. I can send someone to help out while he's off his feet. Make sure everything is running smoothly. He'd do the same for me."

"You're a good man, Luke Adler."

He smiled and shrugged. "Enough of the compliments. Show me these ideas."

I opened the first file. "Okay."

A short while later, he shook his head. "You got all this done in a day? The plans, ideas, and sketches?"

"I had some done before I got here, based on the measurements Rachel sent me. I also had ideas, but I had to see the ranch for myself. I'll do more exploring tomorrow and some filming, and then we can talk again."

He leaned closer, peering at my sketches of the cabins. We had discussed the water supply and the wells on the property, as well as the septic needs. Agreed on the maximum number of guests that could be on the ranch without putting a strain on the entire system and structure. He'd been informative and knowledgeable, and my notebook was filling with our discussion. "Why do you have notes that say 'Ask Dad' scattered all over the place?"

"Oh. My dad was in construction. I can ask him questions about load-bearing walls and things." I took in a deep breath. "I was thinking about asking him to come out and help refit the bunkhouses."

He frowned. "Why would he want to do that?"

"Because I asked him to. He'd bring a few other family members, and they'd do an amazing job. Save some money on construction costs."

"I wouldn't ask him to do it for free. I don't need handouts."

I shook my head. "He would love it. So would Hunter. Some time on a ranch? Ride the horses, breathe in the fresh air—see the beauty of this place?" I grabbed his hand as he started to shake his head. "Besides, my mom and aunts want to come here when it's ready—you can comp them in, like a trade. My dad would be so amazing here. He is such a great builder."

He blew out a long breath, and I held mine. "Do you involve your father in other projects?"

"No," I answered honestly.

He studied me. "Why?" he asked quietly.

"Because I want this to be great for you."

He shifted, bringing his chair closer. "Why?" he asked again.

I shrugged, unable to tell him. To say out loud how important it was that this be successful. That what I planned and my ideas helped him keep his ranch. Made him happy. I didn't understand it, so I couldn't explain it to him either.

He reached out and ran his finger over my cheek. He tucked a stray piece of hair behind my ear, brushed my earlobe with his fingers, tugging at it. "You're going to be trouble for me, aren't you, Lady?" he murmured. "Big trouble."

"I'll try not to be."

He lowered his head, and he came closer. "I don't think either of us can stop it."

I felt his breath on my face. Smelled his clean scent, the heat of him. I lifted my hand, covering his that now cradled my face, his callused skin rough on mine. My gaze fixated on his lips. I wanted to feel them on mine. To taste him again. I leaned into his caress, and he pressed forward, his mouth descending.

"Hey!" A voice rang out.

We pulled apart as if we were on fire. I almost fell off my chair in my haste. Luke grabbed my arm, steadying me as he rose from his seat. "Rach?" he asked. "What are you doing here?"

Rachel was tall with blue eyes like her brother, although her hair was lighter. She looked weary, although she beamed in welcome as I shook her hand. I smiled as I watched Luke pull her in for a hug.

"What's going on?" he asked. "How's Tyler?"

"Grumpy and bossing me around. So, in other words, on the mend," she replied. "His mom is with him, so I came home to get some sleep and fresh clothes. What did I interrupt?"

"Um——" Luke looked uncomfortable as he scrubbed the back of his neck.

"I was showing him some ideas. He was asking questions," I said smoothly.

Her brow furrowed. "Oh. I'd like to see too."

"Why don't you relax for the night, and I'll show you in the morning?" I suggested.

She smiled. "That actually sounds good. I need a soak in the tub and some sleep. Food, too, if there is any." She sniffed the air. "I smelled something good when I walked in."

I jumped up. "Let me get you a plate."

She sat with Luke, and they talked quietly as I heated some casserole for her. I observed the way he acted. Listening carefully, rubbing her arm, reassuring her in his low voice that everything was going to be fine and he would make sure the farm was okay and the project moved forward so she could concentrate on Tyler. He was in big-brother mode—one I recognized because of the way Reed was with me at times. Caring, protective, and loving. It was nice to see that side of him.

I turned and stirred the casserole on the plate, popping it back in to finish heating.

Rachel had interrupted more than us talking. A shiver ran through me as I wondered what she would have seen if she had been a few minutes later. Would I have been on Luke's lap as he kissed me? Wrapped around him as his mouth devoured mine? God knew I wanted that to be the case. Internally, I shook my head as I pulled the plate out from the microwave. I couldn't decide if it was a blessing or a curse she had arrived when she did. I only knew I was torn.

Rachel finished her plate with a satisfied groan. "That was delicious. Thank you."

I smiled. "You're welcome."

She nudged her brother playfully. "We hired her to help advise us on the business, Luke, not cook your meals."

"Hey," he objected. "I didn't ask."

I laughed. "I just did it. I was hungry, and I assumed he would be too, given how hard he worked all day. I don't mind. I like cooking."

"And I appreciated it," Luke said. "I agree, it was delicious."

"I hope you thanked her properly?" Rachel teased.

"What do you mean by that?" he sputtered.

"I mean, said thank you for dinner."

"Yes, he did. Several times," I assured her.

I might have gotten an even better thank-you if you hadn't shown up, I thought to myself.

I lifted my gaze to Luke, who was watching me. He winked subtly, and I couldn't help but wonder if he had been thinking the same thing.

Rachel stood, taking her plate to the sink. "I am going to go shower and head to bed."

"You want to use my tub?" Luke asked, his voice rough-sounding.

She looked surprised by the offer. "Um, no, I'm actually too tired to soak. I need sleep more." She smiled at him, brushing a kiss to his cheek. She looked at me. "We can sit in the morning before I head back to the hospital, if that's okay?"

"Sure."

"Great. Oh, and there is some aloe vera in the fridge. I keep it in there so it goes on cool and helps right away on a burn. It might feel good on your neck."

"Awesome, thanks." My neck did feel warm.

She smiled and walked down the hallway, her shoulders slumped in exhaustion. Luke sighed and rubbed a hand over his eyes.

"She's going to be fine," I assured him. "She has so many people rallying around her."

"I know," he replied. "I hate seeing her upset." He smiled ruefully. "This is one of those times I miss our mom the most. She'd know what to say or do to make things better for her."

"You're doing a great job, big brother."

He stood and put Rachel's plate in the dishwasher, then opened the fridge. I piled up the files on the table and plugged in the laptop for the morning. I was shocked when I felt Luke behind me.

"Lift your hair," he instructed.

"What?" I half turned and saw the tube of gel in his hand. "Oh, I can do that."

He smirked. "If you couldn't reach it with sunscreen, you can't reach it with this either."

He had a point. I reached up and wound up my hair, holding it with one hand. He brushed away a few stray hairs, making me shiver.

"This might be cold," he murmured.

I gasped as the aloe gel hit my skin. Luke's touch was gentle as he rubbed the aloe into my neck, the cool soothing and the gel taking the edge off the slight ache the sun left. He glided his hands over me and the areas on my nape I hadn't reached with the sun block. He pulled away my shirt, getting the pink skin that was under the edges.

"Better?" he asked quietly.

"Yes."

He lowered his head to my neck, his face right beside mine. "Thank you for dinner," he murmured.

"You're welcome," I managed to reply.

He pressed closer, his lips right at my ear. "It was the second most delicious thing I tasted today."

"What was the first?" I asked, trying not to whimper at his closeness.

His lips touched my skin, leaving a fiery path of their own. I expected him to say the stew Callie had made, his coffee, something, anything but the one word he uttered before he straightened and left me alone, sitting and gripping the edge of the table.

"You."

CHAPTER EIGHT

SAMMY

I barely slept that night, tossing and turning. How the mere brush of his lips could wind me up so tightly, I had no idea. But every time I closed my eyes, I felt his mouth on my skin. His hot breath by my ear. His voice whispering, "You."

In the morning, I dragged myself into the shower, got dressed, and after squaring my shoulders, headed to the kitchen. Rachel was alone, sipping coffee. She offered me a smile.

"Morning."

"Hi," I greeted her, pouring a coffee. "You look more rested today."

She nodded. "A good night's sleep does wonders. You look like you need one this morning."

I waved her off. "When I'm in the beginning stages of a project, I have trouble turning off my brain."

She laughed. "I get that. How's your head? Luke told me what happened."

"It's fine. The bump is going away, and the pain is almost gone."

"Good."

She tapped the files. "You want to bring me up to speed, so when Luke shows up, we can move forward?"

"Sure." I pulled the files toward me and went over everything I had talked to Luke about. Unlike her brother, Rachel was enthusiastic and asked lots of positive questions and gave me some other ideas.

"There are some wooden bunk bed frames in the storage barn. Some other pieces of furniture, tables, chairs, and such." She grinned. "Even some light fixtures that might fall into the western slash outdoor theme you're going for."

"Great. Paint and elbow grease are always cheaper than buying new."

"There are a couple of great thrift stores in a town not far from here."

"Awesome. We could do some filming, looking for stuff."

When I mentioned my dad coming out to help, her eyes widened. "Really?" she breathed out. "He'd do that?"

I nodded. "I spoke with him last night and mentioned it. He got quite excited and told me to figure out dates. He was gonna talk to Hunter and a few cousins."

"And they want to come as guests?"

"I thought you could use them as trial guests. Get their honest feedback, and you can tweak or add to the experience before actual paying guests show up."

"That would be incredible."

"Luke didn't seem to like the idea."

"Luke doesn't like owing people."

"But he wouldn't," I insisted. "My mom and her crew want to come sometime for a girls' weekend. They'll fill the big cabin at least. We can trade."

"I like it. I'll get Luke on board."

"On board with what?" Luke asked as he walked in. He removed his hat, dragging a hand through his hair.

"With whatever I say," Rachel responded.

I tried not to stare as he rolled his eyes, shrugged off his denim jacket and walked to the sink to wash his hands. His jeans hugged his ass, and his T-shirt was stretched tight over his broad back. He glanced over his shoulder, catching me ogling him. A half smirk pulled on his lips, then he addressed Rachel. "Not so fast, sister."

She huffed and went over to the oven, pulling a pan from it. I could suddenly smell something savory and delicious, making my stomach rumble. A few moments later, I was tucking into a breakfast casserole Rachel had put on my plate. The sausage was spicy, the hash browns lining the pan crispy and golden. The eggs, peppers, mushrooms, and more hash browns made it filling and tasty.

"Add this to the menu," I instructed. "The guests will love it."

Rachel laughed. "Already is. Callie makes this a lot. I grabbed one from the fridge in the cookhouse this morning."

Luke didn't say much, but he ate two huge platefuls. Every time our eyes met, I saw something flare in his stare—something that made me quiver a little. Made the desire I felt for him burn a little hotter. Every time, I was the one to look away. I was afraid I might spontaneously combust if I didn't.

After breakfast, we talked more. Rachel was, without a doubt, far more enthusiastic about the project. Keen on all the ideas. Luke was accepting but reticent, even with my assurances of making sure the work on the ranch was met with little disruption.

"You'll be over at the farm, playing wife. I'll have to deal with this," he groused.

Rachel shook her head. "Stop it. You know as well as I do, Tyler and his family have the farm well in hand. They're a well-oiled machine over there. He knows I've been dying to get this up and going for a long time and that I'll be here overseeing this until it's operating smoothly. And I built a manager into the budget, so there'll be a second person if I have something else to do."

He hmphed, and she shook her head. "Callie wants to step up as well. Be part of this. So does Rob's wife. They'll all be great at pitching in. It gives them something else to do—something different. And the hands we trust are on board. The bottom line is, if the ranch is a success, they have a job. A place they love to work. It's a win-win for everyone, Luke." She paused and tapped the table. "Tyler's willing to let people come on his farm and play gardener. The hands will guide them on some rides and camping. I'll oversee it all. You should be willing to let them bunk here, eat some cowboy food, and ride a damn horse."

"I'm willing," Luke sighed. "I'm just not happy about it."

Rachel began to laugh. "I give up."

"But you're still going full steam ahead."

She nodded. "Yep."

I watched with amusement. "I think what needs to happen is we agree on the levels of guest involvement, then I'll try them out. What might seem easy to you could be too hard for someone who has never ridden a horse before."

Rachel nodded. "Good idea."

"So, we agree on the basics. Sleeping in the bunkhouse. Three meals a day. Access to the swimming hole. There'll be nightly campfires. Horse rides. They can choose their level of involvement. Some will want to participate in everything—herding the cows, mending the fences, helping with other tasks. Some might want to help collect eggs and nothing else. And some might want nothing but to have their meals prepared and sit by the fire at night."

"Then why come here?" Luke asked.

"The scenery. The peace. Perhaps their partner always wanted to be a cowboy or cowgirl. So, they come, and the partner gets to live their dream. They get to sit in the sun, read, relax, enjoy the tranquility, and watch their partner enjoy the time."

He shook his head. "I swear this is all beyond me."

"Haven't you ever wanted to give someone you loved something they wanted?" I asked. "Something you can't give them?"

A dark look crossed his face, and he stood. "No," he snapped.

Rachel's eyes went wide, and she stood as well. "Maybe you should take Sammy around with you today. Show her what a day on the ranch is like for you."

He shut his eyes and drew in a deep breath. "Fine. I'll get a horse ready for you. Be at the stable in fifteen." He strode to the door, grabbing his jacket. "Dress appropriately today, for God's sake."

Then he stormed out.

"I touched on a nerve there," I observed.

Rachel nodded, looking sad. "His ex did a number on him. She came across as the right kind of person for him, but the truth was, she was anything but. Nothing he did was enough. This ranch, the lifestyle he offered, even his love. No matter how hard he tried, it was never enough."

"Oh God, I put my foot right in my mouth, didn't I?"

"You didn't know. Luke will be fine once he calms down. He just doesn't like to be reminded of her. I don't think he's ever come to terms with the fact that it was her, not him, who was at fault. She left him jaded and angry, and he hasn't believed in love since then. At least not for himself. He doesn't trust easily."

"I see."

"You'll see my goats today."

"Luke mentioned there were some."

"I've been working on making my own goat cheese," Rachel said, looking nervous. "Tyler thinks it's delicious. So does his mom. I thought it might be an add-on for some people to watch the process. Participate."

I sat forward eagerly. "You could sell it. What a great memento. Take back cheese you helped to make."

She nodded. "I have the license applied for. The kitchen at the farm is graded for commercial. Tyler's mom runs a business there already. It's really very simple, but the milk is so fresh and I use herbs from the farm."

"I love that idea."

"I make beeswax candles too, and I have honey from the hives I keep at Tyler's farm. I also use the wool from our sheep to knit. My mom taught me how, and I love it. I send the wool away to be processed, and when it comes back, I knit things with it." She held up her arms. "Like this sweater."

"It's gorgeous. I was admiring it."

"I work with the company that processes the wool, and they custom dye it with the colors I want. The hues are slightly different, but they are all on the blue and gray theme. I always have a project on the go."

I tapped my lips. "If you could display a couple things, you could take custom orders."

She blew out a long breath and frowned. "They'd be expensive."

I smiled. "There will be people coming here who would spend that sort of money. On a custom sweater or a blanket. Handmade goat cheese or your beeswax candles. Maybe down the line, you can open a shop. Display not only your wares, but other local artisans as well. They get a spot in the store and pay you to have it there, plus a small percentage of their sales."

"Oh, I would love that."

"Something to think about, for sure."

She nodded. "Another thing I was thinking about—every Friday, there is a barn dance in town. Admission is a canned good for the food bank. Local bands, lots of cowboys. Hayrides. Town businesses provide refreshment. It's always popular. Maybe guests would like that?"

"That would be awesome."

Rachel stood. "Okay. I will see what else I come up with. Luke will take you around the property today on horseback. Tomorrow, you can live the guest experience of fun in the sun. Then you can do the hands-on experience. After that, Luke will let you be involved with the be-a-cowboy package. You can do everything but sleep in the bunkhouse. Once you give us feedback, we'll tweak."

"Great. That gives me enough time to talk to the architect about the drawings. It'll go fast since we're just adding a few walls."

"And the bathhouse."

I grinned. That was my idea. A small wooden structure behind the bunkhouses with a deep trough for a tub. Just like you would see in a cowboy movie. Except this one would be situated under a skylight. You could book the space for two hours at a time. Soak in the tub, looking at the sky or the stars. Drainage and plumbing were already there from when it used to be a small cleanup building. It would be cozy, relaxing, and a great feature. Luke had rolled his eyes and looked at me strangely when I told him, but he didn't object.

"I'm surprised Luke approved that," she murmured.

"Oh?"

She shrugged. "Not my story to tell. But he must listen to you."

I laughed. "When he chooses to."

"Sounds about right." She chuckled, then became serious. "We'll work on getting all the approvals and permissions. It won't take long to get the permits here."

"Great."

I grabbed my jacket and added the rain poncho Rachel had loaned me. I slid on a pair of boots I had brought, grateful for the thick soles and the extra socks I had added, and headed to the stable. The sky was already breaking, and the air smelled crisp and fresh. I looked around at the various structures, ideas cropping up in my head. I knew Rachel would love them. Luke, on the other hand, would resist. I had a feeling he was going to resist every idea. I would have to figure out a way of talking him into it. My dad always said I was good at that.

At the stable, I found Luke speaking quietly to his horse, Maverick. Another horse was ready, and I drew in a deep breath, tamping down my nerves. Although smaller, it seemed large to me.

Luke looked up, still somewhat on edge. His mouth was set in a frown, and his tone was impatient. "You do have experience riding?"

I lifted my head. "I have been on a horse, yes. It's been a while, but I can handle it." I walked over, letting the horse sniff my hand. "What a beauty."

"Her name is Dusty."

I stroked along her velvet nose. "Hello, Dusty."

Dusty tossed her head, whinnying low in her throat. I looked at Luke. "What did I do?"

He snorted. "She can tell you're green. She's asking me why I'm subjecting her to you."

I crossed my arms. "Are you going to be snarky and rude all day?"

He shrugged. "Maybe sarcastic and indifferent. Haven't decided. Get in the saddle and find out." He paused, his impatience showing through. "Now, Lady. I don't have all day."

I tried to recall everything I had read on getting into a saddle. The videos I had watched so I wouldn't make a total fool of myself in front of him. I slipped my foot into the stirrup and, stretching on my toes, grasped the pommel, confident I could swing myself up into the saddle.

I failed. Twice.

He watched me, his face impassive, saying nothing. Dusty huffed an impatient whinny through her nose.

"I think I'll try using the fence," I muttered. "I think I'm a little short."

Except Dusty didn't want to move when I tugged on her reins.

"How do you get her in reverse?" I mumbled, looking over my shoulder. "Is there, like, a key word or something?"

Luke's lips twitched. "When exactly was the last time you were on a horse?" he asked, his tone mild.

"I was eight," I muttered, turning back to Dusty. "Can you back up a little?" I asked, somehow not shocked when she ignored me.

I gasped as I was suddenly lifted—as if I weighed nothing—up and over the saddle. I gripped the pommel, shocked at how far away the ground was. Luke adjusted the stirrups and shortened the reins, not speaking until he had swung himself back onto Maverick and led us from the stable.

"I imagine a lot of people who come here won't have the wealth of riding experience you have," he stated dryly.

I tossed my head, much like Dusty was doing, ignoring his sarcastic undertone. "I am sure many of them will have never been on a horse."

"So, *total* greenhorns, then."

"Yes."

He sighed and shook his head. "God help me."

CHAPTER NINE

LUKE

We rode around the ranch at a slow trot. I gave Sammy some pointers, my earlier ire evaporating in her presence and smiles. That seemed to happen a lot when she was around. I felt lighter—strangely content.

She had been beyond adorable approaching Dusty and informing me she could ride. I knew she was bluffing. Her remark about a command for reverse made me want to laugh. It was odd, but every time I was close to her, I wanted to laugh and smile. Make *her* smile. I wanted to bask in the warmth of her sunshine smile.

"Relax, Lady. Dusty can feel your tension. Loosen your hold on the reins."

"Nudge with your knee gently," I instructed. *"She'll follow your lead."*

"Try moving with the horse instead of keeping yourself so rigid."

Sammy listened to me, and after her fear dissipated somewhat, she relaxed enough to start looking around at the vista and beauty of the area.

"What is that?" she asked, indicating the tree-covered hills.

"The farthest edge of the ranch. Forest mostly going up the hill."

"Can we go up the mountain?"

I chuckled and indicated the mountain range in the distance. "*Those* are mountains. *That* is a hill."

"Where I come from, it's a mountain. You should refer to it that way. Mount Rock or something. People will love it."

I chuckled. "Well, we can take people up Mount *Rock* for their overnight camping. There is a nice spot I go sometimes. A flat area by a stream. We can get the tents and supplies up by ATV earlier, and people can choose to ride up or get a lift on the ATV."

"ATV?"

I glanced over at her. "I hate to disillusion you even more, Lady, but we often use ATVs to herd the cattle instead of horses."

I thought she'd be upset at that statement, but instead, I received one of her wide, sunshine smiles.

"That's great. If someone wants to experience the task, they can be a passenger and watch safely, but get the feel of being part of it." She reached over and grabbed my arm. "How awesome!"

I patted her hand, refusing to admit how much I enjoyed it when she touched me. "Good."

"Can we go up the mountain?"

"Soon. Today, we stick to the ranch. You'll be sore enough later, trust me."

We rode in silence for a while. I kept my eyes on the fence, noting any areas I thought needed fixing, although I only spotted two and even they were small, but it would be good for her to see what we did as part of being a paid client.

I pointed out a small cluster of willow trees that provided shade in one corner of the ranch. "That would make a great picnic spot."

"It's so pretty!"

"My grandmother planted those willows. The ones by the entrance too. They were her favorite trees."

"Oh, I love that."

I showed her a smaller stream you could sit by and eat lunch. Close to it was a long trail that wound around the hill for those more adventuresome. It would make a good afternoon hike.

"Could someone get lost?"

"Not if they stuck to the trail. It winds around the lowest part of the hill, and you end up back by the front of the ranch."

She nodded. "Some signage would be helpful." She pulled out a small notebook and scribbled in it. She'd been doing that a lot this morning. She glanced up from her book, narrowing her gaze at me.

"You're being very helpful, Luke. Why?"

I scoffed. "I am doing exactly what my sister told me to do."

She pursed her lips, not buying it. She looked over her shoulder. "How far are we away from the ranch house?"

I bit back my grin. "About as far as we can get."

"I knew it! You're trying to keep the clients away from you," she accused.

I held up my hands. "You wanted them to see the ranch. I'm simply pointing out places you might want to utilize in your plans to keep the clients happy. While keeping them away," I added with a wink and a smile.

For a moment, she glared, and then her lips quirked. She threw back her head, laughing. The sound was loud and clear, and I joined her. She wiped her eyes. "I have no idea what to do with you, Luke," she admitted. "You are such a curmudgeon."

"Am not."

"Are so."

"Now you're calling me an asshole?" I deadpanned.

That earned me another bout of laughter. She was a vision, sitting on Dusty, her hair a bright cloud around her face, her smile eclipsing the sun. The urge to pull Maverick closer and lean over to kiss her became almost too much to ignore.

Then she froze, waving the air in front of her face.

"What?" I asked.

"Wasps," she said, moving restlessly, waving her hands, her movements causing Dusty to lurch.

"Stay calm," I said. "Walk Dusty this way. Prod your knees gently."

But she panicked and dug in fast. Dusty took off, and I watched in horror as Sammy flew backward off the saddle, landing on the ground with a loud, painful-sounding gasp.

I was off Maverick and beside her before she could blink. "Sammy," I pleaded, worry filling my chest. "Sammy, open your eyes."

Her dark-brown eyes fluttered open, and she scowled. "I hate wasps."

"How many fingers am I holding up?"

"Three, although I'm sure you'd prefer it were just the one."

I chuckled. "Are you hurt?"

She sniffed. "Just my pride." But then she winced as she tried to sit up.

I slid my hands under her, lifting her and carrying her over to the shaded spot by the trees. I didn't question how right she felt in my arms. Maverick followed, and I grabbed the flask of water, hunching beside Sammy. "Drink."

Her hand shook as she reached for the flask, and with a frown, I pulled her into my lap, touching the bottle to her mouth. She tilted her head back and sipped, her rich brown eyes locked on mine. When she was done, she pushed the flask away. "I'm fine. I was just startled."

"Let me look."

"I'm fine, Luke. Really."

I ran my hands over her. "I need to make sure," I rasped, the anxiety gripping me.

She frowned but allowed me to check her out. I gently ran my hands over her head, pulling out some grass and a couple twigs, satisfied there were no new bumps or cuts. I felt her shoulders and upper arms, pleased that everything seemed okay.

"I think I just got the wind knocked out of me," she assured me. "I guess I startled Dusty. Is she okay?"

I looked over my shoulder. Dusty hadn't gone far, grazing in the grass. "She's fine," I said. "I'm more worried about you. You're going to feel the effects later." I frowned as I pulled a little more grass from her hair. "Your poor head had taken some blows since you got here."

She smiled widely. "And still no sense knocked into me. I have a hard head. People tell me that all the time. Besides, I think my butt took more of a hit."

I relaxed at her words. "I think they're referring to your stubborn nature," I teased, wondering why my fingers were tangling in her hair.

"Me, stubborn? Have you looked in the mirror lately?" she responded. "Pot meet kettle sort of thing?"

Of their own accord, my fingers slid down her cheek, drifting under her chin and tilting it up. "Two peas in a pod, then, Lady."

"You keep calling me that."

I flexed my fingers on her jaw, feeling the tight muscles and the softness of her skin. "Calling you what?"

"Lady. At first, I thought you were goading me, but…" She trailed off.

"But?" I prompted.

Her eyes searched mine. "But it doesn't feel that way when you say it." She slid her hand up my chest, her fingers restlessly playing with the hair on my neck. "When I listen, I hear a difference. It feels more…personal."

I bent lower. "It is."

And then our mouths were fused together. Her full lips opened underneath mine. I pushed my tongue inside to connect with hers, groaning at her taste. I explored her with long sweeps of my tongue. Playful nips to her bottom lip. She responded by licking inside my mouth, sucking my tongue, and whimpering. She scored my lips using her teeth with playful bites, buried her hands in my hair, causing my hat to fall to the ground. She twisted and turned until she straddled me, and I slid my hands under the shirt she wore, the skin warm under my hands as I spread them over the silken expanse of her back. My cock was hard, pressing against the denim of my jeans, nestled between the heat of her legs. Sammy moaned, the sound low and needy in the back of her throat.

I dragged my mouth across her cheek to her ear. "Pain or want, Lady? Which one?"

"Want," she gasped. "Oh God, I want you."

"Are you sure you're okay?"

"Shut up and kiss me, Cowboy."

"I can't give you anything but this," I confessed.

"I'm not asking for anything."

I captured her mouth with mine again. Tangled with her hot, sweet tongue. Popped the button of her jeans, sliding my hand under the waistband and down through her damp curls, into the heat and wetness that waited. She bucked against my hand as I touched her, her clit a hard button under my touch.

"Jesus, you feel so good," I groaned against her lips.

"Luke," she whispered, pushing herself into my hand. "Oh God, please."

"God's not going to help you right now," I growled against her throat. "I am. You're going to come all over my hand. You hear me, *Lady*? All over my hand."

I teased her, gliding my fingers over her center, driving her crazy. She fisted my hair, gripped my shoulders, and undulated over me. I pressed my thumb to her clit then slid two fingers inside her, swallowing her cries of pleasure. My dick was a rod of steel as she ground against me, her movements frantic. Watching her, hearing her whimpers, feeling her moving over me was erotic. I couldn't bear to take my mouth off hers, not wanting to lose her taste or the feel of her tongue with mine. I gripped her waist with my free hand, forcing her closer. She wrapped her legs around me, and I groaned as my cock strained and jumped in my pants. This was going to be messy. Fast.

And so fucking good.

She stiffened, her muscles tightening around my fingers, her moans and whimpers constant. I grunted as my orgasm washed over me, the continuous friction too much for my self-control. I rolled my hips, easing us both through our pleasure. Until finally, regretfully, we stopped. The deep, heated kisses turned softer, sweeter. I pulled my mouth away, and she rested her head on my chest, her breathing erratic. I dropped my chin to her head, the silk of her hair tickling my skin. I held her close until she sat up, meeting my eyes.

I regarded her warily, unsure what to expect. Anger? Accusations? Regret? Instead, her gaze was steady, soft, and warm. I wanted to bask in it.

"Is that what you call a bucking bronco?" she asked, smiling.

I returned her smile, pressing a kiss to her full lips. "That was unexpected and not part of the regular tour, Lady."

"I should hope not."

"The only one I'll buck for is you."

"You kinda bucked on your own." She frowned. "Doesn't seem fair."

"Maybe I'll let you make it up to me later."

She met my gaze, her eyes serious. "I will."

"For now, we have to go. I have work. And I need to change. Otherwise, I'm going to be crusty all afternoon."

She giggled. "Crusty the Cowboy."

I shook my head. "We have to go."

She leaned close, peering up at me. "You're still inside me, Luke."

I shut my eyes at her breathless voice. Slowly, I eased my fingers out of her, watching as she winced a little.

"You okay?"

She nodded, her eyes going wide as I pulled out my hand, then slipped my fingers inside my mouth. She whimpered as she watched me lick them clean. I kissed her. "You're delicious, Lady. You taste like honey on my tongue." I paused. "It makes me want you more."

She crashed her lips to mine.

I didn't object.

SAMMY

The sound of a horse approaching made Luke pull away. I watched as he yanked on his shirt I had pulled partially off him, grabbed his hat from the ground, and casually held it low as he whistled to Maverick. The horse obediently came toward him, accepting a stroke on his nose. I marveled at Luke's ability to command the horse with nothing but a whistle or a few spoken words. No doubt, he wished I were as obedient. I was certain he had already realized it would never happen.

I sat against the trunk of the tree, ghosting my fingers over my mouth that still felt Luke's possession. Under his cool exterior, he was passion and fire. I liked that side of him. The way he lost control with me. The feel of his hands on my body. And his mouth. It was highly addictive.

A gray horse drew up, Rachel seated in the saddle, looking relaxed and in control. She frowned as she looked at us. "What are you doing?"

"City gal had a little altercation with Dusty. She's resting."

"What?" Rachel slid off her horse. "You're supposed to be looking after her, Luke." She hurried over. "Are you okay?"

I waved off her concern. "I'm fine. My ass will probably be bruised tomorrow, but I'm fine. It was my fault. I startled Dusty when some wasps startled me."

She shook her head. "You're flushed. Did you get too much sun?"

"No, I was wearing a hat. It, ah, flew off when I fell. I'm fine, really." I brushed off my jeans, grateful I had done them back up before she appeared.

"What are you doing here, Rachel?" Luke asked.

"Tyler is doing so well, he's going to be released as early as tomorrow. The doctor says he can rest better at home. He had a lot of visitors this afternoon, so he sent me home. I came to find you guys and see what was going on."

Luke swung himself up on Maverick, casually resting his hat on his leg. I was trying not to laugh at his attempted cover-ups. "You can finish up with Sammy, then. I have things I need to take care of."

Like changing your pants, Mr. Crusty. I smirked to myself.

"I brought sandwiches and lemonade," Rachel offered. "I thought we could sit and talk more about plans."

Luke shook his head. "I don't have time, Rachel. You discuss your plans and tell me what you need." He directed his gaze to me, his tone impersonal. "Try to stay in the saddle this time." Then he turned Maverick away and took off, breaking into a gallop quickly.

I felt sad as he rushed off, all his fire and passion tightly contained again. I much preferred hot cowboy Luke to the cool, removed version.

Rachel grabbed the bag on her saddle and came over, sitting beside me. "Are you okay?" she asked. "You look upset."

I shrugged. "I'm fine. He—your brother—he blows hot and cold. Every time I think I'm starting to figure him out, he switches gears."

Rachel opened the bag, handing me a sandwich and a flask of lemonade. I bit into the thick filling, humming in appreciation at the flavorful chicken salad. "Delicious."

She nodded in agreement. "Callie is an awesome cook. She makes the lemonade from scratch too. Iced tea blends as well."

"Guests will love that." I chewed and swallowed. "I have an idea —it's simple but I think effective."

She waited for me to continue, nodding around a mouthful of sandwich.

"I was thinking you should paint the various buildings. It would make it so easy to say the blue building for the cookhouse or the red barn to direct people. Plus, it would be appealing and spruce them up. Paint is a cheap decorating tool. And we can paint the cabins too."

She nodded. "That would look nice."

"I was thinking yellow for the dairy barn, a rusty red for the stables, green for the chicken coop, and blue for the cookhouse."

"And the cabins?"

"Red and white—really Canadian."

She laughed. "What did Luke say?"

"I didn't tell him. I wasn't sure how he'd react."

She mulled it over. "We'll bring it up in a couple of days. I like it, though. We had talked about freshening up the buildings last year." She grinned. "Although I am pretty sure his idea of freshening up was a coat of the same color." Her smile faded. "He won't let you touch the house, though."

I shook my head. "That is private. I wouldn't dream of it. Guests aren't allowed in the private areas of the ranch. You can set the boundaries." I rubbed her arm.

And no female guests were allowed in there at all, I wanted to add, but I refrained. I tried not to think about why Luke having a guest in the house would bother me. That would complicate things. I cleared my throat.

"You guys really miss your parents, don't you?"

She nodded. "When my dad died, Luke stepped in. He was brother, father, friend, boss—something to everyone. When Mom died, I know how much he missed her guidance. He became that much more serious and withdrawn. She was the rock for us and especially for him. I had hoped he would meet someone to help share his life with."

She sighed, crumpling up the paper her sandwich had been wrapped in. "But the one time he tried, it was a spectacular disaster, and he closed himself off. He is an amazing man—warm, caring, funny—but he doesn't let many people see that side of him anymore. He's friendly but removed. He gives everything he has to this ranch…" She trailed off.

"…leaving nothing for himself," I finished for her. "He carries a lot by himself."

She eyed me for a moment. "Is something going on between the two of you?" she asked frankly. "I sense some sort of tension between you."

I didn't want to lie, but I couldn't tell her the whole truth. "Nothing of any consequence. A little attraction, but nothing will come of it since I'm only here a short time."

She lifted a shoulder, dismissing my words. "Holiday trysts can be fun. As long as both parties agree to the rules."

I gaped at her. "Are you telling me to have a fling with your brother?"

She laughed. "It might help loosen him up. I notice how he watches you." She grinned. "I also noticed the little scruff marks on your neck."

"Oh, ah—" I stumbled to find an explanation. "He got too close, making sure I hadn't been stung."

"Your lips in danger of that, too?" She teased. "Something made them swell."

I dropped my head into my hands. "Oh God."

She laughed. "I won't say a word. I promise."

I sighed. "There is an attraction. He says nothing can happen, and he keeps pulling back."

"Sounds like Luke."

"Any advice?"

She stood, brushing off her jeans and draining her lemonade. She studied me for a moment.

"My brother likes to be in control. Of everything. This ranch, the people, his emotions. He likes to call the shots."

I nodded. "I figured that much."

"If he says no, you just have to agree. Then figure out a way of making him say yes. Let him think whatever happens was his idea." She winked. "I don't like to think about him that way, but he is a man. They always want what they can't have. Chase after what isn't theirs. Reverse psychology works wonders. You say no, he is going to want you to say yes." She paused. "If, that is, you want him to say yes."

Then she grew serious. "But don't hurt him. He's been hurt enough."

I stood, wincing a little at the soreness in my butt and legs. Between the fall and riding the horse, my muscles were protesting.

"I don't want either of us to get hurt. But I like the man I see under the serious façade. We get along well in those moments." I grinned. "And frankly, I like sparring with him."

She returned my grin. "I think he likes it too. No doubt part of the draw."

"No doubt."

She linked her arm with mine, and we walked toward the horses. "I'll stay quiet. Just remember what I said. Reverse psychology."

"Got it."

CHAPTER TEN

SAMMY

I spent the rest of the afternoon with Rachel. We went over to the farm, and I met her soon-to-be in-laws, Jane and Harry. They were welcoming and excited about Rachel's plans. Happy their son was coming home and open to the idea of helping Rachel launch her cottage industry business. I saw the beehives, petted some animals, and raved over more of Rachel's knitted items. The blankets were warm and soft, the colors pretty.

"These would sell well." I showed Rachel equivalent blankets on other sites, and she was shocked at the prices. "Yours can be even higher, because of the fact that you produce the wool as well."

I tasted the goat cheese, humming at the delicious taste. The honey was unlike anything I had ever had before. "You will sell out constantly."

"Won't that be a problem?" she asked.

"The literature will state supplies are limited. But you might have to keep more inventory than usual for a while."

"I can make more."

"I'll help." Jane squeezed Rachel's arm. "I think it's so exciting."

Jane sent us back to the ranch with covered dishes of fried chicken and homemade blueberry pie. I was grateful we had driven over, my legs sore and aching.

Luke joined us for dinner, but he was quiet and serious as we ate. I felt his gaze on me more than once, but when I lifted my eyes to him, he looked away.

Rachel chatted away about what we had discussed, even bringing up painting the buildings. She never mentioned the colors, though. He grunted and nodded a lot, but otherwise stayed silent.

She sat back, finished, wiping her mouth.

"What are the plans tomorrow for Sammy?"

He pushed away his plate, picking up his glass and draining it. "Thank Jane for dinner. Tomorrow, Tim and one of the other men will take Sammy around, showing her what they do. She can decide if it's appropriate for the, ah, *guests*."

"I thought you were going to do it."

He stood, leaning his fists on the table. I tried not to think about how those hands felt on my body or moving inside me. "Rachel, I'm a busy man. I told you this. If I can join them at some point, I will, but I have things to do. It's not me who's gonna be escorting these people around when you open this place up. I still have to run the ranch, and it's a full-time occupation. So, get used to it. Now, excuse me. I have to check some things in the barn."

"Oh, you're a bear tonight," she mumbled. "What crawled up your ass?"

"Yeah, you are a little crusty," I said, then started to laugh.

Luke glared. I laughed harder.

Rachel grinned. "Private joke, I imagine."

"Not a funny one," Luke snapped and stomped from the kitchen, shutting the door a little louder than necessary behind him.

I tried to control my laughter but failed. Rachel stood. "I won't ask now, but you have to promise to tell me one day."

I could only nod.

One day.

———

Rachel left to go see Tyler, and I headed to my room. I was aching and sore, unused to riding a horse, and my ass did ache from falling off it.

I stretched to help dispel the aches then found an ice bag and sat on the sofa with the cold pressed on my lower back and butt. I called my parents to pass the time and spoke with my dad about the cabins and timing. He was excited at the thought of a project and asked me to send more pictures.

"I sent Ronan the specs for him to look over. I figured with his eye he might know how to maximize the space," I said.

"Great idea," Dad replied. "I think Hunter and Ronan want to come. Maybe others. Bentley is giving us the plane."

"That's generous."

"Emmy wants to come to the ranch."

"She'll be well treated. I think this will make an amazing place to have fun and relax."

"Okay. Send me those pictures and a date."

"Thanks, Dad."

"Anytime, Mouse."

I hung up as Luke walked in. He saw me on the sofa and paused, then hung up his hat and toed off his boots. He headed to the cabinet and poured something into a glass.

"Bourbon?" he asked.

I shuddered. "No thanks."

"There's some sort of girly drink here," he said. "Amaretto. My mom liked it. So does Rachel."

"Sure."

He handed me a glass and sat down across from me. He looked tired.

"Get done what you needed?" I asked.

He nodded, rubbing his eyes. "One of the ATVs broke down. Needed to be fixed for tomorrow."

"So, you're a mechanic too?"

He shrugged and tossed back his bourbon, setting down his empty glass. "I'm whatever I have to be to get the job done."

"You're tired," I observed.

He grunted, leaning his head back and shutting his eyes. "I'm always tired."

For a moment, I watched him. I set aside my drink and stood, going behind his chair. "Lean forward," I said.

He startled, looking up. "What?"

"Lean forward."

He did, and I placed my hands on his shoulders. I felt the tension under the firm muscles. I began to rub, shocked when he groaned a little. I spied a bottle of hand lotion on the table.

"It would help if you took off your shirt. And if you sat on the floor, I could reach your back better."

His shoulders tensed, then he leaned forward, dragging his T-shirt over his head and sitting back, moving to the floor. I sat behind him, admiring the broad expanse of his well-muscled back and shoulders. His skin was warm under my fingers. I began to knead and rub, finding the tense muscles and soothing them, the lotion helping my hands move over him easily. He had broad shoulders and a strong back, and I worked away quietly, moving to the middle and back out toward his arms. His tattoo was high on his shoulder, and I admired it as I worked on his upper arms, not daring to go lower. It was the same logo I had seen over the entrance to the ranch with a weeping willow behind it.

"Nice tattoo."

He grunted, his head hanging low. I moved my hands to his neck, gliding and stroking. Using my thumbs in a stubborn area, I felt his tension releasing. I wanted to touch him forever. To feel the give of his muscles as I helped him relax. I had the strongest desire to crawl into his lap and hold him. Kiss him. Help him unwind in a totally different way. Then hold him as he slept.

I had a feeling he needed that.

I shook my head. *Where the hell were those thoughts coming from?*

I stood, letting my hands drop. "That should help," I said brightly.

I returned to the sofa and picked up my glass, draining the Amaretto in one swallow. "I'm off to bed."

"Thank you," he said.

I dared to look over at him. Our gazes locked and held. I felt the current flowing between us, live and hot. "That felt incredible," he said.

I swallowed the thickness in my throat. Refused to let my feet head his way.

"You should drink some water and go to bed."

He nodded and stood, still watching me.

I turned and walked toward the hall.

"Why are you limping?" he asked.

"It's nothing," I called over my shoulder. "A little stiff from today. I'll be fine in the morning."

I kept walking, not stopping until I reached the safety of my room.

Hours later, I gave up. I sat up, once again trying to stretch out the muscles that were keeping me awake. Tylenol hadn't helped. The ice pack I had tiptoed down the hall to get from the freezer barely took the edge off. My ass and my lower back hurt from falling, and the thought of getting on a horse again in the morning made me shudder. I padded to the bathroom, searching the cupboards for some liniment or a heating pad. Anything that might help. I came up empty-handed. I went to the kitchen, trying to be quiet, and poured some cold water, walking to the front of the house and staring out the window as I sipped.

Outside, the trees bent to the breeze, the darkness deep and quiet. It was so peaceful here. I shut my eyes, swaying slightly. I was tired and going to be more tired in the morning. With a sigh, I turned to go back to my room, jumping in fright when I saw Luke leaning against the table, his arms crossed and watching me.

"Holy— You scared me."

"Sorry."

"What are you doing?"

"Wondering why you're roaming the house at one in the morning."

"Oh, I was thirsty."

He nodded. I hesitated, then had to ask. "You don't by chance have a heating pad, do you?"

"Yep. Back sore?"

"Yeah."

He headed down the hall toward his room. I followed, stopping as he switched on the light and opened a cupboard. He rummaged for a moment, then pulled out a heating pad and handed it to me.

"Thank you," I said gratefully. "This should help."

"Have you taken Tylenol?"

"Yes. Didn't help much. This will, I'm sure."

I headed back to my room, clutching the heating pad like a prize. I plugged in it and lay down, sighing as I felt the heat begin. I startled as Luke walked into my room, and I sat up.

"What are you doing?"

"Helping you." He turned on my bedside lamp, setting down a bottle of something. "Roll over."

"I beg your pardon?"

He chuckled, the sound low and deep in the room. "Relax, Lady. This stuff will help with the pain. Roll over."

I should tell him to get out. That I would rub whatever that was on myself. Instead, I did as he asked. He slid his hand under me, lifting the heating pad away. "Once I'm finished, I'll put this back on, and you'll get some relief." Then he cursed. "You've got some bruising from your fall this morning."

"Not surprised," I muttered.

Before I could say anything else, I was rendered speechless. Luke ran his hands over my thighs, his touch light and gentle. He added some cream and began to rub it into the aching muscles, and I couldn't help the moan that escaped my lips. He faltered for a moment, his hands stilling, then he began again.

"You should have said something."

"I thought I'd go to sleep and it would be fine."

"You're not getting on a horse tomorrow."

"Yes, I am."

I startled at the unexpected feel of him smacking my ass. "No, you're not. We'll use the ATVs tomorrow."

He slid his hands higher. "This is going to hurt. You're bruised here."

I felt a rush of tears as he went over the painful area. He probed gently, stroking and kneading. "Nothing is broken, but no wonder you can't sleep. This will help."

"What is it?"

"I have no idea. It works on the horses."

I spun my head, meeting his teasing gaze.

He shook his head in amusement. "It's like Voltaren, but stronger. My doc prescribes it."

I could already feel the ache diminishing. He kept rubbing the ointment in, and I felt myself relax as the pain subsided. I stayed on my stomach, sighing as he situated the heating pad over the affected area and drew up the covers. I drifted as he left, hearing the water as he washed his hands, returning. He stood by the bed and I felt his gaze on me, but I was too tired to open my eyes or talk much.

"Thank you," I mumbled.

"Just returning the favor."

I hummed and burrowed deeper into the pillow, the liniment and heat doing their job.

He turned off the light, and I felt the soft brush of his mouth over my head.

"Sleep now, beautiful Lady."

I must have dreamed that part.

The next morning, I still felt some soreness, and I traced the bruise on my tailbone and hip with a sigh. I wasn't going to object to the ATV today.

The kitchen was empty, and I grabbed a cup of coffee then headed to the barn. I found Luke with two other men, and he stopped what he was doing as I approached.

"Sammy," he greeted me. "How are you this morning?"

"Good."

He lifted an eyebrow, and I smiled. "Better."

"Okay. This morning, you're going with Callie. She's helping feed the animals that stay close to home, plus some other chores. We're herding some cows, and after lunch, you can be part of the next move. We'll be using the ATVs for that."

"I can probably ride."

He met my eyes. "Not today."

"But—"

"*Not today*." His voice brooked no argument.

"Fine."

"Go to the cookhouse and get some breakfast. Callie will tell you what she needs doing." He turned, effectively dismissing me.

At the cookhouse, I met a couple other hands who were just leaving, grinning as they tipped their hats and said hello.

"Ma'am."

I had to smile. Obviously, word had gotten around.

I ate a couple of Callie's breakfast burritos, the tortillas stuffed with sausage, egg, cheese, plus peppers and onions. Her homemade salsa was delicious. She grinned as I finished my second.

"On the menu," she assured me.

"Perfect."

I spent the morning feeding and spending time with the animals. I played with the goats and a couple of sheep that were there. Helped gather eggs. Visited the stable and fed Dusty a carrot plus a sugar cube I had snuck. In the barn, I watched as the dairy cows were milked. Cooed and cuddled some kittens in the stable while the momma cat watched me. I was pleased to see the warm, snug space that was made for the family. Callie assured me all animals at River Rock were well treated. There was an entire stall with beds, food, blankets, and lots of straw. They were happy and safe.

Then I helped her make lunch. Today, she was grilling burgers and sausages. She had a variety of salads, and I could smell the rich aroma of baked beans. I chopped veggies, sliced buns and cheese, and set out all the condiments. I captured most of it on film, already knowing the direction I would go with the program.

"Lunch is eleven to one. The later you come, the slimmer the pickings." She smirked. "Unless you're Luke. I always save him some since he is usually the last in. The man would never eat, otherwise."

I nodded, not surprised.

"The hands help themselves. They stack their dirty plates, glasses, and utensils into the dishwasher racks when they're done. I cook. I'm not their maid."

She had two chocolate cakes already made, and I cut them into slices and watched as the men and women trailed in, filling their plates, and enjoyed a break. Some came, grabbed food, and wrapped it to go, heading back to whatever they were doing. Some sat and ate, and I chatted with them, learning about what they did and how long they had been on the ranch. No one lingered, but they all ate well, were polite and friendly, and had one thing in common.

Luke had a dozen employees. The number varied depending on the season, but right now, it was fully staffed. They loved working on the ranch. Their respect for Luke and Rachel was obvious and their loyalty strong. Many of them were excited about the new aspect, a few holding back their opinion, but all were ready to accept new responsibilities.

Tim and John finished their lunch, and Tim came over. "Meet at the stable in ten?"

I was disappointed I hadn't seen Luke, but I knew he was a busy man. "Sure."

I ran back to the house and applied some more sun block and grabbed my hat, hurrying to the stable. I was taken aback, seeing the horses saddled and waiting.

"Ah, I thought we were taking the ATV?"

Tim frowned. "Luke never said anything. I can go get one if you prefer."

I squared my shoulders. They obviously hadn't spoken to Luke since this morning. "Nope, I'm good."

"I got you a mounting block."

"Thanks."

He held the reins as I scrambled up into the saddle. The mounting block helped, but I preferred it when Luke lifted me into the saddle. I held in my wince as my butt met the saddle, and Dusty moved forward. I was going to need that liniment again tonight.

We trotted toward the back of the ranch, and for the next while, I helped as they mended a couple of fences, trimmed some bushes that were growing over, and found a few cattle that had wandered away from the herd. John left with the cattle to guide them back to the herd, and I helped Tim with the final repair. He was a nice guy, with a great sense of humor. He told me some amusing stories that made me laugh, and he liked to talk about his mom and girlfriend.

"Are you an only child?"

"No, I have a little sister." A shadow passed over his face.

"What?"

He sighed. "She had a hard day yesterday. She was supposed to get a new kitten, but he was sick…" His voice trailed off, and he shrugged, unable to finish the sentence.

He reminded me of Reed, who always tried to be strong and not let his emotions out. I could see how much Tim loved his sister. I rubbed his arm in sympathy. "Oh no."

He nodded. "I hate seeing her upset. She's ten years younger than me—an oops baby. We all spoil her, but she's a great kid. I can't stand to watch her cry."

"Why don't you ask Luke if you can have one of the kittens in the stable? Bring her and let her choose one."

"I never thought of that. Thanks, Sammy." He hugged me, his eyes brighter. "I think you're right. She would love it."

I hugged him back. I would ask Luke myself—I was sure he would say yes.

The sound of an ATV bearing down on us startled me, and I stepped back. Luke pulled up, his face like thunder as he climbed out of the vehicle.

He stalked toward us, glaring. "Sorry to interrupt your moment. I thought we agreed on an ATV this morning, Samantha?"

I blinked at the use of my full name. So few people ever called me that.

Tim ran a hand over his neck. "Shit. You never mentioned it, boss. You said the full experience, so I saddled her horse." He glanced at me. "You never said anything."

"Because I was fine," I lied. My ass was killing me again, but I wasn't going to let Luke know it.

"Is that a fact?" Luke snapped.

I tossed my hair. "Yes."

"She's done great, boss. Even helped corral that last stubborn cow. Mended one fence all on her own."

I met Luke's glare. "I know how to handle a *tool*," I said slowly. "I've had lots of practice, especially lately."

His glare intensified, the frown lines in his forehead deepening.

"Well, if the two of you are finished canoodling, there are other tasks that need taking care of." He looked at Tim. "Head back to the ranch. Take Dusty with you. Jeff needs some help. I'll take her around and finish the last of the mends."

Tim glanced between us. I smiled at him. "Oh, work with the boss. How fun," I fibbed.

Tim looked uncertain but nodded. "Sure."

He left, and Luke climbed into the ATV. "Are you coming or walking?"

Tossing my hair, I climbed into the ATV, unable to stop the wince as I sat down.

"*Fine*," he snorted with derision. "Right."

"I am. Did you not eat lunch?"

"Yes, I did. That's when I found out you went by horse. Even though I specifically told you not to."

"You're acting awfully hangry for someone who ate. You're not my boss, jackass. I don't have to follow your orders."

Suddenly, I was pressed against the seat, Luke leaning over me, caging me in.

"That's where you're wrong, Lady. *Here*, I *am* the boss of you. The expert. I know more about ranching and what to do than you will ever figure out. I tell you to do something, you do it. Without question. I issue orders for a reason. I'm not telling you for my own health, but for yours. You hear me?"

His gaze was intense, his voice low and angry. His chest pressed into mine, the heat of him soaking into my skin. His words bounced around in my head, one sentence echoing.

Here, I am the boss of you.

That should piss me off. But for some reason, it only made me breathless.

"Fine," I managed to mutter.

He dropped back behind the wheel. "Good. That's settled."

CHAPTER ELEVEN

LUKE

I could barely hold in my anger. I didn't understand it. The woman sitting beside me could rile me up faster than the most obstinate of cows refusing to move. I had hated to see the bruises and her pain last night. It had taken everything in me not to stay with her and stroke her in another way entirely. Turn her moans of pain into pleasure and hold her as she slept.

Somehow seeing her interacting with Tim, however briefly, had set off a maelstrom in my head. I had stopped at the top of the hill, using the binoculars to scan for them. Furious she was riding again today, knowing she had to be sore. They were standing close, talking, laughing. She touched him, a small tap on his cheek, and an emotion I had never felt before exploded.

Jealousy.

I shook my head as we stopped outside the barn. She hopped out and went over to Tim, saying something, once again patting his arm. He leaned down, the brim of his hat blocking her face, speaking to her, and jealousy once again swamped me as she hugged him. Wound her arms around his waist and hugged him.

Again.

In front of me.

I slid from the ATV and stomped over, glowering and ready for a fight. Unable to stop myself from snapping. "Sorry to interrupt —*again*. Don't I pay you to do something around here besides grope the guests, Tim?" I growled. "In fact, I'm pretty damn sure I said to stay away."

Tim stepped back, shocked. "Sorry, boss. Sammy here was just—"

"Sammy needs to learn to keep her hands to herself," I replied and took her arm, tugging her in the direction of the barn. "I need to speak to her. Excuse us. Do your job," I added over my shoulder.

I took her into the barn, pulling the door shut behind me. I was tired, tense, and angry. Not a good combination.

She twirled around, crossing her arms. "What is your problem?" she asked.

I stalked toward her, knocking over a loose bale of hay in my anger, the straw hitting the ground and bursting open, scattering the golden sheaves everywhere.

"Dammit," I cursed, kicking at the hay.

"Now it's your target?" she asked, sarcastic. "Not poor Tim?"

I closed the distance between us, narrowing my eyes.

"Listen, Lady, and listen well. The staff is off-limits."

She furrowed her brow. "Excuse me?"

"Stop flirting."

"I'm not flirting!" she retorted, sounding shocked. "I'm being friendly."

"Looked a lot more like flirting than being friendly."

She snorted, tossing her hair, reminding me of an impatient filly that was getting ready to throw her rider for incompetence. She glared at me. "Maybe because you're neither friendly nor know how to flirt, you big jackass."

"I know exactly what I was seeing. You laughing and chatting with Tim. Rubbing his arm. Hugging him. That was flirting," I snapped, unable to understand my fury. I hated seeing her close to him. Loathed her touching him. I wanted to find Tim and beat his ass for having the audacity to get close to her.

She shook her head. "You are such an idiot. I was laughing with him earlier as he was telling me stories of his mother and *girlfriend* and how they gang up on him all the time. I was comforting him when he told me about his sister not getting the kitten she was waiting for and how awful he felt for her." She pushed on my chest. "You jumping-to-conclusions *jackass*."

I grabbed her hand. "That's twice you've called me jackass. I hope you're better at writing copy than you are at insults."

I should have known better. The last time I'd grabbed her hand, she'd flipped me like it was nothing.

She did it again.

One moment, I was on my feet, glaring down at her. The next, I was on the pile of hay on the ground, blinking up at her. She scrambled and straddled me, breathing hard, her hands in the middle of my chest.

"You are the most irritating, grumpy man I have ever met," she hissed in her fury.

Then she crashed her mouth to mine. I fisted her hair, groaning at her taste as our tongues met, furious and intense. She bit my lip, and I sprang up, surprising her, rolling us so I was over her.

"You are the most vexing, pushy woman I have ever had to deal with," I growled. Then I yanked her up and kissed her again, holding her tight. Her mouth was sweet. Far too sweet for the venom it could spout.

She wrapped her legs around my waist and lunged. Once again caught by surprise, I ended up on my back again, with her on top.

"Afraid I'll show you up in front of your men?" she taunted.

"You need to watch your mouth."

"Seems to me you like my mouth."

"Only if it was wrapped around my dick."

She arched an eyebrow. "Dreaming of me now, are you?"

"More of a nightmare, really."

I sat up, laying her down on the straw, following her and pressing her into the pile again. "At least you'd be quiet then."

She glared, which turned me on more. "You'd hate me quiet."

I had to grin. "Yeah, I would." I traced a finger down her cheek. "Are you okay to do this, Sammy? I mean—"

She cut me off. "More kissing, less talking, Cowboy."

We rolled, the straw going everywhere as we moved. She was surprisingly strong and agile. I finally was over her, pinning her arms down and keeping her under me. My cock was rock hard, my breathing heavy. Her chest heaved, her lips were swollen from mine, and her hair spread around the hay, a softer version of the straw. Her dark eyes were wide and wild with emotion.

Was it anger? Lust? I knew which one I was feeling now.

"You got anything else to tell me?" she asked.

"You're the fucking sexiest thing I have ever seen."

Then my mouth was back on hers. Our tongues dueled and fought for dominance. The kiss became carnal. Deep. Wet. Possessive. Somehow my hands found their way under her shirt, pressing into the satin of her skin. She clawed at my shoulders, tugging on the plaid so hard the seams split. I sat up, so she straddled me again. She moaned when she felt my cock pressing into her. I dragged my mouth from hers, over her cheek to her ear.

"Tell me to stop."

"No."

"Tell me to stop," I demanded, cupping her breast and stroking the hard nipple.

"Fuck you," she replied.

"Tell me to stop, or I *will* fuck you. Right here. Right now."

She grabbed my face between her hands. "Don't make promises you're not going to keep, Luke."

All bets were off.

In seconds, her clothing was gone, disappearing over my shoulder. She tore my muscle shirt, running her hands all over my chest. My fingers met hers as she grappled for my belt and zipper, the sound of the metal opening loud to my ears. I lifted my ass, and she dragged my jeans down my legs, pushing me back into the hay. She stared at me, her hair a mess, lips wet, a mark already showing on her neck from my teeth. I cupped her breasts, teasing her hard nipples. She moaned and stroked me.

"You gonna show me what you got, Cowboy? Ride me hard?" she challenged.

"You're gonna ride *me*, Lady. I'll show you what a stallion between your legs feels like."

Then I was inside her. The heat, wetness, and tightness of her surrounded me. I cursed at the sensations, gripping her hips. She whimpered, tilting back her head, her honey-colored hair brushing my legs as she held my thighs and began to move. Long, slow rolls of her hips, small gasps escaping her lips as she moved. I met her movements, the feeling of her wrapped around my cock incredible. She bent forward, bracing her hands on my chest, driving me deeper inside.

"Fuck," I groaned. "You feel so good, Lady."

She lifted her head, our eyes locking. "Luke," she whispered. "Please."

I sat up, gripping the back of her neck and covering her mouth with mine. I knew she was still hurting, but I couldn't stop. I didn't want to stop, and even more important, she didn't want me to stop. She gave as good as she got. I sped up my movements, the sounds of our bodies colliding over and over, our skin sliding together, our grunts and groans of pleasure filling my ears. She wrapped her arms around me, her breasts rubbing my chest, her fingers digging into my shoulders. The scent of her surrounded me. Light, feminine, warm.

Just like her.

My orgasm hit me, and she shivered, tightening around me. Everything magnified. Became electric and wild. The feel of her. The taste. The ecstasy rippling down my spine. Her muffled screams in my mouth.

And then, there was only peace. Her in my arms, sated and warm. Close.

I released her mouth, pressing a kiss to her head. She dropped her face into my neck, and I lay back, still holding her, into the hay. I traced gentle patterns on her back, her skin soft and damp under my fingers.

She squirmed a little, and I felt the wet between us. I bolted upright, gripping her arms.

"What?"

"Fuck, Sammy. We didn't use a condom. I was so caught up—"

She interrupted me. "I'm on the pill, and I'm safe."

I pulled a hand through my hair. "I haven't been with anyone for a long time, and I'm safe, but fuck. We can't... Jesus, we shouldn't..." I shook my head. "Not again. This isn't happening again."

She narrowed her eyes at me. "Really?"

"You're here to do a job. Nothing else." I lifted her off me, ignoring the flash of displeasure I felt at being separated from her physically. I scrambled to my feet, yanking up my jeans. "We should never... *Fuck*, Rachel is going to kill me."

She stood and calmly reached for her clothing, pulling her shirt over her head and stepping into her jeans. She picked up her shoes and looked at me.

"I don't plan on telling Rachel a thing. We're two grown-ups who gave in to the chemistry we felt. Scratched an itch. Nothing more. I get it."

I searched for my shirt, finding it under a pile of hay. At least it hadn't been torn much. I could wear it until I got to the house. I stopped as her words hit me.

Scratched an itch?

"Is that a fact?" I replied. "Chemistry—is that what you'd call it?"

She shrugged. "Lust, if that helps you sleep at night. Whatever. If you expected me to fall at your feet and beg you for another round, Cowboy, you're mistaken. We both got what we wanted."

It was my turn to narrow my eyes at her. "Really?" I asked as I fastened my belt, noting how her gaze was focused on my hands. I stepped toward her. "The lust is gone now? One round and we're done?"

She smiled—another new one in her arsenal of smiles. It was wide, devilish, and teasing.

"Your decision. Nothing else, you said."

She walked over to the barn door, sliding it open just enough to slip through. She poked her head around the corner.

"Thanks, Cowboy. I did enjoy taming your stallion."

Then she was gone.

I stood in the barn, gaping at the door.

Taming my stallion?

Regardless of my stupid mutterings, the fucker wanted more.

I wanted more.

And I had a feeling she did too.

But it was a bad idea. I couldn't get involved with Sammy. I shouldn't get involved with her. She was nothing but trouble. Her and those damn smiles of hers.

Something caught my eye, and I bent, picking up the material from the hay. Sammy had left behind her underwear. I held them up, wondering if you could really call this scrap of lace underwear.

Then I tucked them into my pocket.

I grabbed a broom, but her words kept swirling in my head.

Scratched an itch. Lust. Chemistry. You'll never know. We both got what we wanted.

I tossed the broom aside and pushed open the barn door. I stalked toward the house, walking past Tim on the way.

"A bale got broken in the barn. Clean it up," I snapped and kept going.

Maybe she got what she wanted, but I didn't.

This was my damn ranch, and I called the shots here.

Not Sammy.

My itch hadn't yet been scratched.

CHAPTER TWELVE

SAMMY

I made it to the house without anyone seeing me. Hurrying down the hall, I shut the bathroom door, leaning on it, breathless.

Holy shit—had I had sex in a barn with Luke?

Sexy, dirty-talking, cowboy Luke?

My God, the man could kiss. Never mind what he could do with his fingers and cock.

He had totally wrecked me for any other man—without even trying.

I walked to the vanity and studied myself in the mirror. Thank goodness I hadn't seen anyone on my walk—or, in this case, run —of shame. My hair was everywhere, and there was straw in it. I had scruff marks all over my neck and chest and a small bite mark at the base of my throat. My cheeks were flushed, and my lips looked as if they'd been sucked on by a vacuum. They were red, wet, and swollen.

My body ached in an entirely new way, and I knew it was going to be worse later. I would feel every bruise, mark, and unused muscle. Yet, somehow, I didn't care.

My clothes were misshapen as if they'd been yanked off my body, and I realized I had no idea where my underwear went. I dropped my head into my hands, imagining having to sneak back to the barn later to try to find them.

And how was I going to face Luke? I had taunted him, teased, and flaunted the "no biggie sort of sex" thing to him. Why had I done that?

Sex to me was a big deal, and he was the first man I had ever lost my head with that way. And I only said that to piss him off. His over-the-top reaction to me being nice to Tim was laughable. Tim was a boy to me. Luke was a man. A jealous man who was undeniably sexy when he was being possessive.

I shook my head. Rachel said he liked a challenge, and in my own way, I was throwing down the gauntlet. I wanted him desperately, and by telling him the opposite, I hoped he would want me back as well.

The bathroom door opened, and Luke stood in the doorway. I tried not to whimper as I realized I had gotten my wish.

Our eyes met in the mirror, his gaze like blue fire. Icy and hot at the same time. His expression was furious, and he looked freshly fucked.

Which, of course, he was.

His hat was missing, and his hair was everywhere, his flannel shirt torn at the shoulders. I saw some nail marks on his chest, and I tried to recall putting them there.

"Lose your hat, Cowboy?" I asked. "I'll save you some time. It's not in here."

I swallowed as he stepped inside, shutting the door behind him. "Let's get something straight," he said, his voice low, raspy, and full of dark promises.

I tossed my hair, pretending not to be affected by him. I ignored the aching feeling in my center, or how my nipples tightened as he came closer, his chest to my back.

"What might that be?" I asked, pretending to concentrate on picking straw from my hair, praying he didn't notice the way my hands shook as I did.

"You don't call the shots here, Lady. My ranch. My rules."

I shrugged, my body reacting to his closeness. Wanting him closer.

What the hell was he doing to me?

"You said no more."

Our eyes locked in the mirror, and he smiled. It was wicked, wide, and made my thighs clench.

"I changed my mind."

Then he spun me, covering my mouth with his and kissing me hard. I threw my arms around his neck, kissing him back with equal abandon. He devoured my mouth, almost frenzied, ramping up my need for him. My blouse was torn from my body, and he pushed down my jeans, stroking me.

"Where are your underwear?" he asked against my ear, nipping on the lobe. "Forgot those in your rush to get away, Lady?"

"Do you have them?" I asked, tilting my neck to give him better access. He licked at the skin, biting down, leaving, no doubt, another mark.

"Maybe."

"Give them back."

He covered my mouth again. "No."

I ripped his shirt, completing the job I had started earlier. Our fingers met as we both reached for his belt, but he pushed my hands away, lifting me to the vanity. He kicked off his boots and jeans, standing naked and glorious. But he barely gave me the chance to ogle him before he wrapped my legs around his waist, then clutched the back of my neck, kissing me again, his thumb and fingers stroking my skin in small, hard circles. His cock pushed between my folds, and he groaned in approval.

"So wet for me, Sammy? All this for me?"

"Yes," I replied, not attempting to deny it.

"You want me to fuck you again?"

"Yes, oh God, yes."

"You're not too sore?" he asked, a flicker of worry flashing through his eyes.

"Shut up and take me," I pleaded. I'd worry about my sore body later. Right now, he had something I wanted far more. It would ease the suddenly needy ache between my legs.

He slid his hand under my ass, angling me, his intense gaze focused on mine, then he shifted his hips. Slowly, he sank in until we were flush. I pulsated around him, already on the verge of coming.

"Jesus," he muttered, flexing, withdrawing, and sinking back in.

I whimpered, desperate and wanting. Wanting him. Needing him.

He moved his hand between us, stroking my clit. I detonated, arching my back, crying out, clawing at his shoulders. He grinned and clutched my neck harder, his mouth hovering over mine.

"So sexy when you come, Lady. Your mouth open, your eyes glazed over, and the prettiest little sounds coming from your throat." He stroked the column of my neck. "I wonder what your lips will feel like around my dick. How your throat will constrict as you swallow all of me," he said in a low tone. "You're going to show me that later." Then he crashed his lips to mine and started to move.

Powerful, hard thrusts. He kept his hold on my neck as he moved, bracing his free hand on the vanity. I clung to him, my body already awash in sensation, ramping up for more.

I whimpered, and he smiled against my mouth. "Two more, Sammy. You're going to give me two more, then I'm going to come all over you. Inside. Outside. You're going to be covered in me. And you are going to feel me for days. Your own personal stallion, riding you to heaven."

It was all I could do to hang on as he drove into me. He hit me in a place that made me see stars. I came again, shaking and moaning his name. He carried on, never relenting. I lost track of everything but the place where we were joined. The intense pleasure. The growing need in my body. His hot, demanding mouth, the pressure and pleasure of his touch. Rough, but not hurtful. Strong, Powerful. Momentum gathered, and I cried his name.

"I can't. Luke, please…"

He pressed his lips to mine, speaking against them, his tone oddly gentle. "You can, Lady. For me. Come with me."

My orgasm hit, and I lost control—crying, begging, the ecstasy overwhelming everything. He grunted and shook, holding me in place as he came, doing exactly what he said. Marking me, inside and out, with his orgasm.

Then with a low groan, he sank to his knees, wrapping his arms around my waist and burying his head into my stomach. I ran my fingers through his hair, feeling tenderness run through me. For a moment, we stayed that way, him on the floor, me rubbing his neck.

He pushed off the vanity and stood, not looking at me. He dragged on his jeans and grabbed his boots.

"*Now*, the itch is scratched," he said and walked out.

I wanted to be upset and march after him, telling him what I thought, but it was impossible. He'd fucked me so well and thoroughly I could barely move.

And besides, he was lying.

I had a feeling our mutual itch was going to flare up over and over again.

I wondered how long until he cracked.

LUKE

I stood under the running shower, letting the hot water pour over me, washing away the remnants of the day. I sighed as the heat helped loosen my stiff neck. The water was doing its job well.

What it couldn't do, though, was erase my thoughts of the day.

My fury and unexpected jealousy.

The blistering passion that arose.

The mad, intense sex I'd had with Sammy.

Twice.

I recalled my parting words.

"Now, the itch is scratched."

What a liar. Simply thinking of her, I was hard. My itch wasn't scratched. If anything, it had taken over my body and mind, a slow, constant irritant I wasn't sure would ever ease until she was gone.

Which meant I had to be careful not to be around her much. I had to stay in control. I needed to be aloof and distant. Contain these odd reactions and let the hands deal with her. I'd make sure to send her out with a couple of the women next time.

I soaped up, trying to think of something else. Tomorrow's schedule. The upcoming auction I would attend. At least that would give me some distance.

I groaned as I wrapped my hand around my shaft, and images of being buried inside Sammy hit me like a wrecking ball. Her heat. The feel of her. The breathless whimpers and passionate moans. The way she moved with me. Kissed me as if I was the oxygen

147

she needed to breathe. It all rushed back, and I was helpless. I braced one arm on the tile wall and stroked myself, moving faster as the images unfolded one by one. The way her head tilted back and how her hair brushed my legs. The taste of her skin under my tongue. How she looked and sounded as she came.

I dropped my head to my arm as my orgasm hit. I bit my bicep to hold in the deep groan as I ejaculated onto the tile, dragging in some deep breaths to steady myself as the water washed away the evidence.

I shook my head in defeat. I couldn't make it through a shower without thoughts of her. How was I supposed to make it through the next six weeks?

I was fucked. Totally fucked.

I was relieved to find Rachel sitting with Sammy when I ventured down the hall. A platter of meat was on the counter, along with a bowl of salad.

I hugged Rachel. "How's Tyler?"

She smiled. "A slight delay, but home tomorrow." She indicated the counter. "Jane sent over some barbecue. I made up the salad."

"Jane doesn't have to keep sending dinners," I remarked, although I was grateful.

"She knows you're on your own, plus Sammy is here. She always makes too much. She was hoping maybe you would join us tomorrow night to welcome Tyler home."

I filled my plate with the ribs and chicken, carrying it to the table and sitting down. "Sure."

She turned to Sammy. "You're welcome too. It's relaxed and easy since it will be just family."

"Oh, that's fine. I don't want to intrude."

"You won't be intruding. Right, Luke?"

I met Rachel's gaze and shrugged. "The more, the merrier."

She frowned at my lack of enthusiasm but kept going. "See? You have to come. Tyler wants to meet you."

"Okay. Can I bring something?"

Rachel laughed. "No. Jane has it all under control." She took a drink and spoke to Sammy. "So, how is everything going?"

"Good. Ah, good."

Rachel frowned. "Just good?"

"No, great. Tomorrow, I'm going to start filming. Some before shots. I want to feature some sunrises and sunsets, pictures of the ranch. Showing it at its best."

"Of course," Rachel agreed.

"I'll film the process and edit it all. Do some candid shots, some interviews—very casual, of course—plus a few scripted parts I'll splice in. When the show airs, I want to capture people's imagination."

"Make sure you have everyone's permission to film them," I said flippantly. "Pretty sure that's needed."

After a beat of silence, Sammy spoke, her voice low and serious. When I looked up, her gaze was frosty.

"Luke, perhaps you don't know the process, but let me explain it to you so you understand."

I lifted an eyebrow in silence.

"I get hundreds of applications for me to take and help a new business. Each one is vetted. Each idea gone through thoroughly. We look at the business plan, the numbers, the validity of the idea. Rachel's was spot-on. Her application was perhaps one of the best I had ever seen." Sammy leaned forward, tapping the table. "It's not only your ranch and money. It's my money, time, and reputation as well. I want this to be successful for you. I will do everything I can to make sure it is. I'll have you know not one business I have helped with the show has failed. Not one. But the difference here is they believed."

I blinked at her direct tone.

She stood, and I noticed the small frown cross her face as she did. "If you don't believe in this venture, if you brush it and me aside, then it is doomed to fail. Your attitude with the development—and, even more so, the guests—will be paramount. You treat them with derision, then we're bound to fail. I know what I'm doing. What needs to happen. And I assure you, that begins with releases from everyone." She slid a piece of paper my way. "In fact, the only person who hasn't signed one is you." She shook her head. "I'll let you and Rachel discuss this, and you can let me know. I can be on a plane home tomorrow if you're not fully on board. I won't waste any more of your or my valuable time."

Then she walked out the front door, closing it behind her quietly. Somehow the soft click seemed louder than it was in the silent room.

I looked at the piece of paper on the table, then glanced up, meeting Rachel's angry gaze.

"All I did—"

She held up her hand. "She's right. If you're not on board with this, it's not going to work, no matter what we do."

"I'm on board."

"Tim tells me you were yelling earlier. You never yell, Luke. What's going on?"

I couldn't tell her. She would be horrified at my actions. "Bad day," I responded. "But I will go find Sammy and apologize. I know how much this means to you."

"I thought you believed in me. In this."

I took her hand. "I do, Rach. It scares me," I confessed. "How it will affect the day-to-day running of the ranch. But I'll figure it out. I won't stand in the way."

"Sammy has so many great ideas. The income will be a huge boost for the ranch and the farm. And we can control the number of guests and where they go. Sammy knows what she's doing. I trust her." She inhaled, the sound shaky. "She picked me. That alone should say something. She is so successful with her show, and it will help us launch this properly. But she's right. If you don't really want it, it isn't going to work, and I won't waste her time."

I stood and yanked her into my arms. "No, kiddo. I'm right there with you. I'll get my head out of my ass and do whatever you need. I didn't mean to insult her or upset you." I pressed a kiss to her head. "Forgive me."

She looked up. "I do."

"I'll go find Sammy and apologize."

"Make it a good one."

"I'll do my best."

It took me a while to find Sammy. I finally found her in the stable, petting the kittens. The hay had been cleaned up, the evidence of our earlier entanglement swept away.

She looked up as I approached, then dropped her head back down. One kitten was sleeping in her neck, nestled in the crook. Two more were on her lap, while the momma looked on indulgently.

I dropped to my haunches, stroking the calico's head.

"You're a hard woman to find."

"I've been right here since I left the house. You walked past me twice."

"You couldn't have called out and helped?"

She looked up. "No."

With a chuckle, I sat down in front of her, smiling as some kittens crawled onto my lap. I stroked their soft fur. "You like cats?"

"Yes." She paused. "What happens to them?"

"We find homes for them. We keep those we can't relocate." I chucked one under the chin. "We take a couple others in at times. We spay and neuter, but there are always cats around."

She pulled her bottom lip in and nibbled, then spoke. "Tim needs one for his sister."

"Sure. I'll tell him to bring her to choose one."

"Not this one," Sammy said quietly, indicating the tiny black-and-white bundle currently buried in her neck. "He's mine while I'm here, and he needs his mom."

"He's the runt."

She stroked him. "I know."

"Okay." I took a deep breath. "I need to apologize."

She met my gaze. "You need to apologize to your sister. Her idea is solid. She put a great deal of thought and time into it."

"I know. I did apologize to her, and now I'm apologizing to you. I am well aware you know what you're doing. I read up on you last night. Your successes. The things people had to say about you. I was being a jerk."

"Because of what happened between us?" she asked.

"Yes," I said honestly. "It threw me. You bring out something in me I don't quite understand, and I react when you're around. I react a lot."

"I feel it as well."

I shook my head. "It can't happen, Sammy. This means too much to Rachel, and I can't risk it affecting your work or attitude. I want this to go well for her."

"And you don't think we can act like reasonable adults?"

"There is nothing reasonable about how I feel when you're close."

"Oh." She stroked the kitten, lifting him off her neck and settling him against his mom.

"Can we just put aside that, ah, whatever you want to call it and work together to make Rachel's dream come true, then?" she asked. "Can you do that?"

"Yes," I lied.

I would damn well try.

She stood and brushed off her jeans. She winced again, and I lifted the sleeping kittens off me and stood with her. "Did I hurt you today?"

"No."

"But you're sore."

She smiled, her cheeks going a faint dusty-rose color. "Worth it," she whispered, meeting my eyes. I had to smile back at her. I liked this smile—shy and sweet as we shared a knowing glance. Then she cleared her throat.

"I'll be fine. Maybe I can borrow a little more of that ointment you have. I'll soak in the tub a bit."

"Not much of a tub in that bathroom. It's on the list of improvements to make."

"It'll do."

I watched as she moved, knowing she was in more pain than she was letting on. She was a strong woman. And stubborn.

I shook my head as I followed her. We had both those traits in common.

I watched her from afar the next day. I spoke with Tim, apologized for my gruffness and told him to bring his sister, Ella, around to pick out a kitten, or two, if she wanted.

"They'll be able to go in a few weeks."

He accepted my apology with the wave of his hand. "We all have those days," he said and went about his day as usual.

Sammy wandered, taking pictures, using a camera to film different places around the ranch. She was still stiff, and I noticed her wince on occasion. I made sure she stayed off the horse today, knowing that would help. There was plenty to see and do around the main area. For some reason, I stayed close as well. I didn't question myself too closely as to the reason why.

We drove to the farm later, Sammy carrying a container of cookies she told me she'd baked.

"You bake?" I asked.

She chuckled. "We all do. My mom and aunts love to cook. When we do our family brunches or parties, we cook for days."

"You have a large family?"

"Well, my family is small. Three of us, plus Mom and Dad. But I have an extended family." She shook her head with one of her wide, sun-filled smiles. "I lost count of how many there are. Close to forty now, I think. I'll have to do a head count."

"Wow."

"I'm sure my dad will tell you all about them," she said. "Or one of my uncles." She used her fingers to make quotation marks around the word uncles.

"So, not blood family, then?"

She was quiet, then shook her head. "No. Closer, I think. Found family. I'm very lucky my dad met my mom and adopted me."

"Oh," I said.

"He's the greatest man I know. All my uncles and cousins are close seconds."

We pulled up to the farmhouse, and I smiled. "I look forward to hearing more about them."

Surprisingly, it wasn't just a polite statement. I was curious about her. Her family.

Again, I didn't question why.

CHAPTER THIRTEEN

SAMMY

Despite his injuries, Tyler Johnstone was a handsome man. Underneath the bruises, the cast that covered his leg, and the sling around his arm, I could see the man Rachel loved. He was tall and lean, his shoulders broad and his body well muscled from the physical labor he did. He had hair that was so blond it was almost white, bleached by his constant time in the sun. His eyes were a soft blue, and I wondered which hue their children would inherit. He gazed at Rachel with utter adoration. He shook my hand and smiled, teasing Luke and me about our first meeting. Luckily, Luke laughed along, and we left it at that.

Dinner was a loud affair, the table groaning with food. I always had a good appetite, but since arriving on the ranch, I was shocked at the amount of food I consumed. It seemed to taste better after a day of working in the fresh air.

Jane offered me the platter of roast beef, and I took more along with the mashed potatoes. Luke caught my eye and winked, making me blush for some reason. Then I tossed my hair and took a piece of chicken too.

"This is delicious," I praised Jane. "I've never tasted such good beef."

"My cows," Luke said.

"Oh."

"We trade," Jane explained. "His beef for our pigs and some chickens, plus whatever else to make the trade fair."

Luke laughed. "It's a good trade. My freezer is full year-round with meat and vegetables from your farm. Never mind the honey and cheese."

Harry laughed. "Your hay feeds our animals. We're a good team."

Tyler squeezed Rachel's hand. "We are."

"Where's Henry?" Luke asked, referring to Tyler's brother.

"Out with Linda. It's their anniversary."

"Speaking of anniversaries, when is your wedding?" I asked.

"September," Rachel said. "You have to come."

"I would love that if my schedule permits." I winked. "I'll pencil you in."

Everyone laughed, and Jane turned to me. "Rachel says your sister is an author."

"Yes," I said proudly. "One of her books is about to be made into a movie."

"How exciting."

"We're very proud. We all love to read. We even have a family book club."

Rachel clapped her hands. "I love to read too. What name does your sister write under?"

"A.M. Archer."

Her eyes went wide. "Oh my God, I love her."

I chuckled. "I'll get her to send you a book."

"That would be awesome."

"Do your family read her as part of your club?"

I laughed. "No. I preread for her, and they all do read her books. But they are, ah, rather steamy, and we have trouble associating those with our Mila. We usually read historical romance. That's kind of our jam."

Luke snorted. "I wouldn't have taken you for a bodice-ripper fan."

I shook my head. "You have no idea. The books are addictive."

"Do you have a favorite author?" Rachel queried.

"A few. Scarlett Scott is one. I'm reading one of hers right now."

"I should check her out."

"You'd love her," I assured Rachel. "The one I'm reading now, the hero is attempting to use the heroine for his own gain, except he falls in love and can't go through with it, even though it would help his family."

Luke snorted again, and I ignored him. I didn't want to say that Hart Sutton reminded me of him. Filled with honor, hating himself for something he did, yet torn because he wanted it again. Luke would never see that and would laugh at the comparison.

Instead, I grinned at Rachel. "I'll call Mila later."

"Awesome."

After the kitchen was cleaned, I went for a walk, taking some pictures and admiring the well-run farm. Rachel joined me, pointing out different buildings. "Over there, that tin roof, is where Tyler and I will live."

"You must be excited."

"It took us a long time to get to this point. We were friends our whole lives, but that was all." She shrugged. "Until one day, we weren't. I looked at him differently and he looked back at me the same way, and I realized I'd been missing what was under my nose all those years." She sighed. "I wish my parents were around to see it."

"I'm sure they know."

"I am excited, but I'm worried too."

"About?"

"Luke."

"Ah."

"He'll be alone."

"Your brother wouldn't want to hold up your happiness," I advised. I had already figured that out about him.

"I know. And I'll see him every day, but it'll be different. I just hate to think of him all alone in that house."

"Maybe he'll meet someone," I offered, the words feeling thick and strange on my tongue.

She glanced to the side then back to the vista in front of her. "Maybe. I hope so. He would be an amazing partner. Loving, giving, supportive."

I had a feeling she was trying to tell me something, but I ignored it. Neither Luke nor I was looking for a partner. He was focused on the ranch, and I had my career.

"I hope he finds the right person."

She nodded, taking my arm. "I think he will. Sometimes we don't see what is right in front of us until we are nudged in that direction. I might have to help him."

I wasn't sure what she meant by that, and the bottom line was, I was afraid to ask. I wasn't sure I would like the answer.

LUKE

Jesus, she was beautiful. I sat on the porch with Tyler, covertly watching Sammy as she walked with Rachel. Sammy's golden hair was bright in the evening sun, and she was sexy as hell. Small and compact, but strong and confident. I had felt her strength, albeit not the way I would have expected, but she was dangerous when angry. She walked with an easy grace, and the sound of her laughter reached my ears. It was low and sultry, much like her voice when she begged me to fuck her.

I had to shake my head to clear those thoughts.

She was still sore, I could tell. She was slow to stand or sit, and on occasion, a grimace passed over her face. She held herself as though warding off pain, and I was shocked at the pull I felt to help her.

How, I wasn't sure.

"You like her," Tyler observed.

"What?" I replied, sitting back, surprised to find how far forward I had been sitting in my chair.

"Sammy," he said, taking a sip of coffee. "You like her."

"She's fine."

He laughed. "So fine you can't keep your eyes off her."

"Whatever," I bluffed, picking up my cup.

"You've been with her."

"What?" I sputtered around the mouthful of coffee.

"You heard me."

I didn't deny it. Tyler and I were friends—we'd known each other our whole lives.

"Keep that to yourself. I don't need Rachel after me with a pitchfork. Sammy's enough to deal with on her own."

"Is this just a fling?"

"It was. It's done."

"I see."

"An itch. It's scratched," I said, using Sammy's words.

"Uh-huh."

"Tyler," I began.

"Yeah?" he said, an underlying tone of amusement lacing his words.

"Fuck off, okay?"

"Duly noted. But you should know, Rachel suspects."

"Dammit."

"Just saying. You might want to tone down the vibes you throw out when Sammy is around."

"And what vibes are those?" I asked, sarcastic.

"*My woman* kind of vibes."

"Again, fuck off."

He laughed. "This is gonna be fun."

Rachel appeared on the porch, Sammy behind her.

"So, the dance on Friday. You're gonna take Sammy, right?"

I felt Tyler's amused glance, and I feigned disinterest. "I suppose. I can drop her off anyway."

Rachel crossed her arms, glaring. "You will take her and introduce her to people."

"Fine."

"Wow, I feel wanted," Sammy muttered.

"I hate those things. All the women pushing their single daughters my way. I'm not in the market," I stated clearly.

"With Sammy there, they won't. She needs to meet people so she can do some filming in town. I am staying with Tyler for the weekend, and I expect you to do this."

I sighed and gave in. "Yeah, kiddo. I'll take her. But I'm not dancing."

"I wouldn't expect you to," Rachel replied. "I'm sure lots of other fellas will step up and dance with her."

"Good," I grated out, draining my coffee. "That works out for everyone."

I stood, fighting down the urge to punch something. Tyler chuckled, and I threw him a look, then grabbed my hat, ramming it onto my head. "I have things to do at the house, Sammy. You coming?"

She frowned but nodded. "I just want to say thank you to Jane and Harry."

I nodded. "I'll be in the truck."

SAMMY

Luke was quiet in the truck, and I followed his lead. At the house, he headed to his office, and I went to my room. I forgot to tell him that I had run out of the liniment and ask if he had any more, but I decided against bothering him tonight. I soaked in the tub as best I could. It was old and shallow, and I couldn't get low enough to soak my shoulder and back at the same time, so I eventually gave up. I slipped on a nightgown, took some Tylenol, and headed to the kitchen to get a glass of water. Luke's side of the house was dark, and I assumed he'd gone to bed.

In my room, I lay down, draping the heating pad over my legs, hoping it and the pills would dull the ache. Then I moved it to the shoulder that hurt, but the heat did little to dispel the pain. I got up and padded to the kitchen, opening the freezer and taking the ice pack, deciding to try the cold instead.

"Still hurting?" Luke's voice in the darkness startled me.

"Oh!" I gasped as I dropped the ice pack. "Um, a little. I thought the ice would help."

"The liniment not doing its job?" he asked, sitting at the kitchen table, a glass of water in front of him.

"I used it all last night. I meant to ask you if you had more."

He stood. "No, but I'll get more at the pharmacy tomorrow. Doc makes sure I always have refills."

He wore sweats that hung low on his hips. Nothing else. His bare chest gleamed in the dim light, showing off his broad shoulders. I swallowed, thinking how it felt to grip those shoulders. How his chest felt pushing into mine.

"Is the pain bad enough you can't sleep?"

"It'll be fine," I squeaked. "Good night." I hurried down the hall, diving into bed. I placed the ice pack on the back of my legs, shivering at the cold, hoping it would numb the ache enough so I could sleep.

Except my door opened, and Luke strode in.

"What are you doing?" I asked.

"Torturing myself," he muttered.

"What?"

"Helping you," he replied, climbing onto the bed, straddling the back of my legs. "Just relax, Lady. I'll rub out the sore muscles."

"I don't think——"

His touch stopped the words. Firm yet gentle, he immediately hit the sore muscles on the backs of my thighs. Instead of words, a groan escaped my lips.

Luke made a sound of distress low in his throat, but his touch never faltered. He stroked and pressed, his fingers going deep into the ache and pushing it away. He moved the ice pack up to my shoulder.

"You should have told me this morning you were out of the cream."

"I meant to."

His voice was quiet. "I hate seeing you in discomfort." He slid his hands higher.

I had to stifle a moan. The ache in my thighs was slowly being replaced by another ache completely. One between my legs that seem to pulsate and grow with each swipe of his hands.

For a few moments, he worked, and instead of relaxing, my body grew tighter, ached in a whole new way.

"I need to lift your skirts," he muttered.

I chuckled. "That's a very regency thing to say, Luke. You sure you don't read bodice rippers?" I teased.

I felt the cool night air kiss my thighs and ass, and I heard Luke's fast intake of air. I had nothing on under the nightgown I was wearing.

"I might have glanced at one of two of Rachel's books," he said, his voice gritty. He stroked the bottom swells of my ass, and I breathed out a low moan.

He froze, his hands pressing on my skin. "I need to stop."

"No," I pleaded, every nerve in my body on fire. "Don't stop."

He paused, his hands kneading my ass cheeks, muttering to himself.

Bad idea. Stop.

Then he moved down, shifting my legs and opening me up to him. He settled between my knees.

"Jesus," he muttered. "I stayed away for twenty-four hours. That deserves a reward." Then he began his circuit again, except his hands went higher, drifting closer to my center. His thumbs brushed my folds, and I didn't hold back my whimper. He pushed my nightgown higher, one hand spread wide across my back as he slipped the other between my legs. He groaned as he touched me.

"So wet, Sammy. Is that what you need to relax? My fingers?"

"Oh God," I cried as he touched my clit, swirling his finger on it in maddening circles.

"I'm going to relax you, Lady. You're going to forget about everything but this."

He was right. Within seconds, everything faded away except him and his touch. He teased my clit, pressing on it with his thumb, sinking in one, then two fingers and moving them inside me with a rhythm that made me clench.

"Lift," he growled in the darkness, pulling me up his thighs. He bent over me, sliding his free hand to my breasts, pinching and tweaking. I felt his lips on my back, his tongue trailing a wet path up my spine. Then he slid back, using both hands to pleasure me. He touched, stroked, soothed, teased, and pressed. His thumbs were magic, the large digits alternately inside me, strumming my clit, circling my ass with just enough pressure to make me shiver.

My body tightened, the pleasure becoming too much. I arched my back, and he lifted my hips, working his thumb and fingers in tandem.

"Now, Lady. Come now," he ordered, biting down on my ass cheek.

Everything blew apart. Ecstasy tore through me. I cried out, screaming into the pillow. He kept going, the waves of pleasure cresting and peaking—one after another.

Until I was spent. Until my body couldn't take anymore.

I collapsed to the mattress, Luke hovering over me, his heat soaking into my body. With gentle hands, he pulled down my nightgown and turned me over. He lowered his head, kissing me, his touch soft, his mouth tender. I pulled him down and turned to the side, our mouths never separating as I snuggled in and he held me tight to his chest.

The last thing I felt was his lips on mine and his breath in my mouth.

What a way to fall asleep.

Hours later, I woke, warm, nestled against a rock.

Except the rock was breathing and making a low, snoring sound. I peered up at Luke's face in the early morning light. I knew he'd be awake soon, and I wanted to take the chance to look at him.

Asleep, the lines of worry were absent, and he seemed peaceful. His long lashes rested on his cheeks as he slumbered. His lips pursed and relaxed as he made deep, rumbling noises in his throat.

I recalled last night. The way he'd brought me to a shuddering orgasm then kissed me until I fell asleep in his arms. I wasn't sure how he was going to feel about the fact that he, too, had fallen asleep and we'd spent the night together. There was a chance he'd be angry.

Except, right now, he wasn't angry. He was quiet. Resting.

Well, most of him.

His cock was awake, pressed between us, hard and ready. He'd certainly given me a release last night, making me forget about the aches and sending me into dreamworld with a smile on my face.

Surely that deserved a reward?

Carefully, I slid from his embrace. He frowned, groaned, and rolled onto his back, falling back into sleep.

His erection tented the blanket, and I carefully pulled back the covers. His sweats had slid down, and I slowly worked them off his hips, biting my lip as his cock was revealed. Heavy, thick, and hard as steel, it was a vision. A vein ran down the length of it, and the purple head was swollen and already glistening. The girth and length were impressive, and I recalled how good it had felt inside me.

Now I'd see how well it fit in my mouth. He'd said he wanted to see that.

I wanted to start Luke's day off with the same smile I went to sleep with. The reward he'd muttered about last night needed to be given.

I wrapped my hand around him.

LUKE

I'd had wet dreams before. Woken up, my hand around my cock, ready to shoot my load. But the dream I was currently experiencing was so good, I didn't want to open my eyes.

A hot, wet mouth was wrapped around my dick. A teasing tongue stroked my shaft, teeth nibbled playfully along the length, and my balls were being fondled. Again, I was engulfed in wet heat that sucked and hummed around me.

I opened my eyes, and the dream continued. Shocked, I lifted my head, meeting the brown eyes of Sammy, her mouth full of my cock, her eyes gleaming with mischief.

"Wh-what the hell?" I groaned. "What are you doing?"

She slowly released my cock, swiping it with her tongue. "If I have to explain this to you, Cowboy, then it has been far too long for you."

"Jesus—"

She ran her fingertip over the head, making me groan. "I'm returning the favor. I knew you would wake up aching. Just some preventive medicine." Then she swallowed me back down her throat.

I reared up in pleasure. I knew I should stop her. Stop this madness, but I couldn't. I wanted nothing more than to feel her mouth on me. To sink into the sensations she was causing in my cock. I arched my back, wanting closer to the pleasure.

"Yeah, Lady. Suck me." I groaned as her movements became faster. "Yes," I panted. "Like that. Just like that."

She played with my balls. Deep-throated me in a way I had never experienced. Stroked me with her tongue. Teased me with her fingers. Wrapped her fist around me as she sucked. I was lost in a vortex of desire, my body locking down. I moaned and cursed. Slid my fingers into her hair and rubbed restless circles on her head while praising her. Begging her for more.

And she gave it to me.

I succumbed. Shouting, calling her name, spilling down her throat, the blistering heat and frenzy of my orgasm washing over me. Until it was over and all I could do was lie there, drifting and sated, unsure if I could ever wake up again and not recall this moment. Crave it again.

Crave her.

She settled beside me, and I turned my head. She smiled, sunshine and Sammy all rolled up together.

"Are you mad?"

I had to smile. I should be angry. I should be furious at this entire situation. But I wasn't.

"Hard to be mad when my cock was so happily trapped between those pretty lips." I traced the full pinkness of them.

"I wanted to say thanks for last night." She paused. "Pancakes didn't seem the way to go."

I burst out laughing. She said the funniest things when I least expected it.

"Sammy, this is complicated. I can't risk——"

She shook her head, stopping me. "I'm not asking for anything. I don't expect anything. It happened—again—and I'm not going to beat myself up over it."

"So, what do you suggest?"

She rolled out of bed, standing beside it. Her white nightgown hid little from me with the sun coming up behind her and outlining her curves under the cotton. "We move on. At this point, I suppose we're even. We carry on."

I sat up, resting on my elbow. "Simple as that?"

She let her gaze wander over my chest, down my torso to where my cock began to stir simply at the sight of her. I pulled on the blanket, covering myself before she could see the effect she had on me.

She smiled, but this one wasn't as bright as it had been earlier. I much preferred that sunshine. "Simple as that. Although I think, tonight, I'll apply the lotion myself." She bent and picked up her toiletry bag. "For now, I'm going to have a shower."

Then she left. I stared at the door, wishing for her to return. To come back and let me have her one more time. Just to get it out of my system once and for all.

But when the shower came on, I knew she had made the right decision. I rolled out of her bed, yanking up my sweats.

I headed to my room before I changed my mind and joined her in the shower.

I had to stop this madness.

CHAPTER FOURTEEN

LUKE

Two days later, I swung my legs out of bed and sat up, rubbing my eyes after yet another night of restlessness.

I hadn't meant to fall asleep beside Sammy the other night. But doing so, and then what happened the next morning, had unlocked something in me. I relived those first waking moments, seeing her looking at me, her dark gaze intense, her mouth wrapped around my cock, was enough to make me hard instantly. I recalled the other brief seconds I had woken in the night, knowing I should let her go and return to my own bed, yet unable to unlock my arms from around her.

I fought every night not to head down the hall. Slide into her bed and make love to her properly. Hold her and feel the way she melted into me.

I made a point of staying away from Sammy. It was more difficult than I expected, even though I knew it was for the best. I was polite, courteous, and helpful. I was also distant, stayed away from the house, and ignored every feeling of jealousy and the urge to push my own workers in front of a raging bull when I would see them stand too close to her.

She was busy, constantly filming, talking, taking pictures. She had set up a small office in the corner of the living room on an old desk my mom used on occasion. The rare times I would stride into the house, she was there, working. I kept our conversations brief and found excuses to leave as fast as possible. I made sure she ate, asking Callie to include her in all meals, and I took my own food at the cookhouse or ate alone on the porch.

None of my behavior seemed to affect Sammy. She was bright and happy, smiling and talking with everyone. I could hear her laughter across the fields or in the stable as she played with the kittens. If I stopped just shy of the rolling door, I could spy her in the corner, the little black-and-white runt curled up on her shoulder as she worked. I tried not to envy the kitten being able to snuggle into her neck. I knew how soft that skin was and how good Sammy smelled right there. Like lilacs and springtime.

Friday afternoon, I was headed toward the stable, Maverick following, when Sammy walked out into the sunshine. My breath caught in my throat, and I had to force myself not to grab her, haul her against me, and kiss her until she was begging me to take her into the stable and fuck her.

Instead, I smiled and tipped my hat. "Howdy, ma'am."

She laughed, a brilliant sound of light which made me smile again.

"Good job, Luke."

I nodded, intending on going past her until she reached out, laying her hand on my arm.

"Luke?"

I stopped, trying not to feel the spark under my skin where her fingers touched me.

"What's going on?" I asked.

"You still taking me to the dance tonight? I can drive myself in if you prefer."

Rachel had loaned Sammy her truck to get around in. Sammy went to see her and Tyler daily, and it was better than the suggestion Rachel had of Sammy driving an ATV. I wasn't comfortable with that idea at all. The truck made me nervous, given Sammy's small stature, but I was impressed by her ability and the ease with which she drove it.

But I didn't want her driving into town alone to the dance.

"I'll take you."

"But you won't dance."

"No. I'll introduce you, then probably walk around and catch up with a few folks. Head out to the field and stargaze a bit. You can text me when you're ready to go."

"You won't dance with me or with anyone?"

"I don't dance—ever."

"Okay. What time?"

"We'll leave at seven."

"Will you have dinner with me before we go, or are you still avoiding me?" she asked, and I heard the underlying note of hurt in her voice.

"I've been busy, Sammy. Not avoiding you," I lied. "But to take you tonight, I have to work straight through. I'll grab a late lunch from Callie."

"Okay," she agreed quietly. "I'll see you at seven."

She walked away, somehow the light around her dimmer than before.

I didn't like it.

I was in the middle of rolling up my sleeves when she appeared that evening. I almost swallowed my tongue. The Sammy I was used to seeing was gone. The woman I had glimpsed the day she arrived was just a shadow of how beautiful she was.

No more jeans. T-shirts. Carefree, straight hair. Boots on her feet.

She wore a dress. A girly, lacy, barely-to-her-knees, pink dress that hung off her shoulders, nipped in at the waist, and exploded into a fluffy skirt that flounced as she walked. Pretty, strappy heels adorned her feet, making her legs look miles long and sexy. She'd pulled her hair up and curled it. Lipstick made her full mouth pouty. Her eyes were large and luminous in her face with whatever she had done to them.

My cock was instantly hard.

I was instantly furious.

She clapped her hands. "You look awesome! I love the shirt—and is that, like, your dress-up hat?"

"It's a clean one. And there is nothing special about my shirt," I said through gritted teeth.

"Oh, but there is," she insisted.

I looked down. It was a plain black shirt. I had put on fresh jeans and my hat was black, but that was it. She was just being over the top.

"Are you ready?" I asked, not commenting on her appearance.

She frowned. "Uh, yes."

I grabbed my keys. "Then let's go."

The ride into town was silent. When we arrived, I did as promised. Introduced her to the mayor and his wife. The local big shots who always attended these things. Anyone else Rachel had mentioned. A few she hadn't thought of. Sammy was polite and engaging, answering questions about her show and saying how thrilled she was to be working with Rachel and me. I ignored the looks I got from some of the women, their surprise to see me here evident. I didn't make eye contact—that would only encourage them.

Finally, I touched Sammy's elbow. "You okay on your own?"

"You're really not staying?"

"No."

She tossed her head in a gesture I now recognized. She was pissed and was done with me. "You can go home. I'm sure I can get a ride with someone."

"I don't think so."

"Well, it's a good thing you don't think for me, jackass," she muttered. "Just leave, Luke. You've ruined enough of my night as it is."

Then she flounced away. She didn't make it too far before one of the many admirers she'd already attracted stopped her and indicated the dance floor. Without a backward glance, she took his hand and kept walking. I pushed my way outside and grabbed a beer, heading away from the building.

I didn't care. Sammy could dance with whomever she wanted. I hoped she had a good time. And if she wanted me gone, that was fine too. I'd finish my beer and leave. I had seen Tim there, and I knew Callie and Jeff were planning on going. She could get back to the ranch easily enough. She wasn't my responsibility.

She wasn't my anything.

Except I couldn't leave. I found myself back inside, standing in the shadows, watching her. Getting angrier as man after man claimed her for a dance. As she laughed and talked, her hair catching the light, her skirt flaring around her, giving me a glimpse of her smooth thighs. I knew how it felt to touch those thighs. How it felt to hold her close. Taste her mouth. Taste her.

Someone walked into the barn, and I glanced over. Tom Hopkins stood in the entrance, looking around. I narrowed my eyes at the sight of him. He was a known womanizer, a sleazy ass, and not well-liked by many. He had just ended his second marriage, and rumor had it he was on the lookout for number three. He stopped at the edge of the crowd, and I saw him zero in on Sammy. He watched her, licking his lips as if he'd spied the tastiest morsel and was dying to bite into it. He began to move toward her, and suddenly, I snapped.

No fucking way was that happening. I was sick of watching her dance with other men, and he certainly wasn't getting close, never mind touching her.

I strode forward, covering the distance between Sammy and me quickly. He had just begun to speak to her when I stepped between them.

"I think you promised the next dance to me, darlin'," I said and yanked her away, leaving the people around her shocked.

On the dance floor, I pulled her into my arms and began to move. She held herself stiffly.

"What are you doing?"

"Dancing."

"You said you couldn't dance."

"I said I *didn't*, not that I *couldn't*. My momma made sure I knew how to dance." I swung her around. "If you relax a little, you might enjoy it."

She sighed, her shoulders loosening.

"That's it, Lady. Move with me," I murmured.

"Why is everyone staring?" she asked.

"Because I never dance. They aren't sure what to make of it."

"Why *are* you dancing?" she asked, looking up at me.

"I didn't want that slimeball touching you."

She blinked. "Who?"

"The guy asking you to dance. He's a piece of work, and I didn't want him near you." She frowned, and I hastily added, "Rachel would have wanted me to intervene."

To my horror, tears filled her eyes. "That's why?" she whispered.

"What else?" I asked, confused.

She pushed back, brushing under her eyes. "You are such a jackass, Luke." She hurried away, heading toward the door. I followed her, dodging the people crowding between us. Outside, I saw her disappear around the corner, and I hurried to catch up with her.

I grabbed her arm, spinning her around. "What's wrong?"

She slapped my chest, furious. "You are!"

"What the hell are you talking about?"

"I want to go home. Take me back to the ranch."

"Not until you tell me what's going on."

"Are you that blind? You've ruined my night, and I just want to go back to the ranch. I'm done."

"What are you talking about?"

"I did this for you," she sobbed. "I bought this dress, I did my hair... I wanted you to see *me*, but instead, you just ignored me."

I ran my finger down her damp cheek. "Stop with this," I begged. I couldn't stand to see her cry.

"I can't–I can't do this anymore. Just take me back to the ranch, Luke."

I couldn't take it anymore. I pushed her against the wall of the barn, caging her in. "You think I'm ignoring you? I'm in hell not being able to touch you the way I want. You think I don't see how beautiful you are? How sexy? Do you know how hard it was to see you dancing with all those other guys? To know they got to touch you and that I can't?"

"Why can't you?" she cried. "What's stopping you?"

Our eyes met and locked in the dim light. "Because I'm afraid once I start, I won't be able to stop." I drew in a ragged breath. "You drive me crazy, Sammy. I want you with every fiber of my being."

"Then have me," she begged.

I covered her mouth with mine, kissing her, letting all the passion and desire I'd been feeling for her sink into that kiss. She flung her arms around my neck, gripping my skin. I plunged my tongue inside her sweet mouth, exploring and frantic. I slipped my hands under her ass, hoisting her up, and she wrapped her legs around my waist. I dragged my mouth across her cheek to her ear. "I fucking want you every second of every day, Sammy. I can't stand not being able to touch you."

"Touch me, then. Anything you want, but for God's sake, Luke, stop the ache."

"It's only now, Sammy. I can't give you forever."

"I'm not asking for it."

"Are you sure?"

She gripped my neck. "Fuck me, Luke. Now."

I crashed my mouth back to hers, drinking her sweetness, feasting on her mouth like a starving man. I slid my hands up her legs, dipping under the lace I found to her wetness. She moaned low in her throat as I began to finger-fuck her, and she rode my hand in desperation.

"So fucking sexy in this dress," I hissed into her ear. "So beautiful as you ride my fingers. You're gonna come, aren't you, Lady?"

"Yes."

I laughed darkly, speeding up my movements. "First on my hand, then on my cock."

She tightened around me, her body shaking. I kissed her screams of pleasure silent, keeping them for me and me alone. I felt her body begin to jerk and throb as she surrendered. While she was still absorbing the pleasure, I fumbled with my belt and zipper and slid her panties aside, sinking in deep. She shuddered, her head dropping to my shoulder. I began to move, my strokes powerful and hard. She turned her face to my neck, licking and biting me, her quiet sounds of passion continual in my ear.

"Oh God, Luke—"

"Please, yes, yes—just like that."

"Harder, more, please," she begged.

I braced my hand against the wood and held her tight, trapped between me and the building. I drove into her mindlessly, the pleasure snapping up and down my spine until my orgasm hit me. Hard. Biting. Blistering heat that made me hold her tighter, groan into her ear, and curse.

"Fuck, Sammy. What the hell are you doing to me?" I hissed. I captured her mouth as I crested, mumbling against her lips. "Beautiful Lady. Beautiful, sexy Lady." I kissed her. "My Lady."

She buried her face into my neck as we recovered. Our breathing evened out, and I shook my head. I had taken her like a rutting animal against the side of a barn. Anyone could have come around the corner and seen us. I pressed a kiss to her head. "I got carried away."

She lifted her head, meeting my eyes. Hers danced and shone with mischief. "Are we ever gonna do it like normal in a bed, or are you particularly attached to hard surfaces?"

I set her down on her feet, cupping her face and kissing her.

"Did I hurt you?"

"No."

"Then let me take you home and show you how much I can pleasure you in a bed too."

"I like the sound of that."

I kissed her pert nose. "I like you." I peered around the corner. "We'll need to get to the truck without being seen."

"Oh," she whispered, ducking under me and peering too. "Like spies. This is a recon mission. I like it." She grabbed my hand. "Follow me, 007. I'll lead."

I chuckled as we stuck to the shadows and ducked around cars and trucks until we got to mine. A couple of times, she pulled me down, kissing me to stop me from laughing at her antics.

When we got to the truck, we slid in and I started it, heading toward the ranch. She reached over and took my hand, squeezing it. "Told you I'd get us out of there safely."

"Good job, Lady."

Our fingers remained intertwined all the way home.

CHAPTER FIFTEEN

LUKE

When we arrived back at the ranch, I followed Sammy inside, frowning as she headed toward her room. I tugged on her hand. "Where do you think you're going, Lady?"

She laughed, running her finger over my jaw. "I'm going to change and get something to eat."

I blinked. "Eat?" I had other ideas for how to spend the rest of the evening, and food hadn't made the list.

"Your sister told me about all the delicious food there would be at the dance. Between talking to people and you sexing me up, I got none of it."

"I've got something you can nibble on," I assured her. "An entire mouthful."

She chuckled, the sound light and feminine. "I have no doubt you do. But I need to eat *food* first. A girl needs her strength."

I brushed my mouth across hers. "Okay. Meet you in the kitchen in ten."

I changed and was back in the kitchen in a few moments. Sammy was even faster, already in the fridge, pulling out some cold chicken and other items. It felt oddly natural to sit with her at the table, having an impromptu picnic and simply talking to her. She was witty and engaging, and I liked to hear her laugh.

"What was the deal with my shirt earlier?" I asked.

She propped her elbow on the table. "You have no idea, do you?"

"Obviously not."

"Your jeans hug your ass. Your shirt shows off your shoulders, and the black looks so good against your skin. Add in the rolled-up sleeves showing off your sexy forearms and the hat?" She shook her head. "That's eye candy, Cowboy. Pure, one hundred percent turn-on."

I glanced down at my arms. "Whatever cranks your engine, Lady."

"Oh, it does. It really does."

Her phone rang, and she answered it on speaker.

"Hey, Dad."

"Hey, Mouse. How are things going?"

She glanced my way with a smile. It was another new one. Sweet, almost shy. I liked it. Then she averted her eyes and spoke to her dad.

"Great. Plans are set and full steam ahead."

"Awesome. We'll be there a week from today."

"How many?" she asked.

"Five or six."

"Really?" she gasped, delighted. "Dad, that's awesome!"

"Many hands, light work, you know. Bentley gave us the plane. Might as well fill it. Aiden arranged transportation and accommodation for us, so no need to pick us up. We'll be at the ranch mid-afternoon, and you can walk us around and fill us in."

"Awesome. Thanks, Dad. You'll love it here."

"I'm looking forward to it. See you soon, Mouse."

"Love you, Dad. Say hi to Mom and Mila."

"I will. Love you more," he responded.

She hung up, and I looked at her, one eyebrow raised in question. *"Bentley gave us the plane?"*

"My uncle owns his own plane. He is very generous."

"Wow." I couldn't compete in that world.

She shrugged.

"And what accommodation?"

"I don't know. I assume a local motel or something. Dad will fill me in when he gets here."

I wiped my fingers, picking up a cracker and a piece of cheese. "So, Mouse, is it?"

She smiled. "Dad gave me that nickname the day I met him. He was so big, he looked like a giant to me." She sighed. "I think I loved him from that moment. He was larger-than-life."

"You mentioned he adopted you."

189

"Yes. He met my mom when I was five, and he adopted me as soon as they got married. He's the only dad I've ever known. My sperm donor was a piece of work, and I've never had anything to do with him. Van—Dad—has been a constant in my life, and I couldn't ask for a better man for a parent."

"And you have siblings?"

"Two. They adopted my brother Reed after they got married. He's my baby brother except he's older than me."

I laughed. "I see. Then they had Mila?"

"No, she is adopted as well. My dad couldn't have kids, but they had lots of love to spare."

"I can't either," I said without thinking.

Sammy's eyes grew round. "You can't have kids?"

I cursed myself for letting that information out. "No. I had an accident in my twenties. The damage was significant."

She reached across the table, gripping my hand. "I'm sorry, Luke."

"I've come to terms with it." I shook my head. "Anne, my fiancée at the time, couldn't. She walked out on me." I had no idea why I was telling her all of this.

She didn't offer me pity or platitudes. "That must have devastated you."

"It did."

"She wouldn't consider adoption?"

I snorted. "She wouldn't consider anything less than her ideal, no. She moved on quickly. Married another guy a few towns over, had three kids. I saw her at a festival some years ago. I don't think that marriage made her happy either, so maybe it was for the best. I didn't feel anything but relief at not being the one getting the disappointed looks thrown his way."

"Best out, then," Sammy murmured.

"So, I can't get you pregnant by accident," I said, wanting to lighten the sudden heavy atmosphere. "My worry about the condoms was more to make you feel safe."

She studied me for a moment. "I do feel safe with you."

"Good." I looked at her empty plate with a grin. "You finished storing up your energy, *Mouse?*" I teased.

She rolled her eyes but smiled. "What you got in mind there, Cowboy?"

"I think you wanted proof I can bed you…in a bed."

"That would make a nice change."

I leaned forward. "I meant what I said, Sammy. I don't do long-term. I don't do the forever thing."

She stood, putting away the last of the food. She leaned against the counter, crossing her arms. "And I'm not asking for it. I'm a big girl, Luke. I can handle sex without commitment."

I wasn't entirely sure I believed her. "Can I ask why? I mean, you seem like the sort of girl who would."

"I like my life. My freedom. I come and go without anyone telling me what to do. There was someone a long time ago, and he thought he could control what I did. Who I was. I learned really quickly that wasn't for me. Don't get me wrong. I think love, the right kind, is amazing. I see it in my family. My parents have it. But I don't need it to be happy."

I stood and crossed the floor, standing in front of her. "I see."

"I also like sex. I like sex with you. I like spending time with you, Cowboy. You're sexy and funny, and when you're not being a jackass, you're sweet."

"Thanks," I said drolly.

"You are." She reached out and trailed her finger down my chest, her touch warming my skin. "You treat people with respect. You're amazing with your sister. Your staff thinks the world of you. You're kind and wonderful."

"I wasn't kind and wonderful when we met."

She grinned. "I kinda liked that too. The sparks and how you refuse to give an inch with me. You turn me on, Cowboy. You have from the second I met you." She leaned up on her toes, her lips next to my ear. "Just being close to you makes me wet."

I wrapped my hands around her arms, my erection kicking up. "Enough foreplay. My room, Lady. Now."

"You gonna make me?" she teased, her eyes dancing.

She didn't expect my move. In a second, I had her over my shoulder, carrying her down the hall, holding tight to her ass as she sputtered and cursed me.

I dropped her on the bed, not giving her a chance to escape. I caged her in with my arms, hovering over her. "You drive me crazy."

She looped her arms around my neck. "Right back at you."

"You ready for more dancing, Lady?"

"Dancing?"

"Mattress dancing. I'm about to rock your world."

"Bring it on, Cowboy."

CHAPTER SIXTEEN

SAMMY

"What's the matter?" Luke's voice was low and raspy in the dim room.

I glanced over my shoulder. He was sprawled on the bed, gloriously naked. Every muscle, sinew, and tendon visible to my gaze. He was cut from rock, hard, rigid, and powerful. Yet his hands touched me with care, and even in our most passionate of moments, I felt safe with him. He had shown he was equally gifted on a mattress as he was on the barn floor, the side of the building, or the top of a bathroom vanity. He played me like a fiddle, and he knew exactly how to draw that bow.

"I thought you'd want me to leave," I confessed.

"Did I ask you to go?"

"No," I admitted. "I didn't want to outstay my welcome."

He reached over, pulling me back against him. "Stay, Lady. I like you beside me." He pressed his mouth to my shoulder. "And I'm not done with you."

"Oh," I breathed out.

He tugged me down, and a small gasp escaped my mouth. He sat up. "What?"

"Nothing."

He snapped on the light beside him, looking at me, aghast. "You're still sore. You're in pain, and you let me—" He stopped talking, shaking his head. "Jesus, I hurt you."

"No. I'm a bit stiff at times, and my shoulder is a little sore." I smiled at him reassuringly. "The barn was really hard."

"Why didn't you stop me?"

"I didn't *want* to stop you. I'm fine," I insisted. "I'll try soaking in the tub again."

"Try?"

I chuckled. "It's not a very deep tub. I couldn't really get much relief from it the other night. A good hot shower will help." I tugged him back down. "Later."

He wrapped his arms around me, pulling me close. I had never been a huge after-sex snuggler, but with Luke, it felt right. I liked being in his arms. He ran his fingers over my shoulder, his touch gentle. "No more wall sex," he muttered.

I pouted up at him. "But you're really good at it."

He smiled, but it didn't reach his eyes. "I don't like to see marks on you or know you're still sore from the tumble."

"Relax, Cowboy."

He kissed the top of my head, and the quiet around us relaxed me. I drifted a little, frowning as I felt him slip out of bed.

"Where are you going?"

"I'll be right back. Stay."

I must have dozed again, hearing water running in my haze. Then Luke appeared beside the bed, drawing back the blanket. "Come with me."

I took his hand and let him lead me. We went through his masculine en suite, and he slid open a door I hadn't noticed the first time I peeked in.

I gasped in delight at the small room I stepped down into. The walls were covered in river rock, the floor cedar. In the middle of the room was an oversized tub—big enough for two people and deep enough to submerge up to your neck. Over the tub was a skylight—you could lie back and see the stars or watch the rain while soaking. I turned to Luke.

"This is amazing! It's absolutely gorgeous. It reminds me of my idea for the bathhouse, except this is so much better. The rocks on the wall—it's like you're in your own little cave."

"Get in," he said, holding out his hand.

I climbed in, sinking down into the water, groaning in delight as the heat surrounded me.

"I didn't take you for a tub guy, Cowboy."

"I'm not." He drew in a deep breath. "In fact, I've never used this room. I hate it."

Something in his tone made me tense. I looked at him, standing beside the tub, and I saw the rigidity in him. Even in the dim light, I could see the pain in his eyes.

"Why did you do this? Let me into a room you hate?"

He looked at me, his gaze softening. "Because I can't stand to think of you in pain. If this tub can help that, then at least it is good for something."

I slid forward. "Come in with me."

He shook his head.

"Luke, please. I would feel better if you were in here with me." I knew he wouldn't be able to say no if I asked for his help.

He hesitated, then slipped in behind me. I lay back against his chest, feeling the tension in his body. He draped his arms over the edge of the tub, and I took his hand, lifting it to my mouth and kissing the knuckles. Then I laid our entwined fingers on my chest, doing the same with his other hand, so he was holding me.

His body lost some of its stiffness, and I let the heat and quiet soothe him for a while.

"Did you do this?" I asked.

"Yes."

"The rocks are from the property?"

"Yes, I carried them here from the stream."

"That must have taken a long time."

"Yep."

"It's beautiful, Luke. What a wonderful room to relax in."

He didn't answer right away. "You really like it?"

"Yes."

He relaxed a little more. "Good."

"Can you tell me why you hate it?"

"It brings up bad memories I don't want to talk about."

"Maybe you should."

"For what purpose?" he scoffed.

"Maybe if you spoke them out loud, released them into this room, you could leave them behind—let them drain away like the water when we're finished."

"Leave it, Sammy."

I kissed his hand again. "Okay."

I felt the press of his lips on my head, and we drifted quietly. The heat felt so good on my sore ass and back. The ache was dissipating slowly.

"I built this room for someone I thought I was in love with." Luke's voice broke the silence.

"Ah," I replied, hiding my surprise. "I thought as much. Your fiancée?"

"No. Someone else—years later. When my mom died, both Rachel and I were grieving. In her will, my mom had left us everything equally, but there was one specific request. She wanted us each to have a set amount of money and take a trip. Rachel went to Scotland with a friend. I had always wanted to see the ocean, so I chose something closer to home. I went to BC."

"It's beautiful there."

"It really is. I decided to make it a trip to remember. I planned to stay at a really nice hotel, eat at fancy restaurants, and sit by the ocean. Rent a boat and have them take me out so I could experience the vast expanse firsthand."

"Sounds like a good plan." I paused. "I assume you met someone?"

He sighed, his arms holding me closer. "Yeah, I did. I'm not going to go into a lot of details, Sammy. I don't want to rehash everything. But you're right, maybe I need to get it out."

"Okay."

"I met Marie, and we hit it off. She worked in one of the bars at the hotel. She was pretty, funny, and we got along really well. I took her with me when I could, and she seemed genuine. She wanted out of the city and somewhere open. She seemed fascinated when I talked about the ranch." He paused, playing with my fingers. "She said all the right things, seemed to want all the same things I did. I told her I couldn't have kids, and she was okay with it. It didn't seem to bother her."

"Hmm," was my noncommittal reply. I didn't want him to stop talking.

"She was so sad when I left, and we kept in touch. I missed her, and one thing led to another and I asked her to come and be here with me. She wasn't happy in the city, I wasn't happy here, I thought it was what I needed. To be together."

"But it wasn't?"

"The ranch wasn't what she thought. What I did on the ranch wasn't what she thought. I had lived it up on my holiday, and she thought my life was that way all the time. Nothing was enough here. She hated the house, hated the dust and the animals, was shocked I expected her to do a few things if she was going to live here. Like cook or help Rachel."

"What did she expect?"

"To live a life of luxury with others doing the work. I told her at one point this wasn't *Dallas* and I wasn't J.R. Ewing. She didn't find it funny."

"And this room?"

"She had told me she enjoyed a nice soak in the tub while we were together in BC. This was part of the original bathroom, and I changed it to make it a private oasis for her as a surprise." He sighed. "She hated it. She wanted white marble and a Jacuzzi tub. Mirrors. The same as the hotel had. Not rocks and wood. Not a skylight to see the stars. She wanted luxury. She never once used it."

I tightened my hold on his hands. "I'm sorry."

"The woman I had met in BC wasn't the woman who showed up. She was rude and condescending. She belittled everything I loved. I thought she needed some time to adjust, and I gave her space. Tried to be patient, but she only got worse. Rachel disliked her intensely, and they were at odds with each other constantly. I realized I'd been played. She wanted a rich man, and what she saw in BC was the man she thought she was going to get, even though I had told her otherwise. She thought I was teasing her."

"What happened?"

"I came home unexpectedly early one afternoon. One of the cows had wandered, and I found her quickly and brought her back to the pasture. I decided to come and have a frank conversation with Marie. I was tired of her tantrums and demands. The sulking and pettiness. Of being told how everything I said, did, thought, or owned was wrong. Her attitude with Rachel and telling me I had to choose between them. That morning, she'd informed me that if she was staying, she wanted the house gutted and modernized. I told her to forget it."

"And?" I prompted.

"I found her in my office, going over bank statements. I was horrified at her invasion of my privacy. We argued again, and she informed me she decided it would be best to sell the ranch, take the money, and go back to BC. She could build the house she wanted." He huffed out a dry laugh. "As if she had the right. Or as if I had given her the idea I would be open to something like that. As if everything had been great until that moment. I told her to pack her things and get out. Let's just say there was a lot of shouting, name-calling, and accusations. In her mind, I brought her here under false pretenses. Promised her a life of luxury. When I told her she had been the one to play me, she got pretty damn angry. That's when things got real. She admitted she'd thought I was rich, given what she'd seen in BC. The hotel, the dinners, et cetera. She wasn't overly attracted to me, and she spent some time telling me why and how horrible the ranch was."

"What did you do?"

"Nothing. I listened, watched to make sure she didn't steal anything, then walked her to the truck and drove her to the airport. While she was ranting, I had booked her a seat on the next flight out. I dropped her and her suitcases off and left. Last time I saw her was in my rearview. She was flipping me off and yelling."

"And you never heard from her again?"

"She blew up my phone, so Rachel changed my number and email address. For all I know, she's latched on to some other sucker. I pity the asshole." He sighed. "Learned my lesson. First, Anne tells me I'm not enough, then Marie. I have no idea what I was thinking. I decided I had a good life already, and I wasn't going to try to be enough for anyone else. I'm best on my own," he added, and I heard the forced lightness in his voice.

I wasn't going to let that pass.

LUKE

I had no idea what made me tell Sammy all that shit. There was something about this woman, something soft and safe that made it easier to say the thoughts out loud. To get them out of my head. She was right. Having said them, I felt better. Lighter. But I didn't want to dwell on it, and I made a jesting remark when I was done, thinking that would be the end of it.

I should have known better. I already understood that Sammy wasn't like most women. In fact, I was certain no one else on the planet even came close.

She had remained surprisingly silent as I spoke, her remarks at a minimum. Until the last one. She tensed, dropped my hands, and spun in the tub, the water rising and cresting, hitting the wood floor with a splash.

"Good thing it's a wet room," I remarked.

She didn't laugh. Her dark eyes snapped fire, and she narrowed her gaze, looking pissed.

And so damn sexy with her hair damp from the steam, her skin glistening with droplets of water. I wanted to lean close and lick them off her, but I knew better. I had a feeling she could somehow flip me—even in a tub. I stayed where I was, watching her.

She rose up, gripping the sides of the porcelain, straddling me.

"Listen to me and listen well, Luke Jonathan Adler."

I lifted my eyebrows in surprise at her full-naming me. I wasn't even aware she knew my middle name. Her tone was low and furious. Kinda growly. It was another sexy thing about her right now.

"Your fiancée was selfish. Maybe her youth had something to do with it, but she walked away from a great man. That's on her. You were in an accident. Not your fault. Kids can be adopted and loved. My siblings know that better than anyone. So do I. They become your family. She lost out on that with you. You lost out on that. I hate her for making you feel as if you were no longer enough. Any woman who has you would be so lucky. You are the whole damn package."

Her thoughts about me surprised me. She held up her hand before I could interrupt her.

"As for the gold digger and not knowing what you were thinking? You were grieving. Vulnerable. I have no doubt if the Luke in front of me met her today, he would see through her before she had a chance to play her sick little games. She's a snake. A viper. Not worth your time or energy feeling anything but grateful she didn't sink her claws deeper into you."

The venom in her tone shocked me. "I should have—"

Again, she interrupted. "Shut up, Luke. I'm talking. She played you because that is the sort of woman she is. One who likes to take advantage. Not attracted to you," she scoffed. "Proves she had zero taste. You are the sexiest man I have ever seen. You could walk across the room covered in dust and cow shit, and I'd still do you."

I tried not to smile at her statement, but my lips quirked.

Cow shit?

"I have no doubt she preys on men and will do so until she finds one stupid enough to marry her or make her his mistress. She'll live her life in a vacuum of uselessness, and good luck to her. You are far better off without her."

"Can I speak now?"

"No. Any woman—*any woman*—with a heart would have fallen hard for you with this gift. This wonderful little sanctuary. You are worthy of love and happiness, Luke, but you have to put yourself out there. Love will always find a way. But don't let her or your ex make you doubt your worthiness. Because I think you are worthy of everything. *Everything.*"

By the time she finished speaking, she was almost panting in her vehemence.

"Now are you done?"

"Do you believe me?"

I tucked a loose strand of hair behind her ear and smiled. "I believe that you believe it. I'm shocked you think so highly of me, given how we disagree all the time."

"Don't you see? That's what is so wonderful. You don't belittle or talk down to me. We meet like equals on the field. Neither giving an inch. I like that." She cupped my cheeks, forcing me to meet her gaze. "Don't shut yourself off from love, Luke. You are worthy. Find your person and hold them tight. Don't let her win."

"What about you?" I asked quietly.

"What about me?"

"You say you don't want a relationship either."

"I said I'm not looking—that I don't need it like some people do. I haven't shut the door completely."

The silence between us was tentative. Rife with words and emotions.

I ran my finger over her cheek. "So certain, Lady. All defensive and sticking up for me."

"You need someone to stick up for you."

I pulled her close. "You think I'm sexy?"

"Maddeningly so. I thought so the moment I saw you."

"I thought you'd be high-maintenance," I teased.

She glowered.

"Instead, you're simply a joy," I murmured, tracing my finger over her cheek. "You bring sunshine to my world, Lady. I hadn't realized how much I missed that."

Our eyes locked, something flowing between us. Something so tangible and strong, it made me blink. Words were on the tip of my tongue, but I couldn't say them. An abstract idea formed in my head, and I had to tamp it down before it bloomed and took hold.

I crushed her to me and kissed her.

The words *"Are you my person?"* were never spoken. I had no right. She didn't want it either. She wanted free and easy.

So, I bit back my words, carried her back to my bed, and fucked her.

That was all I could offer.

CHAPTER SEVENTEEN

SAMMY

Muted voices met my ears, and I opened my eyes. I was still in Luke's bed, bundled under the covers. His pillow smelled like him, and I inhaled deeply, smiling and stretching, pleased to feel the soreness ebbing. The soak in the deep tub had a lot to do with it. So did the massage Luke gave me around three, before he took me from behind, driving me to another blissful orgasm.

The man had incredible stamina.

I got up, pulling on my clothes, peering out the door. Luke was at the table, sipping coffee, alone. Whoever he was talking to must have left. I sauntered down the hall, staring at his profile, his thick neck and arms highlighted by the tight black T-shirt he wore. The corded muscles. He looked delicious, and I really wanted a taste of him.

"Cowboy," I murmured.

He turned his head sharply, meeting my eyes, shaking his head no. Too late, I realized Rachel was at the counter. She met my eyes, her gaze flitting between me and Luke and widening.

I froze, then tossed my hair and kept going. "Hey, Rachel. I was hoping to see you today. Thanks for the use of your tub, Luke. It really helped. Now I'm gonna get ready for the day. I'll be right back."

"Yep," he said easily. "No problem."

In my room, I closed my eyes, wondering if she bought it. I brushed my hair, got ready, and headed back to the kitchen. Luke was finishing his breakfast, looking cool and collected.

I poured a coffee and sat down, trying to act nonchalant.

Rachel cleared her throat. "Rumor has it you danced last night, Luke."

"You know how I feel about rumors," he replied.

"You left the dance early, tugging Sammy with you."

"Tom Hopkins was sniffing around. Couldn't let him get his hands on her." He indicated me with a lift of his chin.

"Her has a name," I said dryly. "And I am right here."

He rolled his eyes. "Whatever, Lady."

"So, what did you do the rest of the night?" Rachel asked innocently, hiding her smirk behind her coffee cup.

"Came home and had something to eat. Your brother yanked me away before I got to taste anything. Then we went to bed."

"I see."

"Alone," I mumbled.

She nodded.

Luke stood. "Is the inquisition over? I have animals waiting and a thousand other chores to take care of."

"Yep. Your schedule is clear for tomorrow, right?"

"Yes."

"Everything set for you leaving the next day?"

"Yep. Loading the cattle in the morning and heading out. I'll be gone three days."

I knew he was going to an auction to sell off some steers and buy others. He was also meeting with other ranchers and owners. The thought of him off the ranch felt odd, and I somehow knew I was going to miss him, but I forced down the sensations. I had lots of plans to keep me busy.

"Okay."

"You'll—you'll keep an eye out, right?" he asked.

Rachel grinned. "Yep. I'll handle it."

He nodded. "Good." He picked up his hat. "Later." He turned, catching my eye and winking before he walked out. For a moment, there was silence. I finally lifted my gaze to Rachel's. She was watching me, her head tilted.

"Handle it?" I asked.

"Watch over you."

"Oh. Whatever," I mumbled. *Jackass.*

"*Cowboy?*" she questioned.

"He calls me Lady. I had to call him something."

"You call him that in the throes of passion too?"

I lifted my chin. "I am not talking to you about your brother."

She burst out laughing. "You don't have to. Question answered."

"What?"

"You have a bite mark on your neck, Sammy. Unless Tom Hopkins got closer than Luke wanted, someone gave you that. Given the way my brother was smirking and relaxed this morning and you tripping down the hall after 'using his tub,' I'm pretty sure the answer is yes."

"I did use the tub."

"When?"

I gave up, defeated. "After the dance. I was sore, and Luke offered."

"And one thing led to another?"

I met her eyes. "Again."

She began to laugh. "I knew it. I saw something between you."

"It's just sex," I said. "We both agreed. And it won't interfere with the project."

She grasped my hand. "You know why he never uses the tub?"

"He told me the whole story."

"Really?" she asked, astonished.

"I know about her, the fiancée who walked away, his accident…" I trailed off at the look of shock on her face. "What?"

"He never talks about the past. Ever."

"He did with me."

She shook her head. "You have no idea how big that is."

"We're just enjoying the moment," I told her. "We know it's not forever."

"Are you sure?"

"He runs a ranch. I travel and help businesses grow. We live thousands of miles from each other. We have our own lives. This is for the moment. Your brother has been very clear on that. And I'm good with it."

"When I walked in this morning, he looked—different. Lighter somehow. I think a lot of that has to do with you."

"Or maybe the sex we had," I pointed out dryly.

She pulled a face. "Ugh—that's my brother. I'm just going to pretend it was spending time with you."

I smiled and lifted my coffee, ignoring the little voice in my head that wished that was the reason too.

I wandered to the stable, stopping to get Oreo. He meowed as I went toward him and let me pick him up, nuzzling into my neck. I patted his momma on the head. "I'll bring your baby back."

Then I went toward the rhythmic sound I could hear behind the stable. I sat down on an old bench and took in the sight before me.

Luke, his shirt pulled off, skin glistening in the sun, chopping wood. It was mesmerizing. One bend of his body and a log was balanced on an old, thick stump. Another lift and the ax was poised, driving down hard, splintering the wood. Repeat. His movements were powerful, the strength of his upper body evident. Sweat rolled down his chest, beading on his face and arms. If he noticed me, he gave no indication, intent on the task at hand. I couldn't stop staring, remembering how those arms held me. The way his torso pushed into mine, the hardness of it forcing my softer curves to align with it. He was a machine, and soon the pile of split wood towered high. He raised the ax one last time, driving it into the stump, then picked up his discarded shirt and a thermos of water that he drank from, then poured over his head, like my own private Chippendales show. He sauntered toward me, a smile playing on his lips.

"Lady," he greeted me, lifting one leg to rest it on the bench beside me. "Enjoy the show?"

"Absolutely."

He chucked Oreo under the chin. "Brought a friend, I see."

"He needed some air." I fanned myself. "Although it's pretty damn hot right now."

He threw back his head in laughter. "You're good for my ego, darlin'."

"Just telling it like it is."

"Rachel figure us out?" he asked mildly.

"Yes."

"She got a problem with it?"

"Not really."

"Good."

"Were you looking for me, or just happened to end up here?"

"Well, I came for the friskies, but the show was pretty good too."

He paused before taking another drink. "Friskies?"

I waggled my eyebrows.

He laughed again. "Ah, *friskies*." He licked his lips. "You didn't get enough last night?"

I shook my head. "Nope."

"Well then, today is your lucky day," he murmured. "Neither did I. I'm heading to the creek to cool off. If you want to join me..." He trailed off.

"I don't have a suit."

"Neither do I."

"Oh. *Oh*." I stood. "I have to put Oreo back."

He leaned close, his breath on my neck. "You do that, Lady. I can only handle one little pussy at a time, and frankly, I'm rather addicted to yours." He straightened. "I'll grab the ATV. Hurry."

He didn't have to ask me twice.

The next day, I went with Luke and his men, filming the day as a ranch hand. I insisted I was fine to ride Dusty again, and I made Luke laugh as I swaggered close to the horse, tipping my borrowed cowboy hat at her. "Ma'am," I drawled. "It'll be my pleasure to ride you today."

I gasped as Luke stood behind me, lifting me into the saddle. "I had my own pleasure last night," he murmured.

I grinned down at him. "And this morning," I replied pertly.

He smiled, his dimple showing. I loved that smile. It was rare, and it felt like mine. Even if it was just temporarily so.

I helped herd the cattle, staying close enough to film but not get in the way. It was a beautiful day, the sun high, the breeze light. I caught as much as I could with my camera, both as video and stills. Jeff guided me, showing me how to hurry a stray cow along, nudging them in the right direction. I stopped to watch Tim repair a broken pipe, amazed at how quickly he worked. Luke suddenly tore past, bending low over the saddle as he and Maverick covered the ground fast. I was mesmerized as he used his lasso, catching a horse that had gotten away from the stable earlier and was wandering. He trotted back, sitting high in the saddle, grinning.

"Stubborn little filly," he said. "She does this a lot. Likes her freedom."

"What's her name?" I asked.

He winked. "Lady."

I had to laugh.

I spent the rest of the morning following different hands, filming, asking questions, making notes. I got a good idea of what tasks a guest could be part of and which they should not be allowed to partake in. After lunch, I was back in the saddle, pleased that I wasn't as sore as I'd worried I would be. Luke came alongside me. "Okay, Sammy?"

"Fine," I assured him. "Getting used to it."

"You can call it quits anytime."

"I'm fine."

"I don't want you sore again."

"Worried I won't be able to handle your stallion later?" I asked.

He glowered, his gaze becoming dark.

I rolled my eyes at him. "I said I'm fine, Cowboy."

"Stubborn."

I tugged on the reins. "Stop fussing."

"A section of the fence broke the other night, so we're heading to fix it. Nothing much to see. Jeff has the supplies and is heading there on the ATV."

"I want to come. Maybe I can help. And no, not via ATV. I'm fine."

He shook his head but stopped arguing. I followed him, still filming, the vistas so beautiful. I had no idea how I was going to choose which photos or videos to put in the ads.

When we arrived at the damaged section of fence, Jeff and Luke got to work, resetting the broken post and fixing it. I filmed them working with the intricate wire, seeing how the nasty metal dug into the gloves they wore. A piece was frustrating them, the space small. I stepped closer. "I can help."

Luke glanced up. "No."

"My hands are small. I could reach it better."

Jeff grunted. "She's right. This whole piece is going to be a bitch."

Luke sighed. "Did Rachel give you gloves?"

"Yes." I dug them from my bag.

"You wear gloves. This wire will cut your skin easily."

He showed me what to do, and I carefully took the heavy pliers, following his instructions.

"Perfect," Jeff praised.

I met Luke's eyes.

"Good job, Lady."

"I learned from the best. Now I have to do this all the way down?"

"Yes."

"Okay, you can do whatever. No need to watch over me."

Jeff went to the next section, leaving Luke with me. He watched me do the next two joins. I was slower than Jeff, but I did them.

"You know, you watching me isn't getting the job done faster."

"It can be tricky. The wire can snap or—"

I cut him off. "I'm wearing the gloves."

"Don't take them off," he growled and stood. "I'll be right over there if you get into trouble."

I didn't say anything, concentrating on the job. I worked quietly, one piece at a time. The fence tautened as it was nearing completion, and my hands grew sore from the efforts. Inside the gloves, they were hot and sweaty, and I had to stop to wipe them and take a break. I took a sip of water. I only had two more joins to go and I was done. I slipped the gloves back on and finished them, pleased with my efforts. Done, I discarded the gloves, wiped my sweaty palms on my jeans and took a couple of pictures, then frowned. One of the joins looked as if it was going to give way.

Slipping on one glove, I grabbed the pliers, planning on giving the join one last turn. I leaned on the post for stability and twisted it. It happened fast. The wire broke, the tension causing it to snap. It bit into my ungloved hand on the post, blood starting to pour from the cut instantly. I felt no pain, and I stared down at the cut in shock. But I must have gasped because suddenly Luke was beside me, furious.

"What the——?" he hissed. "I told you to wear the damn gloves, Sammy."

"I did," I protested. "It just needed a final twist. I didn't think——"

He cut me off. "Exactly. You didn't think." He grabbed my hand, examining it. "Fuck, this is deep." He lifted his head, calling for Jeff. "I'm taking the ATV."

Jeff hurried over, looking at my hand. "Okay. I'll finish. You did good, Sammy."

"She didn't listen. You never fucking listen to me," Luke snapped, his anger directed at me.

I stayed quiet, not wanting to argue with him right now. I should have put both gloves on, but I'd thought it was fine.

Luke wrapped my hand in a bandanna he had in his pocket and stood, lifting me up.

"Um, it's my hand, Cowboy. I can walk just fine."

"*Shut up.*"

"Okay," I muttered. "Grump."

He deposited me in the ATV and swung himself in, driving like a madman.

"Luke," I gasped. "Slow down."

"You're bleeding."

"It's a cut. I won't bleed out, for God's sake."

He didn't listen, and I held on for dear life with my good hand. At the ranch, he got out, and I scrambled from the ATV before he could reach me. "You are not carrying me again," I hissed. "It's a *cut.*"

He grabbed the front of my shirt, hauling me close. "And here, a cut can become a problem. The dirt, the dust, the animals. Infections set in easily."

"I'll clean it." I pushed him away, annoyed. "Go away, Luke."

I went inside, going to the bathroom. I held my hand under the running water, wincing when the cut kept bleeding. I examined it —Luke was right; it was deep. I recalled seeing a first aid kit in the kitchen, and I went there, hoping for some Band-Aids and antiseptic cream. As I was searching, the door opened and a man walked in, carrying a bag.

"Um, hello."

"You must be Sammy. I'm Doc Weathers. I hear you have a cut that needs looking at."

I gaped at him. "Luke called a doctor?"

"I was already here. Can I look?" he asked with a frown, seeing the blood.

I sat down, and he checked it out. I wondered if someone else was ill, which would explain why he was here.

"Everything okay on the ranch?" I asked.

"Yep," he replied.

"Luke calmed down yet?" I asked.

He chuckled. "He's still simmering." He glanced up. "It's deep but clean. You're lucky the wire didn't go in more or twist under your skin. I think I need to do a couple of stitches, though."

"Can't you put some glue on it and call it a day?" I had a feeling stitches would send Luke over the edge.

"Bit too deep for that. It just needs a couple small ones. If you trust me."

"Sure."

"When was your last tetanus shot?"

"Last year. I fell off a ladder and sliced open my leg." I showed him the side of my knee. "The doc did a good job."

"I'll try to copy him."

He was quiet, concentrating on the task at hand. He was also fast, and it was over quickly. I studied the neat, tiny stitches on my skin.

"You're good."

"I hope it doesn't leave much of a scar. Luckily, it's in the fleshy part between your thumb and index. Easily hidden."

"I doubt it will. I guess it was my lucky day you were visiting when I cut myself."

"I'm here a lot."

"Really? You do drop-in visits for patients just to check on them?"

He sat back and rubbed his forehead. "I'm not exactly a people doctor, Sammy."

I frowned. "Not a people doctor? What are—" It hit me. "Oh my God. You're a *vet*. You're here for the animals." I shook my head. "That idiot Luke made you come and see me, didn't he?"

"He was insistent. I've had experience with humans."

I began to laugh, the absurdity of the whole situation hitting me. Luke freaked out over me cutting myself then he made the vet stitch me up. That overprotective, overblown idiot of a cowboy whom I could see pacing outside. Upset, irritated, and irrational.

Over a cut.

"Does he always overreact like this?" I wondered aloud.

The vet stood, cleaning up his impromptu medical area. "He's usually cooler than an iceberg. I get the feeling you mean a lot."

I shrugged, refusing to acknowledge the ripple of pleasure his words gave me. Meaning a lot to Luke would be amazing.

I scoffed. "He's probably worried I'll sue him for getting injured on the ranch."

He laughed. "Okay, then. The stitches need to come out in a week. Keep it clean and bandaged. If it starts to look red or swollen, there's a clinic in town."

"Vet or people?" I asked with a grin.

"People. You can certainly drop by my clinic if you'd like. I'm always happy to see a pretty lady."

"Won't be necessary," Luke snapped, walking in. "I'll take it from here, Brian."

Brian looked at me with a wink. "Iceberg," he said, walking past Luke, clapping him on the shoulder. "She's fine, big guy."

He shut the door behind him, and I turned, busying myself making coffee. It was a little difficult, given my hand was bandaged and slightly numb, but I refused to stop. I felt Luke's gaze burning into my back, watching me, and I ignored him.

I moved to the cupboard to grab some mugs, but he came behind me, leaning his arms on the counter, blocking me in.

"Excuse me," I said, hating my voice sounded squeaky.

"Are you all right?" he asked.

I set down the mugs and turned, meeting his intense blue gaze. "You made a *vet* look at my hand."

"He was here."

"A vet," I repeated.

"He's stitched me up a couple of times. I trust him. You were bleeding."

"Do you do this if Jeff cuts himself?"

"No."

"What about Rachel?"

"No."

"Then why?" I waved my hand. "It's a small cut. Clean. I could have driven into town and had it looked at. You had to drag a *vet* in here to look at it?"

"Yes."

"Why?" I asked.

He snaked his arm around my waist and dragged me to his chest. He dropped his head, capturing my mouth, kissing me. It was long, intense, and fraught with emotion. Then he broke it off, hugging me tight.

He pulled back, looking down at me.

"I don't know," he confessed, then turned and walked away.

"Your time as a ranch hand is done, Lady. Stick to your plans," he called over his shoulder. "At least I know you're safe while I'm gone."

And he walked out.

I blinked, unsure what had just happened.

Rachel and Tyler came for dinner. It was nice to sit at the table and listen to them all talk. They had their own language, a way of seeing things. Simple and direct. There was a job to do? You did it. A building needing repair? You grabbed your tools. A sick animal? You settled in for the night and helped it. They gave everything they had to the job. Because the job was also their home.

"After you get back, my dad and crew will arrive, and the bunkhouses will be done fast. I'll have everything complete, and we'll go through the options. I'll start putting the show together, and you'll have final approval of all of it," I said to Luke and Rachel.

Luke nodded. He'd been quieter than normal, and I hoped he wasn't still upset about my hand. I barely felt it, and I had been through many other injuries while filming these shows.

"You have enough things filmed?" Rachel asked.

I smiled. "I've filmed constantly. You just don't see it. I'll keep filming until it's done."

"That's your plan while I'm gone?"

"Mostly."

He frowned but didn't say anything else.

Later, he found me in my room, curled up in the chair, looking out the window. He sat on the bed, his hands clasped between his legs as he studied me.

"You planning on staying in here tonight, Lady? You're pissed at me about earlier?"

"I thought you were angry with me, but no. I was going to come to you," I confessed.

"I filled the tub," he offered. "I thought a soak might ease any aches."

I stood, dropping the blanket I had been snuggled under.

"Well then, Cowboy. Take me away."

CHAPTER EIGHTEEN

LUKE

The light behind her showed me her curves under the thin cotton of her nightgown. How something so simple and innocent-looking could be so sexy, I had no idea. But the lace on her shoulders and the way the fabric hung were erotic. I could see her nipples, the curve of her hips, the space between her legs. I held out my hand, and she took it, letting me pull her close. I rested my head on her stomach, groaning as she sifted her hands through my hair, lightly stroking the nape of my neck. I frowned at the feel of the bandage on her skin, and I looked up, meeting her dark gaze.

"I hate that you hurt yourself."

"I'm fine."

"I still hate it."

"Then take me to your room and stop thinking about it."

In the tub, she leaned into my chest. I made sure she kept her hand dry while we enjoyed the warmth of the water around us.

Never having been much of a bath person, it surprised me how much I liked having one with Sammy.

"No stunts while I'm gone," I admonished.

She huffed a little but remained silent.

"When I come back, we'll do the overnight camping trip. We'll take your father and uncles and see what they think."

She hummed. "They'll love it, but I think I'd rather go alone with you."

I chuckled. "We can do that too."

She nestled closer, and I held her tight.

"I guess we go back to client and boss when your family is here."

She sighed. "In front of them, at least. I'm good with the status quo, but I'm not sure my dad would agree."

"Probably not."

She lifted her head, meeting my gaze. "You gonna give me something to remember, Cowboy?"

I lowered my head to hers, my mouth hovering over her full lips. "Totally."

She pulled me to her mouth. "Good."

I sat on the bed in the hotel room, looking at the sterile décor. I scrubbed a hand over my face, feeling weary. It had been a busy two days, barely time to think, yet at every possible moment, Sammy popped into my thoughts. I would see something amusing, and I would think about how she would smile and laugh if she were there. The dessert at dinner last night was rich and decadent, and I knew she would have eaten her piece, then tried to snag mine. A woman on the street had the same color hair as Sammy did, and it made me feel a strange longing. And last night, the bed felt empty, and when I woke up alone, I felt an odd melancholy.

It was as if I missed her.

I resisted calling her, even though part of me wanted to hear her voice. I had texted Rachel, who said everything was fine, Sammy was busy, she was helping, and the ranch was running well. Even stranger than the longing I felt was the sensation that I was more concerned about Sammy than the ranch.

The ranch should be my priority, not the welfare of the smart-mouthed consultant who would be gone in a few weeks.

Still, she lingered in my mind far more deeply than I was comfortable with. Then as if I had conjured her up, a text came through from her.

Sammy: Hey, Cowboy. How's it going? Picked out your new cows yet?
Me: It goes, Lady. Picked them out? It's not a mall.
Sammy: What is the process, exactly? You decide which ones you want, chase them around, and lasso them? I bet you're good with a rope, aren't you?

I began to laugh, her words causing images of me in the auction ring lassoing the cows I'd "chosen." Then I thought about lassoing her. Showing her just how good I was with a rope and knots.

Me: It's an auction. I choose the best breeds to add to the ranch.
Sammy: My idea sounds like more fun.
Me: You're more fun.
Sammy: You lassoed that horse the other day, but I didn't see it. Would you show me?

I grinned as I typed my reply.

Me: How about I lasso you?
Sammy: Oh. And then? What would you do with me once you had me tied up?

Jesus, were we going to send sex texts now? Was that a thing?

Me: Probably gag you and leave you there so I had some peace for a while.
Sammy: Jackass.

I laughed again. Sammy was miles away, and somehow she made me feel better.

Me: I'd probably spread you wide, taste every inch of you, then fuck you until you couldn't recall your name.
Sammy: And now I'm wet. And miss you more than ever.

She missed me?

Me: I'll see what I can do about that when I get back.
Sammy: Something to look forward to, then.

I groaned. Now I had the image of her tied up, writhing on my bed as I did exactly what I wanted to her. My cock felt hot and heavy in my jeans, liking the thought as well.

Me: Go to bed, Lady.
Sammy: Already there.

I hesitated, then typed a final message.

Me: Scream my name into your pillow when you come.

Her text sent me over the edge.

Sammy: I'm in your bed. It smells like you. And I will. x

I dropped my head to the pillow.

Jesus, this woman was going to kill me.

But what a way to go.

I drove the familiar roads, anxious to get to the ranch. It was always the same—a few days surrounded by people and buildings, and I was happy to head back to the peace that permeated the place I called home. The animals I had purchased were already there—sent on ahead with the hands. I stayed and had some meetings with other ranchers and farmers, discussing the future of our industry and the problems and solutions we had to face and implement. My planned three days turned into four, and by the time the event was done, I was ready to go.

I tried to ignore the other reason I wanted to get back on the ranch.

Sammy was there. In the few weeks she'd been with us—with me —she'd become part of the ranch. Part of me.

She had texted a few times since that night with her teasing. Little things. Checking in. Asking about my day. Sharing a picture of Oreo snuggled in her neck while she snuggled in my bed. A picture she took of the fields at sunset. Small glimpses that tied me back to that place.

Home.

As I pulled into the driveway, my pulse picked up. It was late afternoon, the sun high in the sky as I steered the truck up the long, winding road. As the ranch came into view, I felt something ease inside me. That sense of rightness being back here. Everything was in its place, the sunlight reflecting off the metal roof of the deep red barn. I frowned. It looked brighter. I stomped on the brakes, my gaze bouncing everywhere. All the buildings were brighter. All coated in fresh paint.

But not just any paint. None of them were the same color as when I left. The dull, faded hue of the barn was now a deep, rich red. The stable a rusty copper. The dairy barn was yellow. Even the cookhouse and chicken coop had changed. Brilliant blue and forest green met my eyes. It was a kaleidoscope of color that had one name stamped on all of it.

Sammy.

I stepped on the gas and pulled up by the barn, throwing open my door and sliding from the truck. Jeff and Callie came from the cookhouse, both smiling.

"Hey," Callie greeted me.

"What the hell?" I indicated the buildings.

Jeff smirked. "Sammy's idea. I kinda like it. Brightens the place up."

"No one consulted me."

"Rachel gave her permission."

I glowered.

"Where is she?"

"Rachel or Sammy?"

"Sammy."

"Last time I checked, in the stable with the kittens."

Callie held up her hand. "Listen to what she tells you, Luke. It makes great sense. And I agree with Jeff. I like it."

I rolled my eyes. She had them all under her spell.

I stomped to the barn, stopping in the doorway. Sammy was in the corner, surrounded by kittens, Oreo perched on her shoulder. She was taking pictures and cooing at them. For a moment, I drank in the sight of her, then remembered I was pissed and cleared my throat.

She looked up, a wide, bright smile on her face. Pure, one hundred percent Sammy sunshine.

She rushed toward me, excited and happy. Then she stopped about two feet away, and her smile fell.

"Oh," she said. "You hate it."

I hated watching her smile fade away. It made me feel terrible, and I chose my words carefully.

"I agreed we could paint the outbuildings. I never agreed to those colors."

"Rachel did."

"And the reason?"

She tossed her hair, setting Oreo down, making sure he wandered back to his mother. She fisted her hands on her hips, and her eyes flashed. "People coming here won't understand some of the terms. That the barn is different from the stable. Which building the cookhouse is. Now, the hands can say the blue building. The red one. It's easier."

That actually made sense.

"I should have been consulted."

She pushed the hair off her face. "You would have said no."

She was right on that. The movement of her hand reminded me of her mishap.

"How is the hand?"

"It's fine. Doesn't hurt."

"Good." I drew in a deep breath. "How did you do it in four days?"

"I rented paint sprayers and hired a company. We did two buildings a day. It's part of the renovation budget."

"And if I hate it?"

"You are going to live with it for a few days. If you still hate it, we'll repaint." Then she stepped forward and laid her hand on my arm. "But don't hate it, Luke. It looks great, and the cows love it."

"What?"

"I painted the dairy barn yellow because it's a cheerful color. We did the inside too, and I think it makes the cows happier. That'll make better milk, right?"

I blinked down at her. "You think the color makes the *cows* happier?"

"Yes. And the chickens seem very partial to the green. I think we got a few more eggs than normal today. I'm pretty sure Dusty was impressed by the fresh copper on the stable. She whinnied extra loud at me earlier, like a thank-you. Look—" she indicated the horses "—they all look cheerier!"

I wasn't sure what to do next. She was absolutely serious that the paint colors made the animals happier. Suddenly, my ire was gone, and in its place was something entirely different.

This woman was crazy, and I adored her for it. I began to laugh, throwing my head back and letting out the amusement. She regarded me, looking worried.

"Did I just push you over the edge, Cowboy?"

I reached out, dragging her into my arms. I kissed her with everything in me. Passionate and hungry. Hard, soul-wrenching kisses that felt like a balm to my soul.

She flung her arms around my neck, kissing me back. "So, you're not mad?"

I lifted her off her feet, holding her close. "I'm mad, but we'll deal with that later. Show me all the buildings, Lady, and explain them. I want to see my happy cows."

She grinned up at me. "Come on, then."

I let her pull me around the ranch. I had to admit, the buildings all looked good. Way different than I would ever have chosen, but good. Rachel appeared, and I gave her a hard time for the first few moments until she slapped my arm and told me off. I walked between my two favorite women, wondering if I'd lost my balls somewhere. Their enthusiasm and happiness trumped my anger, dissipating it completely. I could barely keep a straight face when Rachel informed me egg and milk production were up. "That happens on occasion," I murmured. "Not sure we can credit color changes with an increase in eggs."

Sammy sniffed, indignant. "Whatever, Cowboy. I researched the colors."

"I have no doubt you did."

Back at the house, we sat on the porch, and I relaxed, leaning back in the rocking chair. It felt good to be home, odd colors dotting the landscape or not. Sammy went inside when her phone rang, deep into planning mode with someone from her team. Rachel watched her, then turned to me.

"She worked really hard, Luke. Overseeing, painting, planning. She's been going nonstop since you left. Try to show some gratitude. She is doing all this for us, you know."

"I'm aware. I didn't tell her to repaint, and I'll get used to the colors."

"You should take her to dinner. Say thanks."

I looked at the bright blue sky, felt the warmth of the breeze. Inspiration struck, and I grinned.

"I've got a better idea. But I need your help."

"You got it."

"Great."

SAMMY

I rubbed my temples and double-checked all the lists I had. If everything stayed on track, I would complete the project on time and, even more important, on budget.

I stood and stretched, then headed out to the porch. I was surprised to see Maverick there, but I assumed Luke would immediately head back to work. The man really needed to learn to take a break once in a while. I had heard him and Rachel talking, and they were in and out of the house as I spoke with various members of the team, ensuring everything that needed to happen behind the scenes was being done. But I couldn't see either of them, so I sat down with a sigh.

Luke accepted the painted buildings far easier than I expected. I was certain we were in for a large blowup and angry words. Instead, he had been more amused than anything. Annoyed that his opinion hadn't been sought, but he gave in fairly quickly.

I heard footsteps and saw him walking toward the house, full saddlebags slung over his shoulder, including what looked like a bedroll. I felt a flash of disappointment. He just got back, and he was going somewhere overnight? I watched as he fitted the saddlebags on Maverick, talking low to the horse and patting his neck. He came over, dressed in jeans, his shirts layered, dusty cowboy boots in place.

He leaned on the rail, frowning. "Everything good, Lady?"

"Yes," I replied.

"You look like someone rustled your favorite calf."

"You're going somewhere?" I asked.

He grinned. "That's why you're upset?"

"I'm not upset," I replied, tossing my hair.

"Then when I tell you I won't be back until the morning, you're okay with that?"

I was shocked to feel my bottom lip quiver a little. He *was* leaving.

"Whatever, Cowboy. You don't owe me any explanations."

He chuckled and flipped up the brim of his hat. "So, I guess you're not interested in a night under the stars—with me."

I sat up. "What?"

"Me, you, dinner, and camping out. Cowboy style. No tent, no glamour. I'll make us dinner and build us a campfire, and we can talk about the colors you chose. How much you missed me."

"I never said I missed you."

He leaned forward, his voice low. "I think you did."

"Maybe a little."

"I missed *you*, Lady." Then he grinned. "I'll show you a rope trick or two if you're good."

The sadness disappeared, and heat set in. Everywhere. "What do I need to bring?"

"Something warm like a sweater or a jacket. Your toothbrush. I got everything else we need. Grab some marshmallows from the cupboard."

"That doesn't sound very cowboy-ish."

He laughed. "It's this cowboy's favorite." He stood, eyeing me. "You have ten minutes, Lady. Move that sexy ass of yours."

I jumped up. "I only need five."

CHAPTER NINETEEN

SAMMY

I nestled back against Luke's chest as we headed up the mountain. Or hill. Whatever. When I asked him why only one horse, his reply had been simple.

"I get to hold you more this way."

I was good with it. He pointed out the trail for hiking, various pretty spots people could visit. He made his way to a location he was obviously familiar with. A nice brook bubbled and danced in the sunlight. Lovely tall trees surrounded the area, and there was a level surface with scatterings of rocks and a well-used fire pit.

He slid from Maverick and gripped me around the waist, lifting me as if I weighed nothing and setting me on my feet. I gazed up at him, and he lowered his head, brushing his lips on mine.

"Welcome to my favorite hiding spot."

"It's so pretty."

He cupped my face. "Yeah, it is. Prettiest thing I've ever set eyes on."

Except he wasn't looking anywhere but at me. I felt myself blush at his words. I wasn't sure I had blushed from someone's flattery since I was a young girl.

He smiled and traced his thumb over my cheek. "You constantly surprise me."

"Back at ya, Cowboy."

He winked. "Come help me set up camp."

———

Hours later, I watched, fascinated, as he cooked us a feast. He was in control and an expert at cooking outdoors. His saddlebags held many secrets, and as he produced them, I shook my head. People would flip experiencing this.

Foil-wrapped potatoes were nestled close to the coals. It was my job to keep turning them. Asparagus was washed and trimmed by the brook, then wrapped in parchment paper, ready to go on the grill when the steak was almost done. He had a lethal-looking knife he used for preparation that he wielded with the skill of a surgeon. And he had thought of everything. We had butter, spices, plates, even forks. An old cast-iron skillet he had shoved into the saddlebags as well. A small metal grill he set into the coals. As we relaxed and talked, he'd whittled two long stakes for the marshmallows.

I eyed the sizzling steaks with appreciation, then indicated his saddlebags. "You have breakfast hidden in there too?"

He laughed. "Some buns from Callie to keep us going. If we were bringing more people, I'd make a trip up in the ATV, and we'd have coolers we'd transport last minute. We have to be careful not to attract wildlife."

"Like bears?"

He nodded. "We're a little close to civilization for them, but on occasion, we see one. If we went farther into the mountains, that could happen. But we'd keep campers close to home."

"Would you bring them to this spot?"

He paused then shook his head. "I'd rather not. There's another spot downstream. Larger. We could fit tents. This spot is sort of special to me. I don't bring anyone here."

"You brought me," I said softly.

"You're different."

I wanted to ask how, but I let it go. The moment felt right left the way it was.

"You gonna chop any more wood for the fire?" I asked.

He laughed, his teeth white in the firelight. "I have lots. I keep a pile here, and I chopped a bunch last time I was up."

"Dammit," I muttered.

He met my eyes. "Don't worry, Lady. You're gonna get an eyeful later. All of me. Promise."

"I look forward to it."

He pushed at the crackling wood with his knife, chuckling. "Keep turning the spuds, Lady."

"Okay, Cowboy. Keep your shirt on." Then I winked. "At least for now."

I set aside my plate, groaning in pleasure. "That was incredible, Luke. I swear it's the most delicious thing I've eaten since I got here."

He waved off my praise. "Everything tastes better cooked over a fire outside."

"No, you were amazing to watch."

"My dad loved eating this way. He taught me. Every weekend, we'd cook outside. This was his fry pan, his knife. That was all he used."

"Would you be willing to cook for guests?"

He scratched his chin. "Small groups, yes."

"Will you do your knife flips and tricks?"

He chuckled. "Sure, darlin'. Whatever you say."

"They'd love to help with prep, even cleanup. But you cook."

"Deal."

After, we cleaned up and sat by the fire. Luke pulled me between his legs, his warmth surrounding me. We roasted marshmallows, drank the strong coffee he brewed, and just enjoyed the quiet.

I glanced up at the stars. They were so bright and clear here. It looked as if I could reach out and touch them. "Are we really going to sleep in the open?"

"You, me, and a sleeping roll." He tucked me tighter. "I'll keep you warm and safe, Lady."

"I know."

He shifted, turning me. We stared at each other, and he lowered his head, capturing my mouth. His kiss was soft and sweet.

Tender. I slipped my hand around his neck, pulling him closer, and it changed. Became deeper. Bolder. Hungrier. He placed his hand under my ass, lifting me to his lap, clutching my hip as he bent over me, devouring my mouth. I shivered as he slid his hand under my shirt, stroking the skin along my sides and back. I moved again, straddling him, our mouths never separating. He wrapped his arms around me, holding me tight to his chest as he ravished my mouth. Dragging his lips to my ear, he bit down. "Ever make love outside under the stars, Lady?"

I rolled my hips against his erection. "No."

"You want to? Part of the whole experience, you know."

I scowled against his mouth. "That better be a one-off VIP ticket, mister."

He grinned, smug. "I guarantee more than one, Lady. But it's only for you."

"Good." Then I yanked him back to my lips, sliding my tongue with his. He lowered us to the ground, his head cushioned on the blanket he had spread out before dinner. We kissed endlessly. Touched and caressed, our hands finding their way under clothing. I sat up, straddling his waist, working his belt open.

"I'm going to ride you, Cowboy. Now."

He groaned in pleasure as I wrapped my hand around him.

"Not objecting, darlin'. Take whatever you need."

He helped peel away my jeans, then guided me down, hissing as I lowered myself onto him, inch by inch until we were flush.

"Jesus, Sammy, you feel good."

"I've been thinking about this since you left. You inside me," I responded, beginning to move. "Feeling your cock fill me."

He gripped my hips, meeting my movements, urging me to go faster.

I whimpered, riding him, pressing my hands to his sternum for leverage. The pleasure came in waves, growing and branching out, filling me with need. He watched me, his eyes glittering in the firelight.

"The stars have nothing on you, Lady. You shine so bright when I'm fucking you."

"Luke," I pleaded, needing more. Needing him.

He sat up, engulfing me in his arms. He hit a new place inside me that made me cry out, and he pushed and pulled on my hips. "I want you to come on me. Let me feel it. Feel you," he growled. "Jesus, I want to feel that."

I gripped his neck, and he covered my mouth with his, guiding me. Grunting his pleasure, whispering words of desire, praise, and longing. My muscles locked down, and I was lost. Ecstasy exploded, and my orgasm hit, hard and hot. He groaned his release, swallowing my cries, sharing his breath with me, and riding it out until I was done. Limp and sated in his arms. Trapped by the feel of him surrounding me. Holding me close, keeping me safe.

He lay back, taking me with him, pulling the blanket over us and holding me. Not speaking, simply holding me, nuzzling my head, stroking along my spine in light passes.

Finally, I lifted my head. "That is not going in the brochure as an extra. Ever."

He chuckled, the sound low and deep in his throat.

"Only for you, Lady. Only for you."

In the morning, I was a little stiff but relaxed when I woke up. The fire was burning low, and Luke sat on a boulder by the water, sipping coffee. As usual, he had rolled me up like a burrito, glancing over his shoulder with a grin as I struggled to get out of the layers. I walked toward him and sat between his legs, accepting the coffee cup he pressed to my lips. The sun was rising, and it was peaceful. I sat enjoying the moment, then spoke.

"People will love this."

"As long as there are tents and sleeping bags," he agreed with humor in his voice.

"Of course. Hot showers would be great as well."

He laughed. "That I can't do. They can have a dip in the brook."

I shivered. "Chilly."

"Invigorating," he insisted.

"I don't think so."

He stood, taking me with him, walking to the edge of the water. His grin was evil, and I clutched his neck. "You wouldn't!"

"Wouldn't I? I think I owe you."

"But I'd be cold and wet!"

"Our clothes can dry in the sun. I'll figure out how to warm you up." He lowered his head to mine. "I made love to you under the stars, Lady. Now I want to watch you glow in the sun."

Then he plunged us into the cold water, never taking his lips off mine.

LUKE

She had fought me like a wildcat as we went into the water. Furious and dripping, she cursed at me, wet and cold in the stream. Until I led her to the shallows I had dammed up years ago. The water was warmer, soothing her chill, and she sat down with a long shiver, lifting her face to the sun. I lowered myself beside her, nibbling on her neck, rubbing my hand up and down her arm until her cold tremors turned into shudders of desire. I kissed her until she forgot the cold, the wet, and everything else but us. I carried her out of the water and did what I promised on the phone. Stripped her of all her clothing and tasted her everywhere. The sun played over her lovely skin, dappled and teasing. I kissed and caressed every inch of her. Touched her gorgeous body with my hands, my mouth, and my tongue until she was begging me. Then I sank into her, watching her eyes grow wide with pleasure as I rode her, her legs over my shoulders, our bodies pressed together in the most intimate of acts. Her cries of bliss echoed in the trees that surrounded us. I had been correct. She was as sexy and beautiful on fire in the sun as she had been under the moonlight with the stars surrounding her.

I was certain there wasn't anything on earth as beautiful as Sammy when she orgasmed. Smiled. Cried my name. She was simple and perfect beauty.

And I knew I was fucked when she left.

But until then, I would get my fill.

After, I wrapped the blanket back around her, and we drank coffee and ate the sweet buns Callie had given me when I'd raided her kitchen for our meal last night. Our clothing was almost dry, and we slid it back on, the process taking a long time between kisses and touches of our hands. We packed up the few things left into the saddlebags, and I lifted her into the saddle, swinging myself up behind her. I liked how she nestled back against me, her softness melding into my hard chest as if made to rest there. I took the long way home, pointing out more things for her to see. She was quiet, not taking pictures, simply in the moment with me. She had been the whole time. The overnight camping had nothing to do with the project, the guests, or anything else. It had been for us. A memory we could both cherish. I realized neither of us had even glanced at our phones when we got closer to the ranch and the message app beeped on hers.

"Reality," she muttered. "It can wait until after I have a shower."

I tucked her closer, wishing I could have stayed in that little spot with her for days. Talked and made love to her. Cooked for her and watched her come alive in the sun and the stars. But I had responsibilities, and she did as well.

I guided Maverick toward the stables, frowning when I saw a large RV parked on the property. It was silver and black and had extensions open, as if it planned to stay where it was. I stopped Maverick's forward motion.

"What the..." I trailed off as the door opened, and two men came down the steps.

Sammy sat straighter, suddenly tense. "Oh my God. Turn him around. Put Maverick in reverse, Cowboy. Now!"

"We've been through this before, darlin'. There's no gearshift."

"Move him!" she pleaded.

But it was too late. One of the men stepped our way, shielding his eyes. He waved, a wide smile breaking out on his face.

"Mouse!" he shouted.

Sammy groaned, then waved back. "Dad!" she called. Then she whimpered, her shoulders falling forward. "Oh God."

I swallowed. Her father was here. A day early. We'd just spent the night together, and there was no doubt what we'd been doing. We both looked freshly fucked.

I was, quite possibly, a dead man.

I slid off Maverick and, without thinking, grasped Sammy's waist and lifted her off. I squeezed her slightly, then stepped back. She hurried forward, throwing herself into her dad's embrace.

"What are you doing here? We were expecting you tomorrow!"

The other man beside him smiled widely. "Bent had to go to BC to see Thomas, so he dropped us off a day earlier." He indicated the large RV behind him. "Figured we had our own accommodation, so arriving earlier wouldn't make much difference." Then he held out his hand to me. "Aiden Callaghan."

His grip was strong and firm.

"Luke Adler."

"Quite the spread you have here, Luke," he said. "It's spectacular."

"Thanks."

I turned to Sammy's dad and held out my hand. "Mr. Morrison. A pleasure to meet you, sir."

He studied me a moment, then gripped my hand. I resisted a strength contest and smiled. "Your daughter had been a whirlwind here."

He pursed his lips with a nod. "She usually is." Then he turned to Sammy. "Why are you wet?"

"Oh, we did the overnight camping thing, and I fell in the water. Luke dragged me out."

"You went alone all night?" he asked, his tone mild.

She tossed her hair, and I tried not to smile. Obviously, I wasn't the only one who was on the receiving end of that warning.

"You would rather I spent the night alone with four or five cowboys, Dad? I was perfectly safe with Luke," she replied, her tone tart. "He was giving me the chance to grade the experience."

"Grade it," he mused. "And?"

"A solid A," she replied.

"Only one horse?" he questioned.

"Sammy isn't big on horses," I interjected smoothly. "She got thrown on her first day. It's a short ride, so we took the one horse. She was able to take pictures along the way."

For a moment, he studied me, then he grinned. "I did warn you, Mouse. You weren't crazy about them as a kid either."

"Dusty and I have made friends since," she protested.

The door opened, and two more men came down the steps. They looked remarkably like Aiden, and I wasn't surprised to find out they were his sons. I shook their hands, wondering what they fed their children in Ontario. They were all large, imposing men. Then the door opened again, and another man came out. Not as large but still tall and broad, he moved with an easy confidence. Sammy was thrilled to see them all, and hugs and introductions were exchanged.

"Ronan and Liam are Aiden's sons," she explained. "Hunter is Aiden's son-in-law. He's married to his daughter, Ava. He and Dad work together a lot."

"I can't express how grateful we are that you came all this way to help."

Van shrugged. "I'd do anything for my daughter. And she was so enthusiastic about this project, I wanted to see it for myself."

Aiden chuckled. "Many hands make light work. And I want to come back and be a cowboy for a few days."

"I'm sure we can help with that."

A woman appeared around the corner with Rachel, and Sammy gasped, running toward her, throwing her arms around her. "Mom! I didn't know you were coming!"

"Mila left early for LA. There was an empty seat on the plane, and I wanted to see this place. You know I love to watch you in action. I thought maybe I could help."

Sammy hugged her again. "I would love that! I'm so excited!"

I watched her with an indulgent smile on my face. I liked seeing her happy. Then I saw the way her dad was watching me, and I schooled my features. Sammy looked like her mom, small and pretty, with the same-colored hair. The main difference was their eyes. Her mom's were a light caramel color, warm and soft, and Sammy's were dark and snapped fire.

Sammy brought her mom over and introduced us. She refused my hand, insisting on hugging me, and laughed when Sammy repeated the story about falling in the water.

"Nothing changes," she mused. "Always getting into scrapes, falling off ladders, into trouble." Then she grinned. "All while wearing pink tulle and glitter."

"That's our Sammy," her dad mused.

"I haven't worn glitter since I was twelve. Tulle either," she sniffed. "And I don't get into that many scrapes."

"What did you do to your hand?" Van asked.

"Oh, cut it on a piece of wire." Sammy grinned sheepishly. "Luke had the vet stitch it up."

"The vet?" her mom asked, looking shocked.

"He was awesome," Sammy said. "Very fast. And neat."

Everyone laughed at her description, and even I had to chuckle.

"I'm sure you must be hungry," Rachel said. "Maybe Sammy and Luke want to change, and they can join us at the cookhouse? Callie is rustling up some breakfast for you."

Van clapped his hands. "Awesome. Then you can show us around, Sammy. We can make our plans. We already ordered a bunch of supplies that should arrive this afternoon. I'll add anything we need, and it'll be here in a day or two. We can get going."

Sammy beamed at her family. "Awesome."

I walked out of the bathroom to find Sammy on my bed. I bent down and kissed her. "Hi."

"Sorry about that."

I waved her off. "No big deal. Although I think your dad is already onto us." I chuckled. "I thought I was a dead man."

"You're fine." She chewed her lip. "I think."

I dragged on my boxers and a pair of jeans, tucking in a T-shirt and adding a plaid shirt over top. Sammy watched me intently.

"What?" I asked.

"You make putting on clothes as sexy as watching them come off, Mr. Adler."

I sauntered over and rested my hands on the mattress, caging her in. "Is that a fact, Lady?"

"Uh-huh. You are so sexy."

"Don't start that right now. If I show up for breakfast with you looking ravished again, I will not have any balls left to speak of. And me sporting an erection won't help the matter either. *Behave.*" But I kissed her anyway, unable to resist. Her lips were warm and full underneath mine, and I groaned as I pulled away. I wanted to lock the door. Forget the RV full of her relatives. Push aside the responsibilities I had and spend the day with her, right here in my bed. I had never known anything like the draw I had to her.

I shook my head and pulled back. "You head over. I'll be along in a few moments."

She grinned mischievously. "Okay."

"And stop smiling like that."

She cleared her throat and tried to look serious. Instead, she only looked more adorable. I pulled her back into my arms and kissed her until she was breathless. Until I was light-headed and dangerously close to giving in to my unusual thoughts. I pushed her away.

"Go."

I heard her laughing right until she closed the front door behind her.

I sat down and tried to think of the worst things I'd ever seen. I didn't dare walk into that building right now. Her father had access to far too many knives.

The cookhouse was full. Callie was in her glory, serving up her breakfast casserole, talking to everyone. Sammy sat between her parents, and I filled my plate, sitting across from them.

Van paused in between mouthfuls. "You gonna feed your guests like this?"

"That's the plan."

Aiden lifted his plate for more food. "Sign me up for a month."

Everyone laughed.

"Or I'm kidnapping this little woman and taking her back to Ontario," he teased, nudging Callie. "You can cook for me. Less work than this place."

She laughed. "I bet you eat as much as the entire crew most days."

Ronan and Liam laughed. Ronan let Callie fill his plate again. "My mom says we're empty pits. Dinner for us takes her all day."

I met Sammy's amused eyes and winked. She had a good appetite too, and I liked watching her eat. She burned it off quickly enough the way she darted around all day.

"Do we get to go camping too?" Van asked, meeting my eyes.

"Of course, sir. Sammy wants you all to spend a day being cowboys, tagging along with me and my crew, and as long as the weather holds, we can do a night out."

"Sounds good."

"Your daughter did the whole experience. No tent, just a bedroll, the stars, and a campfire. You up for that?" I challenged. "Or do you want the glamorized version Sammy has in mind for some people?"

"I want it real."

"Done."

"Does that mean I get to ride on your lap too?" he responded.

I blinked, then he began to laugh. "Teasing, son. And stop calling me sir. It's Van. Liv and Van. We're not formal."

I felt as if I had passed some test, and I breathed out a sigh of relief.

Crisis averted. At least for now.

CHAPTER TWENTY

LUKE

I had always prided myself on my ranch hands. I ran a tight crew, and we worked well together. Nothing prepared me for Sammy's family. After they finished eating, they got down to business. Rachel and I followed them to the bunkhouses, watching as plans were rolled out and the men bent over them, listening to Sammy. She was in her element, and they all paid attention. Rapid-fire questions were answered calmly. Ideas were discussed, accepted, or dismissed. Tasks were assigned, steps were laid out, each man taking on a different aspect to be in control of. Ronan had had a hand in drawing the plans, but he let Sammy run the show, only speaking when a question was directed at him.

I looked over at Rachel, lifting my eyebrow in subtle admiration. She grinned like a loon, knowing her dream was about to come to life in front of her. Liv chuckled. "I've lost Sammy for the next while. She'll be in there with them, hammering and nailing."

"Is that, ah, safe?" I asked.

She patted my arm. "As soon as she expressed interest in building things, my husband taught her. She can hold her own, even with the odd mishap." She turned to Rachel. "I understand there're some great shops around. Once Sammy tells me what she's looking for, I'll start some recon. In the meantime, if you can tell me how to get to the closest grocery store, I'd like to make dinner for everyone. You two included. And your fiancé, of course."

"Oh, we'd love that. I'll drive you to the store. Although you might want to check the freezers here. Luke has to get to work on his chores. And you're going to make sure the crews can help too, right, Luke? Whatever time they can spare?"

I had a hard time taking my eyes off Sammy. She was a wonder to watch as she drew a picture with her hands, demonstrating something to her dad. She was bright, alive, and in the zone. I hated to walk away, but Rachel was right.

"For sure. Sammy can tell me what she needs, and I'll make sure it happens."

"Awesome."

They left, and I stood, observing for another few moments. The sun shone on Sammy's hair, the color lighter than when she'd arrived from her time outside. Even her pale skin was touched by the sun. In her shirt and jeans, which were tucked into a pair of boots, she looked at home. At ease. Bossy. Sexy as hell.

I had to walk away before I did something stupid like drag her into my arms and kiss her in front of everybody.

But I wanted to.

I wiped my brow, looking around in amazement. What Sammy's family had accomplished in a short time was nothing short of incredible. Walls were up. Plumbers that Sammy had hired locally worked on the plumbing. Electrical work was almost complete. The living room in the ranch house looked like a model home. Swatches of fabric, décor pieces, bedding, lamps, all sorts of items were piled up. There was a keep section, a return one, even a maybe pile. In one unused building, furniture and fixtures were being painted, repaired, reused. And Sammy ran it all. She helped build. Paint. Shop. She filmed. She interviewed. She was a wonder. Even I felt the stirrings of excitement. Whatever ideas Rachel had, Sammy had expanded and taken to the next level.

Liv tapped my arm, offering me water. I drank it gratefully. "Thanks, Liv."

She smiled at me, warm and motherly. She was everything maternal that I missed about my own mom. She had taken charge of cooking for her crew and mine every night. The house was full, as many chairs as possible gathered around the table. It reminded me of when I was younger and the hands stayed on the ranch and ate with us. My mom would cook for hours, and everything would disappear, the men showing their appreciation in their hard work and extra efforts. Sitting with Sammy's family, the laughter and teasing were constant, the jokes risqué, and the love evident. I understood Sammy even more now. Her drive and passion. Her love for her family.

Rachel and Tyler joined us most nights. His parents on occasion. Callie and Jeff. I never knew who would be there, and I didn't mind. It brought the house back to life, and I knew my parents would approve.

Aiden leaned over to me one night. "How does one buy one of your cows?"

"I don't think one would fit on that plane of yours."

He waved me off. "Not mine, Bentley's. Well, the company's. But not to take home, although…" He trailed off. "How much land does a cow need?"

Ronan laughed. "Forget it, Dad."

"Fine. I want to buy a cow. To eat."

I lifted one eyebrow. "All by yourself?"

Everyone laughed.

"No, for the family. To send back to Ontario. I have never tasted beef this good." To prove his point, he sliced off another mouthful of steak and chewed it with a groan.

"I'll give you the name of the local butcher. He can package, dry-ice it, and ship it."

"Awesome."

Rachel spoke up. "Friends and family discount, of course."

Aiden grinned. "What if it's both?"

Sammy blushed, shaking her head. Rachel chuckled.

"We'll look after you, Aiden."

"I figured you would. I might need two cows. We feed a lot of people on the weekends."

She laughed again. "I'll hook you up."

"I knew I liked you."

"The weekend," Ronan snorted. "Mom has to feed you every night too."

"Whatever," Aiden sniffed, making everyone laugh again.

It felt good to be part of it.

Callie beamed constantly, the cookhouse full all hours of the day. I walked in with Van, hungry from a morning of moving walls and building frames.

"What smells so good?"

Callie grinned. "Homemade tomato soup, and grilled cheese and bacon sandwiches. Made by Sammy and Liv."

Van grinned. "Our favorite lunch, right, Mouse?"

Sammy laughed and set down bowls of steaming soup and a platter of sandwiches.

I sat down, tucking in, not talking until I had finished an entire sandwich.

"So," I began. "Mouse?"

Van laughed. "The day I met Sammy, she thought I was a giant. I told her she was as tiny as a mouse. The name stuck. It suited her. Still does."

I met her eyes across the room, trying not to smile at her subtle wink. "I see."

"I took her and Liv to lunch and introduced her to grilled cheese and bacon sandwiches. Liv added the tomato soup a few weeks later. It's a standard in the Morrison house."

I finished off my second sandwich. "I can understand why."

He smiled. "Mouse fell in love with these, and I fell in love with her and Liv." He met my eyes. "Family isn't always blood. My kids mean as much if not more to me than if I had made them with Liv. They're a gift to me. To us. I treasure them."

I nodded, unsure what to say.

I had a feeling there was a hidden meaning there.

The best part of the days, though, was when it was late and dark and I would hear the soft footfalls, then Sammy would slip into my bed. I eagerly reached for her, anxious to feel her body molding to me, her mouth moving with mine as I kissed her with a hunger I'd never known was possible.

I craved her. Seeing her in the day, hearing her laughter, wasn't enough. Sneaking to the stable or catching her behind the barn to hold her, kiss her, or even listen to her tell me the progress only eased the ache temporarily. It never faded entirely until I was alone with her.

I refused to think of how empty the house and my life would be once she left.

Because she would leave. She had her life, and I had mine. She traveled and looked for new landscapes. New adventures and people to work with. My life was this ranch and the people I employed to keep it running. Her family was wealthy, powerful. I was simply a rancher.

"Where're Hunter and Van?" I asked, bringing myself out of my thoughts.

"Arguing with Sammy over the color of the floors."

I chuckled. "Why? She's going to win."

"You and I know that. They just like to push her. And she enjoys the tussle."

"She would. She loves to argue."

"Found that out, did you?"

I laughed. "Quickly." I leaned down, lowering my voice. "She flipped me onto my back the first day I met her."

She bit her lip. "Oh dear. My daughter does have a bit of a temper. Did she apologize?"

I shook my head. "I deserved it. She did it again."

"You must rile her up well."

I had a feeling there was a double entendre there, so I simply shrugged. "We strike sparks on occasion."

She laughed. "All the best, most passionate relationships do. Van and I have had our share of sparks."

"Oh, ah, no—we're just friends."

She glanced up at me. "Really," she murmured.

"Yes."

She pursed her lips, looking thoughtful. "You remind me of Hunter."

"Hunter?"

She nodded. "You should get to know him a little better. You might find you have a lot in common."

"Such as?"

"Denial is not only a river in Egypt," she said, then walked away.

What the hell did she mean by that?

I walked into the bathhouse the next day, where Van, Hunter, Liv, and Sammy were talking.

Van was shaking his head. "It's too time-consuming, Mouse. Lining the walls with the river rock is a heavy load job. We have to think scaled back."

"I don't like that." She pointed to a sample Hunter was holding. "It's cold."

"Do all cedar, then," Liv offered. "It would smell incredible, and it's easy to maintain."

"I wanted some contrast."

"What about a few niches lined with the rock? Where you can put, ah, stuff?" I suggested. "I can set it. Two or three of those would look nice on that wall—" I indicated the biggest one "—and it would only take me a few days. I'll just line the inside and three sides so the bottom shelves are smooth."

Sammy tilted her head, studying the walls. Liv smiled. "That would look lovely."

Sammy smiled. "I like that idea."

Hunter looked down at the floor. "What about a small border running along the edge of the floor? I can help with that. Tie it all in."

"You know," Liv mused, working on her phone. "There is this lovely preset rock. I know it's not from the property, but it would make the job easier and is very pretty. It's cut, so it's level and smooth, no chance of tripping."

Sammy looked at it and nodded. "That would work."

I took the phone and studied it. It was nice but not as nice as the rock we had here. But Liv was right. It was practical and would do the job.

Liv frowned. "The only problem is you can only get it in Calgary."

"I'll drive in," Hunter offered.

"I have to get some supplies that are waiting there. I can pick it up," I said. I had hoped to steal Sammy away with me and spend a little alone time with her, but my hopes were dashed fast.

"We'll drive in together," Hunter offered.

I had a feeling I had just been set up, but I was fine with it. I liked Hunter—he was no Sammy, but he was a decent guy.

"Sure. Order it, and we'll make plans."

We left early in the morning a couple of days later, wanting to get the supplies and head back. I had paused before walking out of my room. Sammy was curled up in my bed, still asleep. I didn't have the heart to wake her or carry her back to her room in case someone came into the house. I set her alarm, giving her another hour of sleep—she'd still be up before anyone else. I made sure she was wrapped up tight, and she was burrowed under the blankets, clutching my pillow. I liked waking up with her beside me, slowly coming into awareness with her warmth wrapped around me, her breath on my chest, and our legs intertwined. I'd never been much of a cuddler, but Sammy seemed to bring that out in me.

Hunter sat in the passenger seat, sipping a thermal cup of coffee. He'd brought me one as well, which I appreciated. We hadn't spoken much aside from our greeting. His phone rang, and he answered it with a smile.

"Hey, little dragon."

He listened a lot, asked a few questions, and caught her up on the progress.

"I'll be home soon," he said.

She replied with words that made him smile.

"I know. I miss you too. I'll be there soon. I love you, Ava."

He hung up, looking out the window.

"So, you're married to Aiden's daughter."

"Yep. My little dragon."

I huffed a laugh. "Cute nickname."

"First time I met her, she was going to town on some low-level city clerk who was trying to bulldoze her. She took him down brilliantly. Breathed fire. I was a goner right then, although I fought it. It suits her."

I felt his side glance. "She was everything I didn't want to want. She had a big, rich family. She was sweet, funny, sexy. Loving. Grounded. I was a wanderer. No roots. I didn't believe that love was real and certainly not for me. She became my anchor. My home."

"Ah."

"I almost gave it up. The best thing that ever happened in my life. All because I didn't know how to move away from my past."

I grunted.

"To me, our relationship was a huge, insurmountable obstacle."

I had to ask. "And to Ava?"

"A challenge we could overcome together. And she was right. Her love, our life, is everything I ever wanted or needed."

"And her family?"

He laughed. "You've met them. Some of the best people on this planet. When they have your back, nothing is impossible. Their money doesn't make them what they are, their hearts do."

"Sammy and I are just friends."

"I never said anything about Sammy," he replied dryly. "I was talking about my little dragon." He leaned his head back. "I gave her that nickname the day I met her. I should have known right then. I had never done that before." He paused. "With Ava, I did a hundred and one things I'd never done before."

I concentrated on driving, trying to ignore how his words resonated. I gave Sammy a nickname. She made me do and say things I had never experienced. She brought out feelings I hadn't known existed.

But our situations weren't the same.

Not at all.

Two weeks later, Rachel grabbed my hand. "Oh my God, Luke, can you believe it?"

I slung my arm over her shoulders, giving her a hug. "It looks amazing."

The bunkhouses were done. Simple. Rugged. Befitting the locale. Each one suited to a certain need. All painted red and white, each numbered. Guests would be comfortable. Good mattresses, soft sheets, and fluffy towels would be the added touch of luxury to the accommodations that was necessary, Sammy assured us.

"This is more than I imagined," Rachel murmured.

I looked around, still awestruck by Sammy's vision and the end result. A fire pit with benches placed around it was centered in front of the bunkhouses. A gazebo with tables and chairs had been added for guests to read, eat, or relax. The bathhouse was spectacular, and the other piece of luxury Sammy insisted the spot needed. The family cabin had a small deck with a couple of rockers she had found and painted. She had reused stored items, dug around thrift stores and secondhand shops in the area to add pieces, and turned the unused cabins into useful, good-looking additions to the ranch. Liam had added to the outside space with some new trees and shrubs, making it look inviting. We'd set up a small area for archery, Tim's favorite hobby. He was eager to teach the sport. There was another building that housed the archery supplies, fishing poles, and lots of outdoor games for people to use if they chose to do so.

"I can hardly wait to see her marketing ideas," Rachel said.

"I have no doubt they'll be brilliant."

"Everything set for tonight?" she asked.

"Yep."

Tonight was the overnight camping trip for Sammy's family before they departed tomorrow. My guys had gone ahead and set up the tents, brought up the supplies, and I would be cooking dinner for everyone. There was a fire planned, Jeff and Callie were coming, along with a couple other hands for practice.

"I'm going to miss having them all around. It's been great."

"Yeah," I agreed. "Good people."

"Especially Sammy," she added.

I swallowed the thick feeling in my throat. Her family left tomorrow, and Sammy would be gone soon to do the editing and put together the show. She'd be back for the soft opening, but I knew Rachel would miss her. They had grown close.

I couldn't articulate how much I would miss her. When I tried, my throat closed up, and the words wouldn't come. Instead, I steered the conversation away from that subject.

"Let's go listen to the guru tell us her ideas. Then I'll head up and make sure everything is ready."

"Okay," Rachel agreed. "But Luke, you and Sammy…" She trailed off when I shook my head.

"Don't. We all have our path," was all I could say.

She shook her head and walked away. "And some people refuse to admit when they're lost."

I followed her, unsure how to reply.

Sammy was all smiles when we walked in, talking to someone via Zoom. She looked up as we sat down. "They're here now." She moved the computer so we could see the person she was talking to. He was a good-looking man, with an easy smile and warm hazel eyes. Silver strands highlighted his dark hair, and he waved. "Richard VanRyan," he said simply. "One of Sammy's many uncles." He leaned closer to the camera with a wink. "But no doubt her favorite."

Laughing, we introduced ourselves, and Sammy spoke. "Richard's a huge marketing and ad guy. I ran some things past him, and he helped me nail down the overall look and streamline the packages." She smiled fondly, and he grinned at her and winked again.

"Your ideas, kiddo. I just added a little more flair. That's what I do. This feels like a winner to me. Great concept, fabulous ideas…" He paused. "My biggest piece of advice is an old marketing expression. Underpromise and overdeliver. With Sammy's help, you'll knock it out of the park."

He glanced offscreen. "I have another meeting I have to get to. Luke, Rachel, you're in good hands, and I'm looking forward to joining my family when they come for their stay. I've always wanted to be a cowboy." He grinned widely. "I think Katy would like to see me in a cowboy hat and boots. Knock her socks off."

I smiled. "We'll be happy to help you with that."

He signed off, and Sammy smiled. "He's awesome."

"His name is familiar," I mused.

"He's with the Gavin Group. Semi-retired, but still working."

Once again, she surprised me. "Wow, Lady. You *are* connected. BAM, the Gavin Group—I had no idea."

She shrugged. "Most people don't. I'm my own person, my own business. I only utilize them occasionally." She met my eyes for a moment. "Only on projects I feel passionate about."

I tried not to smirk. I knew how passionate she was. Still, my lips curled into a smile, and I threw her a wink. Rachel laughed softly.

"I can't wait to see your plans."

Sammy flipped open a file. "Let's go, then."

"I love these names!" Rachel enthused.

I had to agree. Little Partners for the kids, Ranch Hands for mid-level involvement, and Branded for Life, which was the highest level of involvement, were catchy. There was also Sidesaddle which was geared more toward women and offered a gentler experience.

"You might get a larger group that wants to pick and choose different options," Sammy added. "I called it The Rustler. You can work with them on a price, but remember to value it high. If they are taking over the entire capacity, they pay for that. I made some suggestions in the file."

She had thought of everything.

"None of the tasks are dangerous or unattainable. Guests have to fill in all the forms, sign a waiver, and I have a file of insurance needs. I got some quotes." She pushed a file in my direction. "This is a mock-up of the brochure. I'm working on the web page and interest form."

We studied it all. Crisp, clean, bright pictures that showed off the ranch in its unique beauty. Clear details on the packages. Even pictures of the bunkhouses. She had everything covered.

"These photos are spectacular," Rachel exclaimed.

I agreed wholeheartedly. Sammy had a good eye.

"I have budgets laid out, expenses, and expected returns. You'll have your soft opening as planned."

"Where are these guests coming from exactly?" I asked.

Sammy smiled. "We ran a contest, and the winners will be here for a three-night stay. It's part of the show, so all expenses are covered. We chose the guests based on the form they filled out. One set of winners from each category so you can try out the various experiences on them. So, we have a family, some guys wanting the whole package, and even some wives. We handled it all. Ten people. Three nights. Doable."

"Ah."

"The program will air in six weeks, and hopefully, the bookings will roll in for the summer. You can start small with numbers and grow next year. But I expect it to be a huge success."

Rachel reached across the table, grasping Sammy's hand. "Thank you, Sammy. This is beyond anything I dreamed."

I opened the file, shock making my eyes widen at her projected numbers. "Is this right?" I asked.

Sammy nodded. "By the end of the summer, you'll be in the black. We saved a lot on labor costs and supplies by reusing what you already had."

"I want to pay—"

She cut me off. "I told you. My family wants to come here. They are happy to take their labor in trade." She smiled softly. "They've had such a good time. They love it here. It's going to be hard to get some of us on the plane."

Her wording caught me. "Some of us?"

She took in a deep breath, and for the first time, I noticed the trace of sadness in her eyes. "I'm going with them tomorrow. I have everything I need to create the show. But I need my equipment and staff to put it together so I can make the deadline. I can't do it here, and I want it to air on the date I chose. Timing is important."

Something tightened in my chest. A dull ache I couldn't identify seemed to take hold. A low roar started in my head.

Sammy was leaving. Tomorrow.

I stared at her, unable to even speak.

"But you'll be back, right?" Rachel asked.

Sammy nodded. "For the soft opening. I'll help with whatever you need."

She'd be back, but only for a few days. Then she'd be gone. Out of my life. Nothing about this was new or different, yet somehow knowing it was about to happen was like a bolt of lightning to my brain.

I stood, unable to stay anymore. I had to leave before I said something. "Well then, that's that. This is all great, Sammy. I can't thank you enough for what you've done for Rachel."

She looked at me, her voice quiet. "It's for you too, Luke."

I waved my hand. "Not my dream. I'm still not sold. I'll hold off on the celebrations until the real numbers come in and we weigh the work against the profit. If there is any."

I ignored Rachel's gasp of indignation and the hurt look on Sammy's face.

"I'm going to go and make sure everything is ready for the camping night. The project is complete, you can head back to your world, and life can get back to normal around here. I'll see you later."

I hurried out of the house, my legs eating up the distance to the barn fast. I had to get away. My eyes burned and my stomach churned.

I cursed the day I ever agreed to this.

CHAPTER TWENTY-ONE

SAMMY

L uke slammed out of the house as if being pursued by the hounds of hell. His dismissive words and cold tone echoed in my head.

"I'm not sold. Get back to normal."

Rachel looked at me, stricken. "He didn't mean it, Sammy. He was upset."

"He knew I had to leave to create the program. It only makes sense to catch a free flight with my family. I'll be back soon." I rubbed my neck, trying to ease the sudden tension in my muscles. "Why is he so upset?"

She smiled sadly. "Because he cares about you. More than he can admit." She regarded me. "And I think you care about him as well."

"I like your brother a lot," I admitted. "But he made the rules, and I agreed to them."

"How much?"

"Pardon me?"

She leaned closer, her expression serious. "How much do you like him?"

I opened my mouth to tell her I felt the same as Luke. This was temporary. We'd set the boundaries, and I was happy with them. But I couldn't. The words died in my throat. I stared at her as realization hit me.

I loved him.

I had fallen head over heels with my cowboy, and the thought of leaving him, even for a little while, twisted my heart into a ball of misery. When my dad had pointed out it made sense to fly home with them, a small part of me had protested even as I agreed with him. The few extra days would give me that buffer I needed to make sure our timelines were adhered to. Still, I felt an ache I couldn't explain until this moment.

I didn't want to leave Luke, even for a couple of weeks.

"I..." I shook my head and tried again. "Um, I..."

"You love him."

Tears filled my eyes. "Yeah, I think I do."

"Tell him."

"He doesn't want this, Rachel. He's made it very clear."

"He doesn't want to be hurt again. Loving him won't hurt him. Let me ask you a question, okay?"

I wiped my eyes. "Sure."

"Could you do what you do from here?"

"Yes."

"If he told you he wanted you to stay here—with him. What would your answer be?"

I thought about it before I spoke, even though I already knew the answer.

For the first time in my life, I saw myself living somewhere other than Port Albany. That elusive something I had sought all my adult life was here. It was Luke. This place.

I wanted to stay on the ranch. I loved it here. The rhythm of life here was different from what I knew, but it suited me. Luke suited me. I liked how he challenged me. Teased me. How it felt to make love with him. His strength and protectiveness. Even his over-the-top worrying at times. He'd stood over me, silent and intense, as Aiden pulled out the stitches in my hand, worried that it would hurt me. I felt his anxiety, the way he rested his hand on my shoulder, only relaxing once Aiden was finished.

I also saw how he hid his emotions, showing only calm detachment to his staff, running the ranch with efficiency. He stayed strong for Rachel, for everyone. What had happened with his fiancée and Marie had hurt him deeply, and he refused to open himself up to that emotion again.

But I still felt the same way. I loved him. And I wanted him to love me back. I wanted to build a life with him.

"I would stay."

"Then tell him. What have you got to lose?"

"My heart."

She stood. "I think you already lost it to my idiot of a brother. He's buried his emotions deep so he wouldn't be hurt again. And by doing so, he is hurting himself even more. I see how he looks at you. The way you make him laugh. He's…lighter, for lack of a better word. Happier. And I think he'd make you happy. He'd love you the way Tyler loves me. The way my dad and mom loved each other." She smiled and lifted her shoulders. "And I'm selfish. I'd love to have you as a sister. Have you around here all the time."

She sighed and shook her head. "Whatever happens, I'm grateful for everything you've done. Your vision and your friendship. I hope we can stay in touch once this is over. As long as it wouldn't be too painful for you."

I reached over and squeezed her hand. "For sure."

She took the files I'd made and left, closing the door behind her.

I sat at the table, thinking of all the evenings we'd spent gathered around it. I had loved every moment of it. I had loved every moment of being here in this house. Of being on this ranch with Luke.

I stared at the floor. The past while had been nothing short of amazing. Having some of my family here. Watching the bunkhouses come together. Planning and working with Rachel. Spending time with my mom, shopping and sketching, her knowledge and eye for detail such a help on this project. The shared meals, the laughter.

And Luke.

He was different. The serious, stern cowboy I had met disappeared. He was constantly smiling, his laughter ringing out. He chose to spend time with my family, working alongside them, seemingly as invested in this venture as Rachel or I were.

Until today.

I hadn't expected his abrupt shift in demeanor. His dismissal of the project. I wasn't sure what to do next.

All I knew right then was my heart was aching. I had to talk to him.

I headed to the stable, glad when I saw Maverick still there. Luke came around the corner, carrying his saddle. He stopped when he saw me, then brushed past me.

"What do you need, Samantha?"

"Samantha?" I repeated. "How formal you're being."

He shrugged as he lifted the saddle over Maverick. "Just being polite. It's a professional relationship after all."

I crossed my arms. "It's more than that, and you know it."

He straightened from adjusting the saddle. He met my eyes, his frosty and aloof. It reminded me of the first time I met him. Distant, uncaring.

"I realize that. Fuck buddies and all. It was fun. Thanks for that," he said, his tone flat.

"You bastard," I hissed, balling my hands into fists. "Don't you dare dismiss what we've shared that way."

"And what have we shared exactly?"

"We've shared our souls."

He barked a laugh. "Well, your soul is leaving tomorrow."

"And I'll be back. You knew I had to go back home and create the program. It has to be done in the studio with the right equipment."

"And you knew this was only temporary."

"Why can't you admit it, Luke?"

"Admit what?"

"That you care about me?"

"Of course I do. The same way I care about my ranch hands or Callie."

"Liar."

He narrowed his eyes. "Don't create a scene, Sammy. I should have known not to start this."

"But you did."

"We did. And I won't lie. I enjoyed it. Every bit of it. But it's over. You're leaving, and it's time to get back to reality."

"Ask me to stay."

He froze. "What?"

"Ask me to stay. Tell me to come back and stay."

"No."

"Why? Afraid of what I'll tell you? Afraid you'll have to admit you have feelings for me?"

"The only feeling I have is a healthy dose of male lust. And you eased that."

He turned and finished adjusting the straps on Maverick. He began to walk past me, then turned.

"I am sorry I was dismissive of your work. Thank you for all you did. I won't forget your efforts."

"But you'll forget *me*."

"That's the way it is."

"It doesn't have to be."

He walked away, whistling softly for Maverick.

"Luke," I said loudly.

He stopped in the doorway, not speaking.

I drew in a deep breath. "I love you."

His shoulders jerked as if he suddenly felt pain.

And he kept walking, never looking back.

I faltered as I folded some clothes to put in the case, my mind going a hundred miles an hour. I thought of all the ads and marketing around love. How it showed happy, adoring couples. Smiling, carefree, their futures set.

Obviously, none of them had ever fallen for a hardheaded, stubborn cowboy who didn't believe in love. I kept seeing him walk away from me, not even acknowledging my words. As if I hadn't even spoken.

I blinked away the sudden moisture in my eyes and wiped it away in anger. I was being ridiculous. Luke didn't love me back. Or he refused to admit that he did. His silence and walking away said it all. It was over. We were over.

We'd never really had a chance.

Heavy footsteps heading down the hall made me turn my head, hopeful. But it wasn't Luke coming to talk who appeared in my doorway. My dad was there, looking worried, a frown marring his face.

"Hey, Dad. What's up?" I asked, forcing a smile on my face.

He sat down on the bed, the springs creaking a little under his large form.

"I came to ask you the same thing. You were supposed to come tell Mom and me how it went with your presentation to Luke and Rachel."

"Oh, I forgot. I wanted to pack up."

He regarded me in silence. "I saw Rachel. She looked like someone had kicked her cat. Luke is in a bear of a mood, and his horse is taking the brunt of it. They were galloping away at a breakneck speed toward the campsite. All I did was ask him how everything was. His response was rather, ah, surly."

"What did he say?"

"That the project was almost done, and he was glad. He needed his ranch back."

"He basically said the same thing to me."

"What happened, Mouse?"

I didn't say anything. I couldn't with the lump in my throat.

"Did he hurt you?"

I shook my head. "No." I sighed. "He didn't mean to."

"But you have feelings for him."

I hung my head. "I tried not to."

Dad lifted my chin, meeting my eyes. "You can't help who you love, Mouse. I hate that he hurt you. I didn't think he was that sort of man to play with someone's emotions."

I shook my head. "He didn't." I defended him. "We agreed on the rules." I sniffed. "I just broke them."

Dad smiled, shaking his head. He cupped my face. "There are no rules with love. That's a hard lesson to learn, my girl." He pressed a kiss to my forehead. "I'm glad you're coming home with us tomorrow. Maybe some time away will help him see what he's giving up."

I gripped his wrists. "Don't be mad at him, Daddy. He's been hurt. I think he's scared."

He smiled. "You haven't called me daddy in a long time, Mouse. I missed that. I won't punch him or challenge him to a gunfight at noon—as much as I would like to, at least the punch. You're an adult, and you have to live your life the way you want it." He tightened his grip on my face. "I want you to have what your mother and I have. That bond."

"I know."

"I watched him around you. I saw something. I saw how you looked at him. In fact, I thought you'd be telling me that I had a little bird leaving the nest and living a long way away from me. And as much as I would have hated that, I hate this more."

"I'll be fine."

"Do you want to cancel tonight? We could leave soon and stop somewhere overnight."

"No. Put this aside and enjoy tonight, Dad. Luke and his men have worked hard on it. People are looking forward to it."

"I don't care about Luke. I care about you."

"Then do it for me. I want to see this through."

He regarded me for a moment, then pulled me into his arms. "You are an amazing, brave woman, Mouse. Just like your mom."

I clung to him, drawing strength from his embrace. I felt six years old again, seeking his comfort. He'd always made me feel safe, no matter what. And that hadn't changed. He let me snuggle close for a few moments, then I drew back and wiped my eyes.

"I have to finish packing."

"Okay, I'll leave you to it."

"Love you, Daddy."

He brushed another kiss to my head. "Love you more, Mouse."

I dreaded seeing Luke. I chose to ride up to the campsite in one of the ATVs. I was grateful it wasn't in the same spot Luke had taken me before. This area was bigger, more open, and the water clear. Perfect for walking or even having a swim on the hot days, the current slow and easy, the middle deep enough to enjoy. Tents were set up, there were foldable seats, a huge campfire in the middle, and a couple of picnic tables they had brought up. Rachel, Jane, and Callie were busy with the food, the crew driving people up from the ranch, and Luke was nowhere to be seen. I went over to Rachel, lifting my eyebrow in a silent question.

"He's getting kindling for later," she explained. "They brought up some logs to split for firewood."

"Ah."

"Did you..." She let the words trail off as I gave her a rueful look.

"What an idiot," she muttered.

"Not here and not tonight," I replied. "This is to give everyone the chance to see how this will work when you have paying guests. Figure out what you need to change or adjust."

"Okay."

"I'm going to step back, and you and Luke run it. I'll make notes we can discuss in the morning before I leave."

"You will come back, right? You won't send someone else?"

"I'll come back." I rolled my shoulders as a sensation of awareness shot through me. "But it might be easier on Luke if I stayed elsewhere."

"You can stay at the ranch," Luke growled behind me. "We're adults."

I didn't turn to face him. "So, as I said, I will observe tonight, and we'll touch base tomorrow before I go."

Rachel nodded, shooting daggers at Luke behind me. I laid my hand on her arm and shook my head slightly. She sighed in resignation. "Okay."

I turned, excusing myself, and skirted around Luke. I could feel the anger rolling off him, but I ignored him, heading toward my dad and Aiden. I knew Luke wouldn't follow.

Aiden clapped his hands. "This is incredible. What's on the agenda?"

I smiled and shook my head, forcing my tone to be upbeat. "Rachel is in charge. I'm observing."

"Gotcha. Grading it, I guess?"

"Yep. I'll be over there, enjoying watching the antics." I leaned up and kissed him on the cheek. "Behave. At least somewhat."

He grinned. "As if I'd do anything else."

Laughing, I sat on the corner of the picnic table. Rachel was quick to organize some games. Aiden, Hunter, Ronan, and Liam all headed into the water for some volleyball, splashing and talking trash. Dad and some of the crew sat around the fire that was already going, a beer in his hand as he chatted with Jeff and Tyler. Rachel was perfect, making sure people were happy and, at the same time, performing tasks that needed to be done without drawing attention to it. She was going to ace this.

I tried not to watch Luke, but my gaze was drawn to him. He chopped wood, his muscles bunching and releasing as the pile grew. He had stripped off his plaid shirt, staying in just the muscle shirt that hugged his torso. I was grateful for my sunglasses and hat. I kept staring, unable to tear my eyes away, aimlessly scribbling in my book, pretending to observe everyone but him. My heart ached, being this close to him yet feeling a thousand miles away. Knowing I would never feel his mouth on mine again. Feel him moving inside me. Hear his voice murmuring my name.

To my horror, I felt tears fill my eyes. My mom slid beside me on the table.

"How are things going?"

"Great," I managed to say. "Rachel is a natural."

Aiden finished the game, leaving the rest of them to swim and cavort. He dried off, watching Luke, then went over, saying something and taking the ax. Luke shook his head, his voice drifting my way. "That's big, Aiden. It'll take a few hits."

Aiden looked at him with a wry grin, lifting the ax and swinging it. The large piece split in two. Aiden handed him back the ax. "That's how we old-timers do it."

Luke threw his head back in laughter, the sound making my lips curl in shared amusement. He clapped Aiden's shoulder. "Lucky strike."

"Oh yeah, youngster?" He rolled his shoulders. "Let's go, then."

The younger guys came out of the water, all eager to get in on the action. My dad stood and joined them. "Let's show them how it's done."

"Four against two?" Luke questioned. "Hardly fair."

My dad took the ax. "I agree. We'll give you an extra swing to make up for it."

"Oh lord," Mom muttered. "Here we go."

I was pleased to see them treating Luke as normal. I was sure my dad had kept what he knew to himself, and I blessed him for his kind nature.

"I got twenty bucks that says the old men beat the boys!" Mom called.

"I'll put twenty on the dads!" I yelled. It felt good to do something normal. Something fun.

Five minutes later, there was a pile of money on the table.

Jeff stood with his stopwatch. "Boys first. Each group has ten minutes."

Rachel sat beside me. "This wasn't on the agenda."

I nudged her. "But what fun."

"The boys" did well, the ax flying, changing hands quickly, the wood pile huge.

Then my dad picked up the ax, rolling his shoulders. "Let's show them how it's done, Aiden."

Ten minutes later, the dads had won, their pile slightly bigger than the boys. There was a lot of trash-talking, shoulder-slapping, and good-natured ribbing, but everyone was laughing. All the men, including Luke, headed back into the water to cool off. I met Rachel's eyes, fanning myself. "Maybe that should go in the plans."

"You took some pictures," she observed.

"Strictly business."

She slid off the table. "I might need copies of a few of them."

I smirked and stood. Mom shaded her eyes. "Where are you off to?"

Now that the moment of levity had passed, I needed to stay busy. "Just going to take a few pictures of the area."

"Okay."

I wandered upstream, taking some photos, then sat under a shady tree. I could hear the sounds of the campsite, but they were muted. I looked around with a lump in my throat. It was beautiful here, and I was going to miss it. Not only had I fallen in love with Luke, but this land. My goodbyes would be doubly painful when I left for good. My family might return for their adventure, but I wouldn't be able to come back. It would simply hurt too much.

I wasn't even sure how I was going to do it this time.

Hours later, the night sky twinkled, illuminated with stars. The fire burned high and bright. Callie, Jeff, and Luke had made an amazing campfire meal that was devoured by everyone. Even the boys were full. I forced myself to eat, to talk, and to smile. I wasn't going to ruin this for Rachel or my family. Luke was quieter than he had been lately, but he put forth an effort, doing his fancy knife flips and talking as he cooked the steaks over an open flame. Tim pulled out his guitar and sang a couple of country songs, getting the guys to join him. Tears welled in my eyes as my dad pulled my mom to her feet and danced with her under the starlight. Then when they sat down, my mom handed my dad the guitar.

"Please," she asked.

Dad strummed, clearing his throat, then began to sing. I had always loved it when he would sing for us. I smiled as he launched into a couple of his old hits, and Luke shook his head.

"I knew I recognized your name. You were with Back Roads."

Dad grinned. "A long time ago." Then he began to play again, and Callie and Jeff got up to dance, and soon others did, laughing and singing along. Dad beamed, watching everyone sing with him. He took requests and entertained for almost an hour before setting aside the guitar.

Rachel clapped the loudest.

"You are hired. You chop wood, beat the young guys, and play your music."

He winked at her. "Done."

Marshmallows and all the makings for s'mores were brought out, and drippy chocolate, gooey marshmallow, and sticky fingers followed.

Slowly, the group dispersed, and I slid into my bedroll in the tent with Rachel, Callie, Jane, and my mom. All the cowboys were around the fire, including Ronan, Liam, and Hunter, the other, larger tent housing the rest of my family. I lay under the covers, listening to the sounds around me. Some rumbling snores, the crackling of the fire, the stirring of the breeze in the trees. I wasn't able to relax enough to go to sleep, and finally, I rolled out of the bedding, shoved my feet back into my sneakers, and slipped out of the tent.

I skirted the fire area, smiling at the snores from the men, and headed to the water. I knew Luke was on the farthest side, and I stayed away from it. I slipped off my shoes, wading into the welcome cool, walking in the shallows away from the campsite. Around the corner was an outcropping of rocks I had seen earlier, and I sat on a flat boulder, keeping my feet in the refreshing stream. I looked up at the sky, still in awe over the brightness of the stars and vastness of the vista. I would never grow tired of such wonder.

A splash to my left startled me, and I looked over to see Luke standing in the moonlight, his hands on his hips as he stared at me.

I shut my eyes and shook my head. "Go away, Luke. I'm not doing anything wrong."

He came closer. "You shouldn't be out here alone, Lady."

My heart clenched at the word *Lady*, but I refused to react. "Whatever."

"There could be animals. You could slip and fall."

"I'm thirty feet from the campsite. If I hear an animal come for me, I'll run. Pretty sure my screaming will scare them away and alert people I need help. Can you please just leave me alone?"

He moved even closer. "Why aren't you asleep?"

"Why aren't you?" I challenged, standing. He wasn't going to leave, so I would.

"You know why," he growled, stepping in front of me.

"Luke," I whispered, fighting back the tears. "Just go. Please."

"I wanted to say something."

I lifted my head, meeting his gaze. In the moonlight, his eyes were glittering and blue in his tanned face. Intense.

"Then say it and go."

"I'm sorry for my anger earlier. What you've done for Rachel and me is amazing. I know it'll be great, and I'll do everything I can to help make sure it is." He swallowed. "I didn't want you to think I wouldn't support her."

"Good. She needs your support."

I went to brush past him, and he grabbed my arms, stopping me. Our eyes locked, his filled with turmoil, mine with tears. "Don't cry over me," he pleaded. "I'm not worth it."

"That's where we disagree. I think you're worth every tear. The fact that you can't see that hurts more than your rejection."

He shut his eyes, his hands tightening on my arms. "What you said—that you loved me. I wanted to thank you for that."

"But you don't love me back."

He opened his eyes, his torment and struggle in them evident. "I-I can't," he admitted.

"You could if you tried," I whispered.

He shook his head, silence falling between us. I felt the same intense connection that flowed between us build, creating an invisible cage around us. His gaze fell to my lips, and I knew if I made one small move, he would yank me close and kiss me. Devour my mouth with the hunger I felt between us all the time. He'd take me down on the hard ground and fuck me one last time, then walk away.

"I can't," he whispered. "I can't..." He lowered his head. I felt his warm breath on my skin. I could already taste him.

Then I stepped back, breaking the spell.

"Neither can I," I said and walked away.

CHAPTER TWENTY-TWO

LUKE

I left the campsite early, heading back to the ranch. I hadn't slept all night, my thoughts and emotions jumping and banging around in my head. I couldn't face Sammy or her family this morning.

I knew Sammy was leaving. I knew she had to go and create the program. Yet somehow hearing her say she was going had set off a bomb in my chest. Then her whispered confession had rocked me to the core.

She loved me.

And as I had realized in some moment of complete and utter soul-crushing clarity, I loved her too.

But I had nothing to offer her. Not what she was used to. Her family was wealthy—her connections and world an entire universe away from the starkness of mine. I worked long, endless hours, and sometimes even that wasn't enough. The ranch would always require my focus. My money. My time. I couldn't be the husband she needed. I couldn't give her children of her own.

Expensive trips away. I had no private jet to whisk her off anywhere. There was little I could offer her. And she deserved the world.

My mood grew darker as I heard the campers come back and the sounds of the group preparing to leave. I had made a point of saying thank you to each of them last night. Offering my sincere appreciation for their time, talent, and hard work. Like the coward I was, I watched from the darkness of the stables as Sammy's family said goodbye to everyone, shaking hands, hugging my crew. Rachel had already been inside the RV, no doubt expressing her thanks, crying, and making sure Sammy would be coming back.

I shut my eyes as the pain lanced through me. I didn't know what I would do when she was gone. When she came back. How I would handle it. The thought of breathing without her seemed impossible. But I had to let her go before she decided to walk away when she grasped the reality of the situation and what a life with me would be like.

"Aren't you going to say goodbye?" Rachel asked, coming up behind me.

"I said my thanks and goodbyes last night."

"And Sammy?"

"She'll be back."

Rachel sighed, the sound impatient and frustrated. The RV slowly started to move, and an incredibly painful ache began in my chest. It took everything in me to keep my feet planted on the wooden floor.

"Sammy isn't Anne. Or Marie."

At the mention of my ex-fiancée and the woman from hell, I shuddered. "I know."

"She's amazing."

"I'm not arguing."

"But you're letting her go."

I turned and looked at my sister. "What can I offer her, Rachel? No kids, a husband tied to a ranch that requires all his attention, a life of uncertainty and hard work? Living in the middle of nowhere, after what she is used to?" I barked out a laugh. "I hardly think so. You've met her family, seen the pictures. She's accustomed to so much more than this." I swung my arm, indicating the stable.

"Maybe that matters more to you than to her." She narrowed her eyes. "This life of uncertainty and hard work you talk about also has a lot of amazing things in it. Family, friends, satisfaction of a job well done. The beauty of living here. Love. Our parents thrived here. We love it. Why can't you allow that Sammy might too?"

"I can't ask that of her. I couldn't stand seeing the regret later."

"Listen to yourself," Rachel snapped. "Who gave you the right to decide what Sammy wants and doesn't want? Did you ask her?"

I furrowed my brow. "No."

"I did. I asked her if you wanted her here, if she would stay."

I swallowed. "What did she say?"

"She said yes. There was no hesitation. She said she could work from anywhere." Rachel stepped closer, gripping my arm. "She loves you, Luke. And if you would stop all this nonsense, I think you would realize you love her too."

I met her eyes, and they widened.

"You do. You love her."

"It doesn't matter."

"Yes, it does."

"But—"

She cut me off. "Stop throwing up roadblocks. Talk to Sammy. Tell her you love her. Work with her, not against her. Don't throw away a chance to be happy." Tears filled her eyes. "I almost lost Tyler. I know that worry, Luke. That fear. Don't let it stop you. Grab it, grab her."

Hunter's words suddenly hit me.

"To me, our relationship was a huge, insurmountable obstacle."

"And to Ava?" I had asked.

"A challenge we could overcome together," he had replied.

I looked out, the dust kicked up from the RV already settling as if it hadn't been disturbed at all.

"She's gone," I replied.

Rachel snorted. "The RV left ten minutes ago and is driving down a dirt road, slowly. Maverick could catch up fast."

"He's not—" I stopped speaking when I saw he was saddled and ready to go.

"Go after her, Luke. Don't let her think this time *she* wasn't enough."

I grabbed Rachel and hugged her. Then I strode to Maverick and vaulted into the saddle. I was about to do something reckless, stupid, and that could possibly blow up in my face.

Sammy was worth the effort.

I guided Maverick to the door and dug in my heels. "*Yah*," I encouraged him.

And we were off.

SAMMY

I scanned the yard of the ranch over and over as we said good-byes to everyone. Surely Luke wouldn't let us leave without making an appearance. He'd been gone when we'd risen this morning, and Rachel said he was taking care of something at the ranch. I hadn't seen him since we got back. I had a terrible feeling I wouldn't.

I knew I was coming back in a couple of weeks, but still—everyone else stopped by to say goodbye to my family and to tell me they were looking forward to my return. Rachel had spoken to everyone in turn, her thanks effusive, her gratefulness abundant. When she hugged me, she whispered, "I'm sorry."

"He's not coming?" I whispered back, fighting down the tears.

"I don't think he can."

I stepped back with a nod, wiping my eyes. "I'll see you in a couple of weeks. I'll be sending you things to approve and look at as well."

She sniffled and wiped under her eyes. "Okay. And we can chat, right?"

"Absolutely."

I couldn't help one last look before I climbed into the RV. My dad looked upset, my mom patting my knee as I sat beside her. Even Aiden was quiet, Ronan looking over his shoulder from the passenger seat.

"Okay there, Sammy?"

"Yep. Let's go. We have a plane to catch."

The RV was silent as we pulled out of the driveway. I looked around at the somber faces and forced a smile to my face. "It's all good, guys. You'll be back. You'll get the royal treatment when you return as a guest."

They all shook their heads, and I was quick to shake mine back at them. "I'm fine. Honest. This place is awesome, and I want you to come back here and support Rachel and Luke."

"Luke—" Liam began.

"He did nothing wrong," I interrupted him. "Nothing. And you will stop looking at me like that. All of you. Luke is a wonderful man, and I adore Rachel. End of story."

They all fumbled with their phones, grumbling. I met Mom's gaze, and she leaned over, cupping my cheek. "He has no idea what he has lost," she whispered.

I focused my gaze outside the window, refusing to cry. For a few moments, I watched the landscape go by, the RV slowly heading down the dirt road. We would pick up speed once we got to the main road and off the dirt, but this road needed careful navigation.

Up front, I heard Aiden mutter. "What the hell?"

Ronan turned in his seat, looking at the side mirror. "Oh boy. You better pull over, Dad."

"No," Aiden said. "He can damn well work for it."

I heard a series of thumps on the RV, but Aiden kept driving. I looked at my mom. "Did we hit something?"

She shook her head, a smile ghosting her lips. "I don't think so."

"What's wrong?" I asked, directing my question to Aiden.

"We've got company."

I glanced ahead, wondering if some cows had gotten loose on the road, but Aiden smirked. "Coming up on the side." He shook his head. "He better not dent this thing."

I turned and looked. Beside us, moving fast, was a horse and rider.

I recognized both.

It was Maverick with Luke bent low over his mane, reaching over and hitting the RV with his fist to get it to stop.

What was going on?

"Stop!" I cried out.

With a muttered curse, Aiden slowed down and pulled over.

My dad stood, his hand on my shoulder, stopping me from getting up. "I'll handle this."

He stepped outside, shutting the door behind him. He met Luke in the middle of the road, his arms crossed. He looked calm and in control. Luke looked anything but. He was talking, pacing, gesturing with his arms. Dad eyed him impassively, asking him something. Luke nodded, pointing to the RV. Dad shrugged, holding out his arm, stopping Luke from coming over.

Frustrated, Luke knocked off his hat and bent to pick it up. Our eyes met through the glass window and locked. He laid his hand on his heart and mouthed a word.

"Please."

I stood, my mom squeezing my hand as I went past her. I opened the door, hearing my dad.

"You've hurt her enough, Luke."

"I don't want to hurt her anymore. I have to talk to her. Please, Van. I have to see her. *Please.*"

I heard the agony in his voice.

"I've got this, Dad."

Luke's gaze met mine. His eyes were tormented and wild.

Dad sighed and walked past me into the RV. "I'll give you some privacy."

I tried not to laugh. Privacy. Luke and me on an open road with my family's ears stuck to the windows to hear every word.

Luke paced then came closer. "You can't go, Sammy. Not like this."

I sighed. "What do you want, Luke? Forgiveness? You can have it. I'm as much to blame as you are. You made the rules, and I broke them."

"Fuck the rules!" he yelled suddenly. "They were stupid and were bound to break anyway."

"What do you mean?"

He closed the distance between us, gripping my arms. "How could I resist you, Sammy? You snuck into my heart and settled there right away. Your fire, your sass. Your beautiful sunshine smile that lit up my life. Everything about you held me in wonder. You made the ranch feel like home again simply by being there with me. I love your mind and the way you make everything around you beautiful. You brighten every part of my life." He shook his head. "I even love how you worry about making my cows happier with your damn yellow paint." He moved his hands to my face, cupping it. "Since you've been here, nothing has been as hard to handle. Knowing I'd get to see you made everything right. My responsibilities seemed easier because you were there." He huffed a laugh. "You made me forget it wasn't forever."

"What are you saying?" I whispered, my throat tight.

"I was a complete jackass. Your words made reality hit, and the thought of you being gone threw me. I wasn't prepared for how it made me feel."

"How?"

His eyes blazed down into mine. "Empty. Lonely. You fill me up, Lady. That beautiful, sunshine smile. Your laughter, how you tease me." He lifted his eyebrows. "How you put me in my place. Even when I piss you off and you flip me. I told myself we were just for now, but my heart knew better even when I refused to listen. From the first, I adored every single thing about you. Every. Single. Thing. Then adoration became more."

"More?" I asked, hardly believing what I was hearing.

"I love you," he said simply. "I love you."

"But?" I asked.

"But I'm worried I can't have you."

"Why?" I asked, my heart racing. "Luke, why?"

His gaze was tormented. "I can't give you children. I can't give you what you have now. I can't compete with BAM and the Gavin Group. I have no planes or RVs. No rich friends to drop by and help me out. All I have is a ranch that needs my attention. A bank account that is in the red half the time. I have *nothing* to offer you."

"Instead of telling me what you can't give me, why don't you think about what you *can* give me?"

He frowned. "What?"

I stepped closer. "Your heart. Your love. Your strength and protectiveness. That's what I need, Luke. You."

He dropped his hands in resignation. "How can that be enough? How can *I* be enough?"

"Because you are." I sighed. "I've always been restless, looking for something. With you, my soul feels at peace." I touched his cheek. "I think maybe I was looking for you. For this place."

"Sammy," he breathed. "You have that wrong. I've been waiting for you. You make me whole."

We stared at each other. "But children—" he started, and I cut him off.

"You know how I feel about adoption. Think of the difference we could make for a child who needs love. And I'm not BAM. I'm not my family. They are wealthy. I am not. I want to keep working. Our bank accounts can help each other. Because that's what partners do. Help each other."

His breathing picked up, his chest moving fast. "You want to be my partner?" He swallowed. "Still?"

"I want to be your everything."

A beat of silence stretched between us, and it felt as if my world hung in the balance. Then he cupped my cheek again, stroking the skin with his thumb. "Lady, you already are."

Happiness welled in my chest. "Ask me, Luke. Ask me to come back and stay. Believe in this. In us."

"Come back to me, Sammy. Come back and stay with me. Let me love you. I don't want to be alone anymore."

Tears rolled down my face. "Yes."

Then I was in his arms, his mouth on mine. He held me tight, his kiss hungry and passionate. It was a kiss of hello and celebration. Of love and a future. It was us.

And it was over far too quickly.

He set me on my feet. "I'm an idiot, Sammy."

"My idiot." I smiled up at him.

"I need your strength. Your love. I need you."

"You have me, Luke."

He yanked me into his arms again.

My family piled outside the RV, slapping Luke's shoulder, lifting me in hugs.

Aiden grinned. "Good groveling, Luke."

I rolled my eyes. "I suppose you were all listening."

No one denied it; they only smirked.

"I tried to stop them," Mom said.

"That's like trying to stop a freight train," Luke teased, wrapping his arm around my waist.

Everyone grinned, not at all put off by his observation.

When my dad approached Luke, he stiffened.

"You gonna do right by my girl?"

"Yes, sir. I want to marry her. I'll do everything in my power to make her happy. I know I don't have much—"

I blinked at the word marry. The Cowboy was moving fast.

Dad interrupted him. "Money and planes don't make a life. Love and family do. If you love her, that's all I ask."

"With everything in me."

"Then we're good."

Aiden cleared his throat. "I hate to break up this little impromptu lovefest, but we have to go."

I turned to Luke, already crying. He pulled me into his arms.

"I don't want to go."

"I don't want you to go either. But you have to," he murmured. "Go and work your magic, Lady. I'll be right here waiting for you. When you come back, we'll plan our future. Together."

Together. I loved the sound of that word.

"I'll call you every day."

"You better," he said. "I want your voice to be the first thing I hear when I wake up and the last thing before I go to bed." He dropped his voice. "That will hold me until I can feel you beside me again."

He kissed me. "I love you."

I kissed him again. "I love you more, Cowboy."

Two weeks had never passed so quickly or dragged on so slowly. I worked on the feature with my team, editing, layering. We went through hundreds of photos, hours of film, condensing it all into an entertaining, captivating episode. I did the voice-overs, bringing the story of the ranch to life.

Finally, all that was left was to add the footage I would capture and add of the first guests. The website was ready to go. The brochures printed for agents. I had been teasing on Instagram, TikTok, and Facebook already. The waiting list for more information grew daily.

And every day, I spoke to Rachel. We had endless meetings. She was gearing up, excited and happy. She'd hired some locals, and the staff on the ranch was getting ready. Often we Zoomed, and when the sounds of heavy footsteps approaching would happen and Luke's face would appear behind her, my smile couldn't be contained.

He'd lean close, smiling at me. "Lady," he'd greet me. I loved how his voice curled around the word. The way his eyes softened when he spoke it.

Then he'd list the number of days until I got back. "Six more days."

"Hi, Cowboy," I would reply. "Six days, five hours, and twenty minutes."

"Not letting you go again."

Rachel would push at him, pretending to be mad. "Business meeting, Luke. Keep the flirting for after hours."

"I'll call tonight when I'm in bed."

"Meet you there," I'd whisper breathlessly.

Rachel always groaned. "Right here, you two. Break it up."

But we'd all be smiling.

I loved our nightly calls. We talked for hours. About the ranch, his plans, my plans. Something cute Oreo was doing. Luke assured me they were both waiting anxiously for me to return. Often, talk turned into something else, and I'd fall asleep with a smile on my face and the echoes of Luke's low groans repeating in my head.

When the day finally came for me to fly back, I found out how Luke greeted someone he loved at the airport.

He was leaning up against the same pillar where I'd first seen him. Tall, serious, with his cowboy hat perched on his head, he looked sexier than someone had the right to in his tight jeans and T-shirt. He held a small bouquet of flowers, and his foot tapped an impatient staccato on the floor. He ignored the admiring looks he was getting, instead staring at the blossoms he held. Then he looked up and saw me walking toward him. The heat of his blue gaze touched me, scorching me everywhere he looked. I stopped in front of him, my heart racing.

"Cowboy."

He handed me the flowers. "Lady."

Then he cradled my face in his big hands, bending low and kissing me. Sweet. Passionate. Hungry. He curled one arm around my waist, dragging me close. I wound mine around him and held tight.

He buried his face in my neck.

"My beautiful Lady. I've missed you. Welcome home."

And with him, I was.

————————

Tyler and Rachel were there when we got to the ranch. Luke hadn't let go of my hand for more than a minute the entire drive. He sat beside me at dinner, his arm slung over the back of my chair. After, I played the almost-complete show for them, watching their reactions as I cuddled Oreo.

At the end, Rachel was crying, and Luke stared at me. "You did that?" he asked in awe. "All of that?"

"It's what I do."

"You do it perfectly."

Tyler shook his head. "This place is going to explode."

"I agree," I said. "But we keep the numbers small to start, grow with it. By the end of the first month, you can add. By the end of the season, you'll be fully booked for next year."

"We'll be fully booked," Luke corrected. "You're part of this now. Part of us."

I smiled at him, cupping his face. We talked for a while, then Rachel and Tyler left. Luke went to return Oreo to his momma, and I padded down the hall, lying on his bed.

Luke came in, standing in the doorway, leaning his shoulder against the jamb. "I can't tell you how good you look in our bed, Lady."

Our bed. I loved how those words sounded.

"I thought you might like a bath," he said, his eyes never leaving mine.

"As long as you join me."

He leaned over the bed, bending and kissing me. "Try to keep me away."

The water was warm. Luke's embrace was warmer. We were quiet for a bit, simply enjoying the peace and being together. Then he spoke.

"How do you see the future, Sammy?"

We'd touched on the subject but not discussed it fully yet.

I turned, pulling my legs up and facing him. He leaned over, tugging me close. "Talk to me."

"I'm freelance and do what I want. I want to keep doing these kinds of shows—helping small businesses, families. The network wants them too. But I want to spend more time here on the ranch being part of 'Home on the Range.'"

He smiled, tucking a strand of hair behind my ear. "I love that name you came up with for the brochure and website. And I love the thought of you here. But I don't want you to give up what you love."

"I'm not. I'm adding to it." I drew in a deep breath. "I was serious about adoption, Luke. We could give a child—or children—a good life here."

"I'd like that. But I want you to myself for a while."

I kissed him. "I'd like that too."

"We have to move your things here."

"I don't have a lot. Mila will be in the house, so she can have the furniture. I have some personal things. Would you come back to Port Albany with me while I get them? You could meet more of my family."

"Yes," he said simply. "When you're ready, we'll go."

"After the show airs and we deal with all the wonderful chaos that will happen."

He smiled, tilting his head. "I love the chaos you brought with you. You turned my world upside down, yet somehow righted it at the same time. You stole my heart, Sammy. It's yours forever."

He shocked me as he held up a pretty ring. "I'm yours forever, if you'll have me."

He looked nervous. Earnest. Hopeful. Worried.

Tears filled my eyes. "Yes."

He slipped the sapphire and diamond ring on my finger, bending and kissing it. "I'll get you something bigger one day."

"I don't need anything bigger. I only need you."

He dragged me into his arms, kissing me. "You have me."

I pulled his mouth back to mine, losing myself in his kiss. It started sweet and warm, and soon turned into blistering heat. He caressed me, his fingers smoothing over my skin, cupping my breasts and moving my legs so I was on his lap. Water splashed over the edge of the tub as we discovered each other again. He groaned as I flicked his nipples, nibbled his neck, and stroked his cock. I shivered as he slid his fingers over my clit, light and teasing. I gasped as he slipped them inside, pressing his thumb on my clit.

"It's been too long, Lady. Too long without you."

"Then take me, Luke," I pleaded.

He pulled me up, notching himself at my entrance. Our eyes locked as I slid down, inch by inch until we were flush. He groaned and cursed, filling me completely. We began to move, our bodies locked together, our motions fluid and fast.

He gripped my neck, his eyes intense and filled with emotion. "Mine, Sammy. You're all mine."

"Yes," I moaned. "Yours, Cowboy."

"And you're going to be my wife. *My wife.*"

His words did something to me, and my orgasm hit me. I cried out, feeling Luke stiffen and fall with me. He pulled me against him, my head resting on his shoulder as we came down from our high.

"We're going to have a great life together. I promise," he murmured.

"I know."

"I love you, Lady," he murmured. "I love you so much."

"I love you more."

He pressed a kiss to my head. "Thank God."

EPILOGUE

SAMMY

THREE YEARS LATER

I walked out to the porch, a steaming cup of coffee in my hand. It was early, the sun barely breaking over the horizon. The air held the predawn chilliness, and I sat down on the swing Luke had made for me, looking around the ranch. It was still and peaceful, but that would change soon. The animals would wake, chores would begin, and the guests would rise, looking forward to another day on the ranch.

Home on the Range hit the ground running and exploded. The soft opening had been a success. By the time the three days were over, Rachel had sold all the honey, cheese, and blankets she had produced and had a waiting list of people wanting more. I helped Rachel hire people from the local towns, and we never looked back. Every aspect of the business was successful.

From May to September, we were booked solid. When the show aired, the website crashed from the volume. The social media pages blew up. The waiting list was enormous. We changed and tweaked the packages and how we made bookings until we found the perfect ratio.

With the help of my family, we built two more cabins set back in the trees. More self-contained, which was big with families. A third, more luxurious cabin was constructed, and it was my family's home away from home but was rented out occasionally as needed. Luke was shocked at the number of honeymooners who wanted to spend their time on a ranch.

For ours, he had taken me to a small cabin in the mountains, and we had spent five days locked away from everything and everyone. Him, me, a bed, and a campfire. Naked most of the time. The outdoor tub had been an added bonus, and I loved it so much, Luke added a private one at the back of the ranch house for our first anniversary.

We had two large corporations that booked all the cabins at once every year for their retreat. Many other guests were repeats. Rachel ran the business like a well-oiled machine. Luke ran the ranch and was still the favorite for the overnight camping. His outdoor grilling and knife tricks were legendary, and his skills at wood-chopping epic. I still got a thrill watching him, although my views were private and shirtless and often ended up with us rolling around in the stable, doing things that shocked the horses.

As if he heard me thinking about him, Luke came out onto the porch, tugging on one of his plaid shirts over his tight muscle shirt. He was still hard as a rock, toned, tanned, sexy as hell with his stern demeanor. Except when he looked at me. His blue eyes softened, and a smile curled his lips—one only I ever saw.

He had been as good as his word to my dad. He loved me so completely, my life was full.

He walked over, bending low and kissing me, then stealing my coffee and draining it.

"You could have gotten your own, Cowboy."

He shook his head, leaning against the porch railing. "Yours tastes better. Your lips were on the mug."

I nudged him with my foot. "Cheesy."

He winked. "Only for you, Lady."

We were quiet for a moment, then he spoke, his voice tight. "Everything set for next week?"

"I'll only be gone three days."

"Three long days."

I chuckled. I still worked, although not as much as I had before. I loved being on the ranch, working with Rachel. I had started helping local businesses, building up the towns around us, which drew our guests there and helped the community thrive. It was a win-win, and the network loved the local aspect of it. I only picked two projects a year that took me away from the ranch and Luke.

He hated my being gone but supported me.

"Maybe we can do a trip to Port Albany when I get back."

"I'd love that," he agreed. Luke had fallen in love with Port Albany when I took him to meet the whole family. At first, he'd been overwhelmed, but he got used to them. He came with me to every family event. We'd been to many weddings, my cousins, Elise, Brandon, and Craig, all getting married in Port Albany. Mila's surprise nuptials. He'd come with me to BC to see Chloe get married. Thomas had eloped, not at all interested in a fancy wedding. Instead, we all donated to his favorite charity that helped whales and dolphins and celebrated with a dinner the next time he came to Port Albany. There'd been babies and retirements. Some surprise additions to the family. So many celebrations. Sometimes, Luke teased me, it was as if he saw more of them than Rachel.

But he loved it.

My loner cowboy was no longer alone.

He sighed. "I can do three days."

"I was thinking of taking a break," I said, watching him. "Trying my hand at something new."

"Oh?" He grinned. "Whatever it is, you'll ace it, Lady. What's going on in that beautiful mind of yours?"

"I'd like to try to be a mother."

He became serious, searching my eyes. "Are you ready?" he asked.

"I am. What about you?"

We had been through the paperwork, done the inspections. But we both had to be ready to bring a child into our lives.

He leaned forward. "I would love to be a parent with you. Call Sandra at the agency, and let's go to the next step."

"Really?"

"I think any child would be lucky to have you as a mom. I know you'll help me be a good dad."

I flung myself out of the swing and into his arms. "We'll be great. I know it."

He kissed me. "Then make the call, Lady."

ONE MONTH LATER

The drive into the city was silent, both of us lost to our thoughts. We pulled up in front of the drab gray building, and I glanced at Luke. The tightness in his jaw was the only tell of his tension.

I unbuckled my seat belt and turned to him. "You okay?"

He nodded. "These kids have been through a lot."

"I know."

"I worry I'll disappoint them."

I smiled and cupped his cheek. "You could never. They need a home, love, and support. What better place to get it than with us?"

He leaned into my caress. "I thought we'd start with one, not siblings. What if…" He trailed off.

"What if it's wonderful?" I asked. "Like us?"

He sighed, loosening the tension in his jaw. "Like us."

"They need love. We have an abundance of it."

"You're right."

"I usually am."

He leaned over and kissed me. "Don't push it, Lady."

He slid from the driver's seat and came around to open my door. My cowboy loved old-fashioned gestures, and I loved that about him.

I glanced down at the file, whispering a little prayer of hope.

One that would give us a family to love.

LUKE

Allison and Jake Martin had been left with a babysitter one evening. Nothing unusual except, this time, their parents never came home. They were killed in an auto accident. The children had no family, and they ended up in the system. Allison was six, Jake was five, and they clung to each other with a grip that made me want to drop to my knees and hold them.

They watched us with fearful eyes as we approached, Sammy's hand tight in mine. The agent told us they had tried sending them to different homes, but it was a disaster. They had to be adopted together. When Sammy and I heard their story and saw their pictures, we knew we had to meet them.

They were introduced to us, and we smiled, crouching down. "Hello," Sammy greeted them. "I'm Sammy Adler. This is Luke Adler, my husband. We've been looking so forward to meeting you."

They remained silent, Jake pressing closer into his sister.

"I like your hair," Sammy said to Allison. "Such pretty curls. Mine is always straight."

Allison looked at her, touching Jake's hair. His was a dark brown, while hers was a lighter, golden color. They shared the same eye color. Sammy nodded. "Yes, like Jake's. Would you like to come sit with us? Both of you?"

Neither responded. I met Jake's eyes, the dark color reminding me of Sammy's. The fear and anguish I saw in them crushed my heart. "Hey, Jake," I murmured. "Do I scare you, Little Partner? I don't mean to."

He was staring at my hat, and I took it off, extending it to him. "You like that?"

"Cowboy," he mumbled.

"Yeah, I am."

"You haf a horse?"

"I have lots of horses." I looked at Allison. "You like horses, Little Lady?"

She shook her head. I smiled and lowered my voice. "I bet you like kittens, don't you? We have some of those too."

Her eyes widened, and she nodded.

Sammy pulled out her tablet. "Do you want to come sit with us? We can show you some pictures."

Allison and Jake shared a look. I could almost hear their silent conversation. Feel their fear—and their longing. I wasn't sure which one would win out. I decided to stack the deck. "Sammy made some sandwiches and cookies to share with you. And we have chocolate milk. I hear that's your favorite."

That made the decision.

We sat at the little table, encouraging them to eat. Jake watched me with fascination, edging closer the longer we sat there. Allison stared at Sammy, listening to her talk, asking quiet questions about the photos. I pulled some coloring books and crayons from the bag Sammy had packed and opened one, frowning as I looked at the page.

I held out the crayon to Jake. "I can never keep in the lines. Could you help me with that?"

I held my breath as he took the crayon then inched closer. Then closer. Close enough to hit my knees. "You want to come up?" I asked, patting my lap. He bit his lip, then nodded, and I lifted him, letting him settle, then picking up another crayon. "Okay, Little Partner. Pick a picture."

He flipped the pages, settling on a basket of puppies. "I like puppies," he mumbled.

"Me too."

He looked up and grinned. He was missing two teeth, which made him look impish. He glanced up at my hat, and I took it off, sticking it on his head. It was way too big, falling down over his face, and I huffed out a sigh.

"Sammy, where did Jake go? He was on my lap a minute ago."

Allison stared at me as if I was crazy. "He's still there."

I lifted my hands. "Where?"

Jake lifted the hat. "Right here!" he said and then laughed.

I began to laugh too, and Sammy chuckled, shaking her head. "Boys," she murmured to Allison.

Allison looked at us and suddenly began to laugh too. "Boys," she repeated.

The sounds almost made me tear up. The agent sitting in the corner looked shocked, a smile of pure relief curling her lips.

I looked at Sammy, and we had our own silent conversation.

We'd found our little family.

And I couldn't wait to hear their laughter ring out at the ranch.

In the car, we were quiet. "Sandra is going to start the paperwork for placement," Sammy said finally.

"I don't want them staying in a foster home," I agreed. "I want them to come with us."

"Me too," she whispered, her voice thick.

I squeezed her hand. "Sandra is going to work with us. She says she hasn't seen the kids respond to anyone like they did to us."

Sammy nodded, unable to speak. She looked out the window, and I wanted to pull the truck over and haul her into my arms.

"We'll get them home, Sammy. Make them feel safe."

She nodded.

"Can you call your parents?" I asked. "Put them on speaker."

She did as I asked, and Liv answered.

"Hey," I greeted her. "Van around?"

"I'm here," he said in the background. "What's up?"

"I got a project I need your and Liv's help on."

He chuckled. "Okay. What is it?"

"We need you to come out and help Sammy and me turn the guest rooms into happy places—" I paused "—for your grandkids."

There was silence, then he spoke. "We'll be there next week."

"Good. I'll be in touch."

I hung up and reached for Sammy's hand. "Hold tight, Momma. We'll get your babies home."

It was still dark as I sat at the table sipping coffee. The rest of the house was asleep. I rubbed my eyes. The past weeks had been stressful, and since we'd brought Allison and Jake home, it hadn't lessened much. They were scared. Worried about being separated. Still not grasping their new life, mourning their old one, and unsure of the future. They refused to be apart, even sleeping in the same bed. The social worker and counselor assured us they would adjust and we just had to be patient.

I had plenty of patience, but their fear broke my heart. They got anxious when one of us would leave, worried, like their parents, we wouldn't return. Sammy and I couldn't be out of the room at the same time without tears from one or both of them. Sammy often cried too.

I sighed, letting my head fall back. I heard a noise and glanced down the hall. Jake was walking toward me, pulling a blanket Sammy had given him the first night. I was shocked to see him out of the room without Allison. I kept my voice calm.

"Hey, Little Partner, you okay?"

"Hungry," he said.

"Okay. Cereal?"

"Please."

I got bowls, cereal, and milk and sat down. He remained standing, and I held out my arms. "You wanna come up?"

He let me lift him to my knee, and I poured cereal and milk into his bowl, then did the same for myself.

He ate steadily for a few minutes, then set down his spoon.

"Had enough?"

He shook his head, and I knew he'd go back to the bowl soon.

He looked up at me and then the hooks by the front door. I laughed softly. "I don't wear my hat in the house. Sammy doesn't like it."

"Outside."

I ran my hand over his head. "Yeah, outside. In the stable."

He played with his lip, one of his nervous tells. "Horses," he whispered.

"Yep. In the stable." I paused. "Maybe you'd like to come see them this morning?"

"Yes," he whispered. "Ally not like them."

"Maybe Ally and Sammy could visit the chickens."

He frowned, then looked up at me. "Then we come here. Back here?"

"Yes," I said firmly. "Both of you."

He nodded, pulling his cereal bowl back and eating.

Sammy came down the hall, stopping in shock when she saw us.

"My Little Partner and I are having cereal," I explained. "He wants to see the horses."

Jake looked up. "Ally see the chickens."

"Sure," Sammy said easily, not giving away her surprise.

The sound of rushing feet came down the hall. "Jake!" Allison cried, skidding to a stop when she saw us. She rushed over, gripping his arm. "Jake," she whimpered, the sound of tears in her voice.

"Hey, Little Lady," I soothed. "We're just having cereal. Little Partner was hungry. Are you hungry?"

She wiped her face. "Yeah."

"Sammy will get you breakfast. You want cereal too?"

She nodded, sliding onto a chair, her gaze fixed on her brother.

Sammy poured her some cereal and got a cup of coffee. We ate and sipped for a moment, then I cleared my throat.

"Jake wants to see the horses with me today, Ally. He thought you'd like to see the chickens and the kittens with Sammy?"

Her eyes widened, fear filling them. Jake put his small hand on her arm. "Back here, Ally," he said, assuring her. "Home after." He patted her again. "Us home. Ally, Jake, Sammy, and Cowboy."

I began to chuckle. Sammy called me that all the time, and he had somehow picked it up.

Ally sighed, the tension leaving her body. "Okay."

"Great. After breakfast, we'll see the horses, chickens, and kittens." I kept my voice calm, as if it was a regular occurrence.

"And cows," Jake said. "Happy cows."

My laughter was loud this time. I ruffled his hair.

"Yeah, Little Partner. The happy cows."

I met Sammy's gaze, the wonder of the moment not lost on us. Ally trusted Jake, and Jake trusted us. Our circle was beginning. And it was only the start.

Three Years Later

Luke

I paused at the foot of the hills, looking down at the ranch. It had changed and grown so much since Sammy had entered my life.

It was thriving. The ranch was in the black. The business was in the black. Deep in the black, despite all the upgrades we continually made. We opened every season up on February 1 for reservations and were booked solid by the end of the day. From May to September, Home on the Range was a bustling, energetic entity. Rachel and Sammy oversaw everything. Between the income from the guests, the cheese shop, the wool shop, and the small crafters' market, business boomed. Rachel and others worked endlessly in the off-season, building up inventory and selling items online. The wool and cheese shop alone needed three full-time workers year-round. I lost count of the number of people we employed in the busy season. The business thrived. The ranch thrived. Our families did as well.

It was more than Rachel ever dreamed and better than I had imagined.

I urged Maverick in the direction of the stables. Inside, I slid down and handed Maverick off to one of the hands to take care of.

"Give him an extra rubdown," I said, stroking his velvety nose. "He worked hard today."

"Will do."

"Dad!" a voice called, and I turned, already smiling. Jake ran my way, flinging his arms around my waist and hugging me so tight his hat fell off his head. "You're home!"

I chuckled. "I was only gone one night, Partner," I teased him. I'd had to drop the "Little" in his name when he started sprouting and insisted he was too big for that.

"But we missed you."

I hugged him back, thrilled to hear that. "I missed you too." I picked up his hat and set it back on his head. "Where's your sister and mom?"

"Over here, Daddy," a soft voice called.

Jake looked up at me, rolling his eyes. "The kittens," he explained.

We went over to the corner, and I bent down, pressing a kiss to Ally's head. "How's my Little Lady?"

So far, she still liked me calling her that. I hoped it never changed.

"Good."

"How're the kittens?"

She grinned. "Cuddly."

I had to laugh. All six of them were curled up in her lap, except one. A fluffy, caramel-colored one was nestled in her neck. It reminded me of Sammy and Oreo.

"Mom said I could ask you if I can keep Taffy," she whispered, stroking the sleeping kitten. "Like she kept Oreo."

"Have they met?"

She looked guilty, then nodded. "Oreo is okay with her."

I lifted one eyebrow. "Did Taffy stay the night last night?"

"Yeah."

"And she was okay?"

"She was good." She looked at me, her dark eyes pleading. "Jake got a dog."

Jake laughed. "Ralph kept trying to take the kitten to his basket."

I had to laugh. The golden retriever we'd gotten him not long after they came to live with us helped him and Ally get over their anxiety. He was a great dog, protective, loving, and loyal. That he'd try to baby a kitten didn't surprise me. He often came to the stable when there were kittens and checked them out. He and Oreo had a good relationship—as long as he remembered Oreo owned the place.

This was the first time Ally had ever asked to keep a kitten, so I knew how important it was to her. I pressed another kiss to her head. "If Mom is okay with it, then I am too. Same rules as Jake, though. You have to care for her."

"I will, Daddy! Thank you!"

I stood and looked down at our kids. They were settled and happy. Did well at school. Loved living on the ranch and especially loved the times the ranch teemed with guests.

It had taken a year before their personalities had completely shown through. Ally was quiet and sweet, but as sharp as a tack. She was a homebody and loved hanging with her mom and Aunt Rachel. She especially adored Liv and Van and was overjoyed when they came for one of their many visits or going to see them in Port Albany. She thought the entire massive family on Sammy's side was the greatest thing in the world.

Jake was outspoken and mischievous. He loved working on the ranch and hated school. Sammy had explained to him it was illegal for him not to go to school, so he did it so "Mom won't go to jail" but informed her once he graduated, that was it. He'd be working on the ranch. And despite his dislike of school, he did well. I had to admit I loved the fact that he was anxious to learn and be part of the family business.

They were both Adlers now, the adoption complete and binding. We slowly went from Sammy and Cowboy to Mom and Dad. We didn't push; it just happened naturally. Once they met Liv and Van, or Nan and Pops as they called them, they became more open, and one day at supper, it simply happened.

"It's parents' day next week at school," Ally announced. *"For both our classes."*

"Okay," Sammy said, looking at me.

"Jake and I discussed it on the bus and decided Dad could go to his class and Mom could come to mine, if that's okay?"

Sammy blinked. Tears filled her eyes, and she had to lift her glass of water before speaking. "Sure," she agreed. "Sounds good, right, ah, Dad?"

"Sounds great," I agreed, my voice thick.

"Is that okay?" Ally asked. "That we..." Her voice trailed off.

"It's more than okay, Little Lady," I answered. "We'd be honored."

Ally smiled. "Good. We talked about it and decided our Mama and Papa would like it too. We like being your kids, so you should be our Mom and Dad. It only makes sense."

I nodded. "Yep."

And that was that.

I left the kids with the kittens and the horses and headed to the house. Inside, I smiled. Sammy had changed the interior, updating it while keeping its old-fashioned charm. I headed down the hall and stopped in the office doorway, leaning on the frame, staring at my wife. The woman who'd changed my life and made it better.

The office was organized now. No more piles or chaos. Sammy was far too methodical for that. She was busy typing on her computer, a cup of coffee at her elbow.

"I know you're there, Cowboy. Stop staring."

"Just looking at my sexy wife, wondering how to lure her away from her work and into my arms."

She lifted her head, her rich brown eyes dancing. Her hair was longer, almost to her waist, and today she had it braided, the thick plait hanging over her shoulder. She smiled, sunshine and warmth, then stood, walking toward me. I pulled her close and bent down to kiss her, savoring her mouth underneath mine. I groaned as she wound her arms around my neck, deepening the kiss.

Moments passed as we said hello. I lifted my head, grinning. "Remind me to go away more often if that's the greeting I get, Lady."

"Wait until the kids are asleep, and I'll show you how much I really missed you," she murmured.

I grinned. "Then I'll go and give them extra chores to wear them out."

She laughed and snuggled close. "Everything good?"

"Yep. Scouted another area for camping and mended some boundary fences."

"Good."

"I hear we have a new family member."

Sammy laughed. "Yes."

"Jake hugged me when I got home. Felt like he grew again."

Sammy sighed and drew back. "I think he did. His dad was your height, so I expect he'll be tall too."

"They're growing up too fast. I feel old."

"You don't feel old to me, Cowboy."

"Somehow when you're close, I don't."

She slid her hand down my torso, cupping me. "In fact, you feel pretty, ah, hard."

I groaned. "Lady, do you remember what happened last time we tried to have sex in the middle of the afternoon? Two kids ring a bell?"

She chuckled, leaning up to kiss my jaw. "But that time I hadn't bribed Callie to keep them at the cookhouse with cake for an hour after you came home."

In a second, I had her over my shoulder, carrying her to the bath. "An hour? Lady, get ready. You have no idea what's about to happen."

"Show me."

I set her on her feet and cupped her face. "I love you."

"I love you. But time is ticking. Less talk, more action, Cowboy." Then she grinned. "And lock the door in case those old bones need a little more time."

I was going to need more time, but it had nothing to do with my old bones. The boner in my pants was raring to go.

I tipped my hat as I flipped the lock.

"Yes, ma'am."

Thank you so much for reading SUNSHINE & SAMMY. If you are so inclined, reviews are always welcome by me at your book retailer.

Grumpy vs sunshine is a trope I love to write. Add in a sexy cowboy, and I fell in love with Luke.

If you would love to read another age-gap/opposites attract story

from me, check out Maxx and Charly's story in REVVED TO
THE MAXX.

Luke decides Sammy should have a few more twirls around the
dance floor. Check out this excerpt to read all about their two-
step adventure. - Bonus Scene SUNSHINE & SAMMY available
at Bookfunnel: https://BookHip.com/KLFZGRD
Enjoy reading! Melanie

ACKNOWLEDGMENTS

As usual, a few thanks.

Lisa, thank you for your humor, your support, and your red pen. I hate the red pen, but it certainly loves me. LOL

Beth, thank you for your feedback and funny comments. Your insight make the story better—always.

Melissa, Trina, Carol, and Deb—thank you for your encouragement, laughter, and support.

Carissa, thank you for your eagle eyes and assistance. So appreciated!

Kim, I never know what to say. I have no idea what you do. I just know it is amazing.

Karen, I have no idea how many books I've written since you came into my life. I know it's never enough and you are always wanting more. I love that. I love you. Thank you for all the wonderful little things I forget to thank you for. You rock.

Nina (Valentine PR). Thank you for your calm, your humor, and your laughter. I appreciate all you do.

To all the bloggers, readers, and my promo team. Thank you for everything you do. Shouting your love of books—of my work, posting, sharing—your recommendations keep my TBR list full, and the support you have shown me is deeply appreciated.

My reader group, Melanie's Minions—love you all.

MLM—for all you do I cannot say thank you enough. I wish I could hug you all. Maybe one day.

Matthew—my own hero. You have given so much joy and love to me. You are my everything. Thank you for your love. For you.

ALSO AVAILABLE FROM MORELAND BOOKS

Titles published under M. Moreland

Insta-Spark Collection

It Started with a Kiss

Christmas Sugar

An Instant Connection

An Unexpected Gift

Harvest of Love

An Unexpected Chance

Following Maggie (Coming Home series)

Titles published under Melanie Moreland

The Contract Series

The Contract (Contract #1)

The Baby Clause (Contract #2)

The Amendment (Contract #3)

The Addendum (Contract #4)

Vested Interest Series

BAM - The Beginning (Prequel)

Bentley (Vested Interest #1)

Aiden (Vested Interest #2)

Maddox (Vested Interest #3)

Reid (Vested Interest #4)

Van (Vested Interest #5)

Halton (Vested Interest #6)

Sandy (Vested Interest #7)

Vested Interest Box Set (Books 1-3)

Vested Interest Box Set (Books 4-7)

Vested Interest/ABC Crossover

A Merry Vested Wedding

ABC Corp Series

My Saving Grace (Vested Interest: ABC Corp #1)

Finding Ronan's Heart (Vested Interest: ABC Corp #2)

Loved By Liam (Vested Interest: ABC Corp #3)

Age of Ava (Vested Interest: ABC Corp #4)

Sunshine & Sammy (Vested Interest: ABC Corp #5)

Men of Hidden Justice

The Boss

Second-In-Command

The Commander

The Watcher

Reynolds Restorations

Revved to the Maxx

Breaking the Speed Limit

Shifting Gears

Under The Radar

Full Throttle

Mission Cove

The Summer of Us

Standalones

Into the Storm

Beneath the Scars

Over the Fence

The Image of You (former title My Image of You)

Changing Roles

Happily Ever After Collection

Heart Strings

ABOUT THE AUTHOR

NYT/WSJ/USAT international bestselling author Melanie Moreland, lives a happy and content life in a quiet area of Ontario with her beloved husband of thirty-plus years and their rescue cat, Amber. Nothing means more to her than her friends and family, and she cherishes every moment spent with them.

While seriously addicted to coffee, and highly challenged with all things computer-related and technical, she relishes baking, cooking, and trying new recipes for people to sample. She loves to throw dinner parties, and enjoys traveling, here and abroad, but finds coming home is always the best part of any trip.

Melanie loves stories, especially paired with a good wine, and enjoys skydiving (free falling over a fleck of dust) extreme snowboarding (falling down stairs) and piloting her own helicopter (tripping over her own feet.) She's learned happily ever afters, even bumpy ones, are all in how you tell the story.

Melanie is represented by Flavia Viotti at Bookcase Literary Agency. For any questions regarding subsidiary or translation rights please contact her at flavia@bookcaseagency.com

Connect with Melanie

Like reader groups? Lots of fun and giveaways! Check it out Melanie Moreland's Minions

Join my newsletter for up-to-date news, sales, book announcements and excerpts (no spam). Click here to sign up Melanie Moreland's newsletter

or visit https://bit.ly/MMorelandNewsletter

Visit my website www.melaniemoreland.com

 facebook.com/authormoreland
twitter.com/morelandmelanie
instagram.com/morelandmelanie

Made in the USA
Monee, IL
14 January 2023

25045398R00193